TACONITE CREEK

John Luthens

Best wishes
and
Fondest memories,
John Luthens

TACONITE CREEK

John Luthens

CABLE PUBLISHING

Brule, Wisconsin

TACONITE CREEK

First Edition

Published by:
Cable Publishing
14090 E Keinenen Rd
Brule, WI 54820
www.cablepublishing.com
E-mail: nan@cablepublishing.com

Soft cover: 978-1-934980-50-7

Library of Congress Control Number: 2014956857

Photo on dedication page courtesy of Scott Wisherd

Cover design by lvmultimedia@wi.rr.com

Printed in the United States of America

This is dedicated to my dad. For many years, we searched together for Taconite Creek. He may have gotten there first, but I know he's waiting along its banks for me.

With Thanks

I owe the bulk of this book to my family. They let me wander away to the furthest corners of Wisconsin without question, always taking me back in when I'd show up at the front door with nothing to show but stories and an empty bank account.

I also owe a debt of gratitude to Dick Ellis, publisher of *On Wisconsin Outdoors*. He is a beacon in the ever-shrinking world of outdoor journalism. He gave me a platform to write. More importantly, he is a friend.

Finally, to Nan Wisherd of Cable Publishing: She is not only the finest editor I've ever met, but she also took a chance with me on the journey to Taconite Creek. This book would have never made it out of the northern wilderness without her.

Praise for Taconite Creek....

A good outdoor writer allows those left behind to live vicariously through the story. John Luthens has taken me along for years to find the most secluded places that Wisconsin's Lake Superior Country can try to hide. I never did leave the desk, but I felt the current push against the waders, too, and caught those browns, brookies, and steelheads from the pristine streams and pools of God's Country. Luthens writes from the field, from the wild places, from the heart...and he takes us along, too. In Taconite Creek, *Uncle Jack and Ernie and an incredible adventure of triumph and tragedy spill from the author's imagination and help a young boy become a man. This is a story for outdoor enthusiasts, trout fishermen, and anyone who loves to read quality writing set outdoors. Expect the unexpected, but don't worry. Those of us who have already been with Luthens know you'll be following a great guide.*

— Dick Ellis, publisher of *On Wisconsin Outdoors*

Trains, mining, and fishing. Obsessions, trade-offs, and spirit. All merge into poetic metaphors that in one instant can take away our breath and then, in another, just as easily draw forth an awe-inspired sigh. This reflective narrative transports us back to a summer in which a young boy tumbles headlong into some of life's greatest mysteries. Under the tutelage of Uncle Jack, the finest fly fisherman he ever knew, and Ernie, Jack's deep-thinking Finnish cohort, lessons are learned amid lightning-like revelations and hard-knock strokes of luck. Author John Luthens champions the sensory nuance of fly fishing as adeptly as he does the unrefined, heavy-booted march along tracks leading into the unknown. Exquisitely written, profoundly woven, and forever memorable, I enthusiastically recommend this magnetic, suspenseful tale where the line between obstinacy and vision lies twisted among the overgrown wreckage along Taconite Creek.

— Jackie Boor, author of *Logan: The Honorable Life & Scandalous Death of a Western Lawman*

Luthens has spun a fun, yet moving, story appealing to anyone who has ever experienced or imagined spending time in wild places. He has also subtly woven in the issues we're faced with today – whether to leave natural places as they are or exploit them for financial gain.

— Bobbi Rongstad, officer of the
Bad River Watershed Association

Taconite Creek is an enjoyable read full of laughs and tears, tying together a historical world of trout and taconite ore like a crafted fly, while conveying a message for all of us living in present-day times.

— Jerry Kiesow, outdoor writer, photographer,
and fly-fishing instructor

In this wonderfully unique and fascinating book, a fatherless boy experiences the priceless importance of older men mentors. Uncle Jack and Ernie (Jack's Finnish pal and the inventor of an exotic sauna train), taconite scouts and trout fisherman, work for the mining companies in the northern Wisconsin wilderness. It so happens that the taconite rocks they seek are often paired with some of the best trout streams near Lake Superior's South Shore. This is a rich, elegiac story about how the power of nature itself, with its teachers, guide a young boy into manhood. It is a must-read for anyone who loves the wilderness, its sunshine and storms, the brooding presence of Lake Superior, giant brook trout, and the mature necessity to safeguard such sacred things.

— Steven D. Fortney, author of
The Cabin: A North Woods Memoir

THE RINGS OF LIFE

The stories once woke me. A wrist flick and a casting arc from the paper boy's creel bag; bicycle tires spitting gravel and dust over the crisp fold headlines. I'd look for the eastern glow. I'd look forward to the stories.

Now, the floods of my past have long ago washed away. I reckon that time eventually blasts the mightiest of rivers forward and gone, nothing left behind but yellowed headlines of old and a rusted bike frame in a gullied creek bed. The dust long since settled on the water; the paper's sound muffled to a dead thump on the porch. I wade from the flow of a long night and swing around the bend of another day and the results are the same no matter the watery perspective. I don't sleep much anymore, and I don't dream, either. I'm too old to do anything but wait out the night. Now, like a tiny pebble fallen off a high ridge and rolled into a stagnant pool, the paper barely breaks the silence.

It isn't the same one...the boy I remember or the paper, either. It's a bigger piece of steel that brings the stories now; no more bicycle spokes and spitting gravel, just a flash of brake lights, the push of an electric window, and a tube of plastic wrapping drives up with a whole lot of shaved-down journalism and advertisement inserts flopping out the sides.

Maybe the new delivery kid is a descendent. That kind of work flows like iron in the blood, and it's hard to judge how far back the current stretches. Maybe it's been long enough that it's a son's son now. Delivery bicycles change into cars, news stories change just as fast. But early-morning time has always been for the boys toting paper stories – no matter what they're driving or what kind of stories they're carrying. Early morning is a premium along the stream of time.

The sun still dark behind the horizon and the twinges of the day starting to seep through; I've seen those mornings plenty, but I greet them all the same now; an imperceptible nod of my head, like to an old neighbor who's lived next door for a lifetime. It's a daily routine, and there isn't a lot that can surprise me anymore. Down the steps with a coffee cup, swaying from side to side like I've got waders full of water; hollering at the squirrels to get the hell away from the paper, stooping hard to pick it up, and kicking the gray rodents all the way to my front-yard reading stump.

Those tunneling thieves love digging under there. I bet it's a generational thing, like the family of paper boys handing off the paper baton to the next one in line. I don't doubt that these modern critters have it engrained between their stubby ears that their ancestors lived above this stump, back when it was still a live oak and leaves were still in nest-décor style. The best the long-tailed offspring can manage is to steal the headlines and wallpaper the ruined foundation of the stump's basement with newsprint.

If I had any trust left in my far-seeing eyes, I'd shoot 'em all. I'd cut off their bushy asses and thread 'em onto a round-shank hook; tied just right with enough of that gray and white tail dangling and streaming through the water; stripping it with just enough wobble in the current seam. Why, any self-respecting trout would clear a half-foot of water after one of those. Ah, hell, maybe I wouldn't shoot one. I remember Ernie feeding chipmunks out of his hand, trading crumbs for all the hackle he cared to spin without harming a hair. I reckon the squirrels probably get as much entertainment out of the news stories as I do.

That's the coffee got me talking now – fresh out of an automatic machine – got me talking fishing and squirrel murder, almost got me feeling a little ashamed to be bashing the local newspaper so early in the morning. I'd warrant that if it was boiled over a battered stove, a dented iron pot bubbling out of the ashes with coffee grounds and spring-fed water spilling across the rocky ground, well, then it would work better magic. There isn't but me and the squirrels and my old stump left now; a place to sit with the paper and wait out the day. No fire and no gurgling stream to kneel down beside and fill the pot in the early morning mist. I reckon I'll take any magic I can get.

This reading stump is like me and my paper. It's only a shredded part of what it once was – sort of reminds me of one of those old Supreme Court Justices who won't retire and have to be darn near led by the hand to find a seat on the bench. Not that I'm any better, mind you. I'm no judge, and this stump isn't much of a judicial bench. We're all just part of a faded core that started a tree to going in the first place.

Concentric rings of an old stump, sucking you in and counting back the ages. If I stare long enough, they start to wriggle around, and I swear that they still retain the life of long ago. There's a rhythm: like casting a fly line forward and back. It starts to take on a bigger meaning. Every cast is different, and every stump is different. They all have a particular story.

Ernie once told me, "Befores you go forvard, you gots to go backvard." Along with feeding chipmunks and tying flies, he spent his whole damn life rolling around those mysterious mantras in his head. Before you go forward, you need to go back. It's a good way to look at the rings on a stump and a good way to look at history. It becomes the basis of a good fly cast, too. Start at the beginning and work your way out.

The more I stare into the rings of my reading and bitching perch, the more they remind me of rings in a still pool of water after the tiniest pluck that got them going. I reckon that's why they remind me of a fly-line cast. Rings, bigger on the outside, slowly spiraling back to the center of the rise. The center ring like the tiny sip of a trout, a sip so small, so imperceptible, that your eyes don't even see it begin. They only see it afterwards as slow-plucked ripples floating outwards, floating like sound waves from a tight string struck in an empty chamber; one quick chord reverberating into nothing.

Uncle Jack, he wasn't a deep thinker like Ernie, wasn't any great shakes at feeding chipmunks or tying flies, either. But he would have gone along with the fly-line cast and the rising trout. He was the finest fisherman I ever knew, and he would have appreciated the sentiment. He wouldn't for an instant have bought the tight-string and sound waves bit. I can hear his voice rising out of the morning: "That has absolutely nothing to do with nothing – just a lot of confusing hoo-ha designed to trip a practical man up."

Trip a practical man up. Ernie knew all too well. Over the course of their magnificent symphony together, through the forest glens and up the whispering pine slopes, and along the roaring crescendo of the wildest streams in northern Wisconsin, Ernie heard enough tight strings and sound waves from Uncle Jack to fill the deepest valleys.

Trip a practical man up. There's more involved and a lot more at stake than what you see on the surface – rocks hiding in the weeds, waiting to send you head-over-heels and flat on your nose. There's always a submerged log below the bank to snag up that perfect cast; waiting to wrap tackle into a nightmare of throbbing rod and twisted leader. There are always such things in every cast and in every story, and if there are not, then someone – while not exactly lying – isn't properly telling.

The rings of life circle both ways. I have only to open this newspaper that the paper boy thoughtfully threw at my porch and the squirrels thoughtfully neglected to chew into a gnarled nest. Like a fly line slowly unfurling and releasing its pent-up energy onto the top of the fold are the columns and editorial stories of a mining company's quest. It's a quest that aims to smash acres from the land, spiraling one way across the ring of stories with a straightforward goal of digging out a bunch of rocks. Of course, they're a peculiar species of rock. Taconite rock spun into solid iron ore, if one is a stickler for details and wants to mold it down exactly.

The stories fly from the pinnacle of the northern Wisconsin reaches. They start a lot further north than the rings on this stump but, ironically, maybe not so far removed from when it was still a tree.

The stories spin, telling of a thousand jobs and tons of fused steel – money thrown into a northern wilderness. That kind of money buys a lot of new toys to drive the morning paper around in. It turns fleets of delivery bicycles into fresh and shining automobiles. A load of gas-price complaining is just waiting in the ground up there, round about the ore-dock city of Ashland, smack dab in that monster of a range that the native Ojibwe people called Gogebic. It's a slice of Lake Superior cut deep into the rawest wilderness Wisconsin has to offer. It's deep in history, deep in legend, cut with iron-stained ridges and iron-stained rivers, with virgin timber running through it all. And running right with it, deep center on the whole mountain of rock that the paper stories are climbing, is the hot-forged money of taconite steel.

Moving across the next ring of the stump, the next fly cast across the river, or the next page of the newspaper, is the environmental talk. Those folks got stories too, and they don't care a whit for any new mine. They're fired up and worried about taconite offshoot waste, worried about what lurks behind the scenes of wresting economy-driving steel from the bare essence of the land. They're worried about cutting the scenery to pieces, busting up the streams, taming the wildness – killing off the animals and killing off the trout.

The Gogebic Range: There's plenty of money and plenty of politics swimming on the surface. But the Ojibwe first spoke it, long before there were any paper stories to print the name. Taconite translates into iron ore, and that translates to fire-branded steel. But the roots of the range itself are uncertain, hidden in the shadows of the past, depending on translation to mean "a place of rocks," or "where the trout rising to the surface make rings in the water." The truth of the Ojibwe translation probably lies somewhere between. Peer deep, and the truth is that the taconite rock of the Gogebic has been entwined in those rings forever.

The Badger State; that's what Wisconsin's forefathers named it, digging in the ground to build an empire out of metal. Maybe if I left some scrap iron lying about the place, then maybe the squirrels would root around after that instead of going after my paper. Who the hell knows anymore? The mines and the iron, the paper stories and the money, everyone with a vested interest; it's not much different from the rings on this stump. Start at the inside and work your way out, or start at the end and work your way back in. Either way, the circling lines take you in and turn you, year after year and story after story. The whole thing isn't even a tree anymore, for God's sake. It's just a confusing history of what a tree used to be.

It swings full circle, whistling like a fly line through the air, singing the tune of a lost steam engine train, shooting smoke and shaking the steel foundations of an entire country. Full circle; when I could still sleep and dream, when the paper was still dropped off by bicycle, and when I drank my coffee from an old tin pot; back when I roamed the morning hatch with Uncle Jack and Ernie, long ago...before I hatched into a rambling old man perched on tired bones and prone to talking all morning about squirrels and trout and iron mines.

I listen every morning now. My ears are like my eyes, not what they used to be, but I don't recall hearing that whistle for quite a spell. Even the rail tracks that ran the field line back of my house are silent. I'm not senile enough not to register the fact that there haven't been too many steam engines running for damn near a century, but the only thing these old eyes can decipher is a fallen sign left at the crossroads that reads "Tracks out of Service."

Those tracks once ripped a part of my heart right out. But they gave something in return. They were a straight-edged lifeline across the rings of life when I needed one. They might not go anywhere now, and maybe they weren't but parallel lines of steel back then. But back then, the rails sang out, and they were built with hard-forged iron, and at least they went forward instead of just stretching silent and standing for something lost.

Listen close. Those tracks... Now, those steel tracks once went somewhere....

CHAPTER 1

Many years ago, across the tracks and the fields and the fencerows of my youth, Uncle Jack and Ernie came to snatch me into their business.

Uncle Jack and Ernie on one end and me on the other, we were opposite sides of a double-tapered line that tangled in the iron rocks of Taconite Creek. But to unfurl that line, to unfold the iron hills, I need to tell how it was after it was over. I'd look over my shoulder and see it disappearing into the cold mists of the Lake Superior hills. It was like waking from a vivid dream. Still a boy, growing slowly into the daybreak of a man, but already I'd lived a lifetime of dreams.

I had a ship's hold full of far-going, impulsive, and chaotic thoughts fostering in my head, and they were inherited from the same family-tree branch that Uncle Jack perched on. Not exactly inherited; inherited implies freely given. I earned my lessons on the taconite range. I'm only a minor player in history, a stump-sitting reporter who has run his course. But I was necessary back then.

It was a junction point in my life. I had changed and knotted, and it seemed I'd need a lifetime to unravel it all. Taconite Creek was a powerful force, emptying me out like a rushing pool behind a dam after it has been shot through with enough explosives to send it back to the rubble from which it was first created. I was of an age when the emotional roller-coaster corkscrews a kid upside-down anyway. It's common. It can be dealt with in any number of ways, both healthy and unhealthy. I dealt with it by wandering as far from society as I could get, searching into the forests of my home for answers to life's mysteries. While that might be diagnosed as melancholic escapism by clinical psychologists, I went with a fly rod in my hand, so it was a free pass from the white room reclining couch in my mind; and my mind was all I was concerned with back then.

I disappeared into scrub tree meadows, out the door, beneath the big red oak in the yard, and gone. I went afternoons, after school let out, or in the early tint of light before school began. I'm morally ashamed to say that occasionally school got left behind altogether. Uncle Jack and Ernie wouldn't have wanted that. They worked hard to teach me. So we'll sweep the school thing under the carpet for a moment and focus on the summer. In the summer I carried a jointed rod and a small cigar box of flies. I'd acquired them, earned them, if you will, from a pair of masters.

A railway track lay in the distance, springing from wherever it is that rail tracks begin, resting comfortably over fields and disappearing at times into tunnels of thorny ash and willows. I'd hack a path up the grade with my fly rod through blackberry brambles. The rails were easy walking compared to the surrounding jungle. I stepped in time across the splintered wood ties. There were shadows dancing in the thickets, and it was like entering a lost world.

At the critical juncture of my adolescence so many years ago, I left childhood behind and followed the rails that Uncle Jack and Ernie started. Maybe the tracks represented a crossroads. I could look at them that way. The sun glinted off rails behind and unknown miles in front. On the other side was the river.

My river across the tracks was not wild, not like Taconite Creek had been. It was awfully fond of running in cow pastures, and weeds grew high on the trampled banks. It was not Taconite Creek, but in the early spring, when the water was cold enough from snowmelt seeping out of the meadows; then there could be trout almost anywhere.

They never grew large in the pasture water. No rainbows or brooks cared to call that kind of water home. They were all brown trout and that was fine, because even a small brown hooked on the end of a cane rod was exiting. It wasn't blue-ribbon water, just a nameless river flowing through swaying trees and pasture. But they were trout, and it was really the river – that's what I was after.

As summer wore hotter, the trout fell back from the open pasture. Then the bass and pike moved in. I took a lot of bass, horsing them from weed beds where they'd smash out at any buggy-looking thing passing overhead. Some of the bass were huge, and I wonder if I might not have held a record for a bass on light tackle sometime in my rail-river wandering. I don't know if such a record existed back then. But if it did, maybe I once held it.

The pike took any streamer flashy enough to imitate a minnow, provided it was jerked ever so slightly through the deeper cut channels of the flowing weeds. I usually couldn't land the pike, because their sharp teeth cut through my leaders. I never thought of using a wire leader. Uncle Jack and Ernie would have chided me for that. But then, they wouldn't have been messing around with cattle pasture bass and pike in the first place. It wouldn't have been near wild enough for them.

I fished it every chance I got. Even when I discovered girls and cars, they weren't enough to keep me from the backwaters of that rail-side farm creek. It helped that most of the girls wouldn't give me the time of day, and I couldn't afford a car. Now it's come full circle, just like the rings on my stump, and I'm too old to drive. I still couldn't afford one of those chrome and steel jobs that run on computers, anyway. I had my cow-pasture river after I had Taconite Creek. That was something.

Where the trout went when it got too hot, that was something, too. It was something I took from Uncle Jack. Ernie helped, because I was using his flies. I absorbed from both of them. I found out where the trout went to hide because of their spirits.

It was a deep run set below a high cliff bank of sandstone, rising out of nowhere at the end of the pasture land. The cliffs had been there long before my river eroded the sandstone in its path, long before the farmers and the pasture makers moved in. No matter how hot the summer, I was apt to hook a big brown trout there anytime. The sandstone cast shadows across the slow current. Pockets eroded from rough faces of rock where the sun never reached, sand pouring from the pockets like entryway carpets. The sand was always wet from springs seeping out of the rock, and some of the ledges hung right over the water.

I never opened the covers of *Tom Sawyer* or *Huckleberry Finn* without thinking of those sand cliffs over the river, and I never went there without remembering Taconite Creek. There might have been a cave with buried treasure. I never found it, but that doesn't mean it wasn't there. The seeping springs cooled the river and placed the real treasure in the water, because the currents below the trickling sandstone were where every trout in the river went to hide after it got to hot for comfort, lurking beneath the ledges to avoid the predators, isolating themselves from the bass and pike that dominated the surrounding pastures.

Uncle Jack knew. While so many others looked on the surface, scraping the ground for every trace of iron ore that could be turned to steel, turning the steel to papered gold; all the while, the real treasure was in the water. Uncle Jack was misled on a lot of points, sidetracked down the banks of tangent streams, but he never once wavered from that one.

I threw countless flies below the cliffs; every pattern tied by Ernie sailed out on the end of my line. It went on like that for days, sometimes days without a strike. But then, I'd hook into one. Then my solitary journey of silence would be broken by thrashing waters and singing line.

One rain-soaked afternoon, a hook-jawed brown trout grabbed a grasshopper fly I was skating beneath an undercut bank. The fish stripped my reel dry, running along the bank before leaping over an alder branch as tall as my head. The trout broke the line off on the branch and the alder twig whipped my face and delivered a nasty scratch. It took me an hour to untangle the line, drops from my face bleeding into the river's flow. A fish like that – one that's mad enough to do that – is worth many hours of waiting.

Through the looking glass of years and across the rings of this stump, it was just a cow-pasture stream. But it was important water, and it was water that I needed. I'd been on Taconite Creek. I was trying to grow up and I was trying to hold on. Trying to forget and trying to hold on at the same time. That's how it was with me. And I think, in the end, that's how it was with Uncle Jack and Ernie.

I could have kept on walking down that river into eternity. I might have ended up just like them. But instead, there on that pasture stream and below the sandstone cliffs with cool springs seeping out and the train tracks for company, I began to let life reel me back in. I was on the tag-end of the line, but not destined to end up pinched and broken in the alders or snapped off in the jaws of a sulking monster to ride into the swirling undercurrent of life. I was reeled to life on the banks of that river.

Uncle Jack, there were no waters big enough to hold him. And, too, there was always Ernie. If I'd had someone like Ernie to help me along the banks when it got too much to handle alone, to study the secrets of the water and the deeper secrets of life, then maybe, just maybe, I would have kept down those tracks and down that river.

I was a simple fly on the far end of the line. They weren't. They were doing the casting, and there was iron in their veins. They played that iron all the way to Taconite Creek.

CHAPTER 2

I made a semblance of a living writing, cutting out pieces and digging the way that Uncle Jack and Ernie dug into beds of taconite rock; not too deep, just deep enough to uncover what I felt really mattered. I dug with a pen instead of a shovel. It never brought me any real fame in the news-reporting circles, but I learned from Uncle Jack and Ernie that it was far better that way.

If you dig really deep, maybe write some good gossip on a controversial subject like a local politician with a hidden agenda, then word spreads like wildfire, and the communities remember your face. You need a killer's instinct and a desire to dig through garbage in the dark to find that single acorn that should have been burned in the fire, but now gets planted by a reporter in a fertile little plot and grows into a tree fast and high enough to hang somebody from its tangled branches.

I had enough garbage of my own to carry around. I chose to go after the stories that floated like newly-hatched bugs on the water. Small stories, but seen in the right light, say, with the sun setting over the pines and the summer wind pushing across a splashing pool, then those stories were intricate in their delicacy. It gave me an inner-satisfaction to find a grain of truth floating by that others, greater writers and reporters, may have thought too ordinary and small to bother with. Not to mention I could tailor my stories to lead where I wanted – and that usually meant out on a river with a fly rod.

Take this very stump, for example, when it was still a tree, before it leaned too hard against time and a big wind storm. It didn't cave in my porch right away. The real collapse came a few days later when an opportune tree cutter came to take the oak down, taking it right through the top of my porch instead, with me and the squirrels watching the whole thing.

There I was, a so-called reporter, and this tree fell right into my porch and gave me a story. The contractor was a storm-chasing fellow who showed up in the wake of disasters, cutting trees, repairing roofs, whatever kind of jobs need doing in the aftermath of a serious squall. He took half my money up front, and I wasn't the only one he got to. My neighbor's roof leaked worse after this guy got up there with a shingling hammer than when the shingles were still wind-scattered to all four corners of the county.

Half the money was good enough for that guy, who likely had no better a handle on a chainsaw and roofing nails than a beaver does cutting down trees and piling them onto a lodge dam. After the damage was done, this guy dove for his beaver lodge with a smack of the tail, and he split town faster than the high winds that caused the damage in the first place.

I could have spun the story down any number of branches: the weather behind the windstorm, the damage to the house, most especially the unscrupulous contractor and the insurance companies who ended having to pay twice for the storm damage. Chance put any number of stories through my porch roof and right into my lap. But instead of sitting down at the typewriter, I climbed up on the caved porch, where one of the biggest oak branches popped down through the porch roof and straight into the front room like an accusing finger of God. That finger was pointing right at me and telling me to write it in the manner of a serious news reporter. Instead, I snapped the finger off and began carving it up.

I honed that cut branch into one of the wispiest fly rods you ever laid eyes on. I didn't just lay my eyes on it. I took the rod to my cow-pasture stream, not knowing what to expect, as I hadn't been back there since my early years; down the railroad tracks that were now mostly silent, with barely a whistle still sounding along the horizon. The river had silted with the years. The cattle were fatter and had taken the run of the place, heavy paths leading in one side and out the other. I fished anyway, moving below the sandstone cliffs that had either eroded with time or else were never as large in the first place as I'd remembered from my youth.

The hours rolled by, and my editors wondered where the hell I'd gotten off to. All the other reporters were working double time and having a field day of stories in the aftermath of the storm. I should have felt guilty. I probably should have been fired. Instead, I just fished and, as the sun slanted over the cliffs, sparkling on the pasture grass that was sheered over from the storm, I caught a brown trout that went five pounds if it was an ounce. Maybe the storm had brought it up from the river depths. For all I know, it may have been the last one left in the river. I wrote about building the rod from the storm. I wrote that it was trout destiny that destroyed my tree and my porch. I put that fish front and center. The editors had doubts. They told me I buried the lead story. I guess it wasn't newsworthy as they saw fit. Turned out, it was as famous as I ever got as a writer, because everyone in a fifty-mile radius wanted to know where in the name of creation I caught a trout that big.

I hinted at it, but I never revealed the exact location. I made sure to bury that lead plenty deep. All the other paper stories I've written in my career…well, I don't remember now what they were about. They couldn't have been that important.

I conquered the actual grammar in hard-fought school-room battles. But the way to write it, how to make it your own, winding a story down an ancient river path whose entrance is so choked tight with weeds and vines that others fail to see and simply walk on by; to write as if you are the only one who has seen the vine-covered opening for what it really is; *that* is something not so simple as memorizing grammar and sentence structure. They don't teach it in newspaper school. *That*, I learned on Taconite Creek.

Stories move on. Sometimes they come back. They come back in storied columns like the ones in this newspaper. The Gogebic rise continues, even as I sit on an old stump that spawned a red oak tree and a great story so long ago. Just like a fly-line cast, there is a rhythm to news cycles – angles that need measuring, and political backs that need scratching. Spanning arcs of false casting must take place before an iron mine can spring to life where before there was nothing – nothing but the endless waves from Lake Superior and the swaying of wind in the high pines standing watch.

There's a rhythm on the inside to what you see on the outside. The front page is not the half of it. But if you get down on your belly, crawl through the weeds to the edge, and stare deep into the water; if you get on the inside and slow down and breathe it in, then you get to know it. Then you see what is not so easily written at a news desk.

Uncle Jack and Ernie went down the path of this political mine debate. You might say that they were there before any path existed to go down. They watched the mine executives and the politicians, the environmentalists and the news-types like me who set the whole thing down on paper. Uncle Jack and Ernie were masters at burying the lead. They ran, and the mine companies ran right after them, 'till they all ran out of breath or 'till the evening hatch came on to barter a temporary treaty. Uncle Jack and Ernie: arguing in dizzying circles about political direction and iron, about anything and everything really – but mostly it was about trout fishing.

I'm nothing but a tired reporter whose time has washed away like spent wings. But I was there when a taconite mine met a trout stream. To go back is to go forward. Perhaps that is why I'm still sitting here today. Maybe, just maybe, that's what my cow-pasture stream saved me for – to tell the story, to show both sides of the cast, to get beneath the rings of the Gogebic rise. This stump spawned a good story through my porch, but it holds another ingrained deep.

Taconite Creek. I was there with Uncle Jack and Ernie. I was there to see it, to report it, to remember; I was there to live it. All that remains are newspaper stories of a northern iron mine, and beneath that, the circled ring of a stump. If I could drive a rail spike deep enough into the wood, there may still be a remnant sap of life. It might be enough. I think it might be told.

CHAPTER 3

Uncle Jack howled, "Trout fishing is the highest order of work, but I reckon if they ain't rising from the fields, then you ain't getting paid. By God, I guess there's nothing left for a man but to go out and invest in his future!" It was raw wilderness, and anything was possible in the land.

His first fish was a stunted bass from the farm pond, and how it rose from there to blossom into the rises of the taconite range is akin to speculating on the origins of the universe. He was hooked. The universe has always been. How and why it spiraled out from the first atomic light is the endless quest of scientists, philosophers, and holy men. Some questions are not meant to be known, like how the stunted bass found its way into the stagnant farm pond to begin with. A universe starts in the water. It always starts in the water.

The cold Lake Superior ranges where he grew was an endless setting. He quickly gravitated from the farm ponds, hoofing the northern Wisconsin hills, poking his nose into deep-cut banks where trout lay hidden. He became obsessed, partial especially to the brook trout. The native fish were the ultimate prize, surrendering, even all those years ago, surrendering to modern pressure and retreating further back into the hidden places. Uncle Jack was native like the first and finest of Wisconsin's speckled brethren. Browns and rainbows were dandy, but he would have wrestled a den of bears for a chance to dangle an offering in front of a brook trout.

Fresh out of a whitewashed one-room schoolhouse, a limit of farm-school book learning to complement his miles of trout-stream searching, with all that tucked under his belt, he began to search his way. That's one part of the early story I'm sure about. Some of the rest is shrouded in the mists of time, whose gates are often chancy. Sometimes they open to reveal a profound truth. But, more often, they are locked tight in the chains of stories.

Only once did I visit the old farmstead where he grew up. It was a cold and windy October day, trout streams long since closed for the season, the brook trout long since moved on. The farm pond was shallow and green and skimmed with first ice. The ramshackle barn had fallen to seed, along with the remains of the schoolhouse where he learned. Even the old country church on the hill, where he claimed to have been forcibly marched every Sunday morning whether the mayflies were hatching or not, even the church with rusted relics of organ pipes and the weathered grave stones of a fenced cemetery had long ago faded to silence. It started there, his universe and mine, too. That was only once. That was long ago. Then it moved on.

"The future it is." Uncle Jack was done howling now. He was, in fact, very stoic about it. "Seeing that my crabby old man told me I had to either start pulling my weight on the farm or get a job," he added, volume slowly increasing. "Took away my rod and flies and buried them behind the barn – said I couldn't have them back until I found something!" He was howling again.

He never took to farm life. Not that he minded getting up early, sweating hard under the blazing sun, or tromping back from some far pasture wood lot under the dark of the moon. He'd keep pace with the heartiest of farm hands as long as there was a winding stream and he pushed a fly rod in front of him instead of a plow. If there had been a trout stream running through the barn, then just maybe things would have worked out differently. But farmland never called to his soul like the wildness of the northern hills.

Along with the daily struggles taking place along the pastured field and cattle grazing valleys of the northern Wisconsin fence farms, the Great Depression was really one of the only other things working at the time. It was rolling into a full and inglorious downward swing, and there was a daunting lack of work in the cities; which wasn't exactly paramount to Uncle Jack. He wouldn't have donned a jacket and tie and sat behind a desk. He would have starved instead.

He was stubborn and lean, a set jaw and a fanatic gleam shining in his blue eyes, cropped hair that may have started light brown but was bleached from the sun until it streaked bone white. He carried the air of a hardened traveler. He'd stalk a country mile on his belly in stinging nettles, crawling into the streambed to wait it out if that's what it took. If he was going to be prodded to hook a job, it would be on his own bullish terms. Having his fishing gear buried under cow manure in the back-forty simply pushed him to an extreme measure.

"Farm life is the path to righteousness," his father said. "Work harder, not smarter, go to church on Sundays."

Uncle Jack furrowed his brow. "I thought it was the other way around without the church part thrown in. I've almost got it narrowed down to the edge of the hayfield or the back of the milk house. I'm getting tired of digging holes."

"Then take a break and get your smart ass in the truck. We're headed to Ashland to straggle together enough seed to keep the place running."

They made the trip from farm country to Ashland, feeling the coolness of Lake Superior before they topped the last rise, coming over birch and maple-lined roads of red clay, ridges looming dark-pined into nowhere on either side. Wooden shipping piers stretched out to meet the cold mist and waves breaking on the shore. The city spread before them like a gray and many-pocketed overcoat on the lake shore, streets winding narrow into mazes of houses and mercantile.

His father speculated over hay seed prices, standing with fallen companions on the foreclosed-farm auction circuit, looking to find anything of value springing from the harshness of a country more suited to growing red clay than to growing crops. Uncle Jack, meanwhile, speculated on three more places to prospect for his fly rod, wandering through the lake-chilled city, wandering from the seed barrels and store-front railings where his father pounded fists and stomped work boots with like-minded brethren.

He literally bumped into fate, running headlong into a neatly dressed man wearing a suit and tie in front of a sporting goods store window, where, insult to injury, there was a fine display of trout fishing tackle. The man scattered sheaves of paper from his hands and across the sidewalk when Uncle Jack bowled into him. "Excuse me, I wasn't paying attention to where I was headed," Uncle Jack said, helping pick up a jumble of papers that were scrawled full of numbers. Not that he noticed the numbers, intent as he was on the sporting display.

"Quite alright, I was rather admiring these fish poles in the window myself," the stranger said. "I was just musing over sneaking out of the office, getting back, and seeing the land and the water, seeing where it comes from. Why, I believe I might put a clearer picture with the margins and profits. I believe there may be something to gain."

"Fish poles? Oh, you mean the fly rods. I know what you mean. Damn things are expensive. I used to have a dandy one. If I could ever find it again, I wouldn't mind getting back into the land and water myself – get a clearer picture on a mess of leaping trout – that's what I'd do!"

"Some of my bosses are quite the anglers themselves. They do fly off to quite exotic locations and have extensive collections of poles – I mean – of rods. I'd say they're quite reasonably priced. Money is really no obstacle, don't you know."

"Money sure isn't an obstacle. I don't have any. My only problems are getting a job and digging through about forty acres of crap to find my own sorry gear. Say, if money's no obstacle for you, what kind of business are you in anyway?"

"Iron," said the man, pointing down the narrow street. "Our offices are right here in town. If you look down the hill, right over the National Bank and through the mist down to the water, you can see them sitting above the docks."

A suite of office buildings hulked above the ore docks, paint peeling and downtrodden as if the offices themselves were slowly shifting, sliding like a bank of iron clay into the waters of Superior. The docks and iron processing station in Ashland were one of many that dotted the northern and southern shores of Lake Superior, from Michigan to Minnesota and like a swath through the tip of Wisconsin. They'd sprung up like brown weeds since the turn of the century, spawning reaping strip mine pits slowly across the logged-over glacier hills.

The easy picking of the open pit iron, like the lumber before it, was running dry. The iron was still there, waiting to be chipped away from the wilderness. It was difficult to locate in the vast reaches, expensive to find and expensive to reach. The leaner it got, the harder the shareholders of mine-held interest pushed, desperate to suck every penny, nickel, and especially every mighty dollar from the mine infrastructure plants that were already in existence along the Superior coast's mining cities. The mine companies reached out to the land in ever-increasing circles.

"I bet you've seen some good fishing out there, digging those iron holes," Uncle Jack said.

"I don't believe it works exactly that way. Don't quote me on it, because I'm seldom in the field. I'm stuck in the office, gauging iron quality, adding up prices, brokering land – quite a dull chore. They just don't make the iron land like they used to. Not that I'm naïve enough to think they make new land, understand. There just aren't any easy deposits left. I bet if I could bring in a few of these trout that you talk about, show them around the office, impress the bosses, why, I'd prove myself above and beyond. Exploring new options, I'd say. Maybe even garner a promotion."

"I can't guarantee you a promotion," Uncle Jack said. "But I know exactly what you mean about impressing the boss. My dad's a hard nut to crack. Tell you what: For an even dollar, I'll bring you to the best trout hole in the area. How 'bout Sunday? You're not a real religious churchgoer, are you? Bring a Bible if you want, Providence will supply the rest. Course, you got to provide the fishing equipment, too."

Possibly believing his father would count a budding fish-guiding career as worthy of unburying a fly rod; or possibly believing that sitting behind a desk all day, the executive pencil-pusher would find the rigors of trout fishing too demanding and surrender freshly-bought gear to Uncle Jack in a face-saving trade to bring home bragging trout for the boardroom table; whatever the motive, Uncle Jack guided the executive back to a lovely chain of hidden beaver ponds. Maybe the timing was right, or maybe he just got lucky. But I believe he sensed it like a trout before a growing storm. The harried front-office iron executive wasn't a fisherman, but Uncle Jack smelled a hatch coming on.

Prodding his rookie through the brush and up over a beaver-guarded pool, Uncle Jack showed him where and showed him how. Leaping, spotted beauties were taken on the lashing casts of a mining official who had never before bent a fly rod and had stolen gaudy-tied imitations from his wife's hatband to boot. Both men skipped church, and there was no Bible, but secretive brook trout changed hands, and a baptism took place in the pooled water of those beaver dams.

The convert couldn't load a cast to save his soul but, with Uncle Jack's help, there would be a limit of bragging rights for the spectacled and bow-tied executive to spill out at the next shareholder meeting. As far as Uncle Jack's budding career was concerned, and fortunately for Uncle Jack's fishing gear (buried right beneath the entrance to the country church, the last place Uncle Jack would be tempted to look), it would be something more than brook trout front and center on the stage.

What Uncle Jack's prodigy lacked in fishing skills, he made up in something else, and it started Uncle Jack rolling down the taconite rails. The mine brass, prodded by the higher powers to reach deep into the ore reserves of the northern hills, was loaded to the gills with the knowledge of a certain rock formation. Iron rocks collided with fate and began rolling down the slopes into the waters of history. While walking home off the stream through a deep and rocky valley in the twilight gloom, Uncle Jack's client excitedly began jumping up and down, his cut-branch stringer of brook trout keeping rhythm and jumping up and down with him.

"What the hell! Is it a bear or a wolf?" Uncle Jack shouted. "Don't let him get at our trout!"

"No, it's nothing like that – it's fiercer than that! Look at that jagged outcropping of red rock. It appears to be pure-grade taconite ore!"

"What's the big deal? I've found a ton of that junk hidden back in the hills. Don't poke at it with your rod, for God's sake. You'll bust the tip off, then I won't – I mean, you won't – be able to catch another limit next Sunday."

The hiring interview was that quick, with Uncle Jack's only references being brook trout on a wood-pole stringer and a pile of red rocks. Trout fable or not, no one knows for sure. Even the gates of time are unclear on the exact location of those beaver ponds or that first pile of taconite rock. But before the week was up, Uncle Jack retrieved his fly-fishing gear from the church yard burial ground. The sunset threw a final glow on the hayfield fences behind him as he walked into the rolling wilderness of the Lake Superior range. Uncle Jack had a gleam in his eye and a plan in his heart. A taconite career was born.

CHAPTER 4

By all accounts, it went well initially; the first operations being nowhere near a trout stream. Uncle Jack carved tracks into arrays of iron rock. He surveyed routes, freighting the ore out. He guided trains to their destination and rode ore-laden boxcars out of virgin wilderness and onto the Ashland ore docks. He scrawled locations on a map, symbols and secrets on taconite-dusted parchment, decipherable to no one else. He cashed in his trout-rambling discoveries and deposited them to the waiting holds of deep lake freighters. But it was only a down payment on his future.

A network of rail routes crept like clutching fingers over the high hills and through the shadowed valleys. Eventually, they branched out to cross some mighty promising water. Uncle Jack rode the boxcars, looking over the high pines and the tangled swamps with a far-seeing eye. That's when the first signs of trouble started. That's when his investment really began to pay dividends.

He bounced atop the trains in a pair of hip boots. He paced across the train tops like a tiger, powdered taconite rising from the freight cars in clouds. The other rail-men and miners chided him. "Aren't you hot in them boots, Jack? You look like a damn fool up there! If you fall and get rolled under the wheels, it'll be just like hitting a stray dog in the dead of the night. The company ain't going to care; they'll get themselves another bloodhound. Hell, we could just as easily go in there and find them rocks ourselves."

Uncle Jack clutched his folded map in his hands. There was a battered copper compass that opened like a snuff box dangling from a cord around his neck. He was seldom seen without either. Clambering around on the ore-topped piles of the freight trains, the map and compass became as much a part of his character as his boots.

"Well now boys," he shouted from the train top. "I don't care to have all this taconite dust clinging to my feet. Don't want to track it all over the countryside and leave a mess of footprints to follow. It would take the fun out of it for you. Pick a direction, put your noses to the trail, and have at it. And say, you best tell your wives not to expect you home for dinner!"

He grew into an iconic figure, hip boots crunching, compass dangling, and map in hand. He waved merrily to residents of small, outland farm towns that the ore trains passed through. Everyone started calling him Hip Boot Jack. It was harmless frivolity. The mine company thought it was great publicity.

No one knows how he secreted his fly rod. He was never seen carrying it to work. But soon, there it was, on any given day, especially when the clouds hung low and the breeze brought in the rich smell of watery places. The fly rod appeared in his hand atop the train like a scepter in the hands of a ruling lord. He'd hang low down the side of the moving train, with his rod tucked deftly and cinders burning black brands along his boot seams.

It happened above pine-pitch river bridges. It happened at deep-bend cuts where the rail grade dropped sharply and dark water wound into floating garden swamps. Uncle Jack was atop the train one moment, and the next he was gone, ore dust floating in the air and an iron-stained boot print vanishing into the stream.

The company started having second thoughts about harmless frivolity. Uncle Jack claimed he'd seen promising visions. "Prospecting, I was prospecting. To see the ore, you have to be the ore," he told his bosses, giving them a mysterious and close-lipped stare that is usually reserved for mystics and liars. Passing shift crews reported hearing phantom whish-whish singing sounds echoing along the rails.

Soft darkness found whippoorwills calling and Hip Boot Jack flagging down a late passing train to catch a ride back to town. Some nights he had a buck-tailed hook or a heavy wooly bugger snagged in his flannels. He'd smell suspiciously of trout. No train crew ever recalled seeing a fly rod when they'd pick him off the darkening rail bridges.

Understandably, the mine powers eventually wanted dividends on Uncle Jack's mystic prospecting. It was inevitable that he was summoned to an accounting review before the company board in Ashland.

It was the height of a sultry wet summer, and humidity hung thick every morning. There were pool-splashing rains. Water levels rose and, at night, the mist rose from the waters where Hip Boot Jack worked his trade. The air could be cut with a knife, and the weather had set the brown trout on a feeding frenzy. They came dark and thick like the humidity, smashing flies from first light till the mist of night pulled blankets over the swirling pools. Uncle Jack was twitching involuntarily when he walked the trains; twitching with the abandon of a marabou streamer pulled sharp and tight along jungle-grown banks.

He was sullen and sorrowful when he pulled out of the field and headed into town. The smaller creeks that held the promise of brook trout had been low and unfishable for a long time. The rain kept coming as Uncle Jack sniffed the wet air. "By God, it sure smells like brook trout in the frying pan," he said, licking his lips as he watched the dark water rise in the swamps. He sulked to town like a man being led to the hanging gallows.

"We've gone over the totals of the ore deposits you've brought in so far," the board members told him. "It's not that they weren't good, you understand. It's just that they're running a little dry. We thought there would be...ah...well...a little more. You know, with all the prospecting."

"A little dry?" said Uncle Jack, "I'd say it's a little wet, but otherwise it's perfect. I think I know a place." He stared out the window at the summer rain. He was lost in thought, and he was concentrating hard. I doubt that any of the board members even suspected he was doing anything but working for the cause.

Not wanting to leave the weather-spun fishing unchecked, Uncle Jack pitched an idea to the company; a stretch of rock down a swamp-tangled stream. The rock cropped up in a red-veined freak of nature from the bottoms, about a half-mile back from the main track line. The stream was usually no more than a spring-fed trickle, but it was rolling in tantalizing glory after all the rain. Uncle Jack had been saving it for just such an occasion.

"I'll take full charge," Uncle Jack told the board. "It can't miss!"

The rock was wallowing in the swamp just like Uncle Jack had foretold: high-grade taconite, too. The initial quality tests came back from the lab, and the company gave Uncle Jack the go-ahead. The iron was there, indeed; sitting for the taking along the creek, with water levels rising just about to Uncle Jack's liking. The taconite was never the issue.

"Really, how many times in our life are trout jumping like that in the middle of the day? I'm not a weather man, mind you, but I sure thought it was a good omen."

That was after the mine company cooled off and decided not to fire him.

"I'm not a biologist – not really a mineral expert, either," he added. "How was I to know that taconite sprouted up over quicksand?"

The dark water from the alder swamp looked promising, brook-trout water if Uncle Jack had ever laid eyes on it. But the mine company was livid when hundreds of dollars in rails and cross-ties went down in the rising bog, not to mention a freight car careening into the muck that couldn't be pulled out until the autumn frost hardened the ground.

Uncle Jack wasn't happy, either. He'd tried everything – coarse-tied egg nymphs to home-plucked chicken feathers wrapped around a hook. He even resorted to canned corn. He overturned logs and rocks looking for bait. He failed to strike a single trout on the creek. He didn't even catch a chub.

The mine company must have had an inkling of Uncle Jack's ulterior motives, but they weren't ready to pull the plug. The lure of the steel-wrought dollar was too strong. Instead, they gave him Ernie. It was like matching a custom fly rod with the perfect reel. Unfortunately for the iron mines of northern Wisconsin, it was also like kerosene on an open flame.

CHAPTER 5

Ernie's first words set the stage for mighty things. It was an innocuous way to start a journey towards a majestic pinnacle.

"I studied dem rocks at da Finlander College."

Uncle Jack was duly impressed. "Well I studied rocks too – if you call picking them out of the back-forty formal training. I hope you studied those rocks in Finland harder than you studied English grammar."

The mine company foreman stood like a referee between the two men.

"Ernie, meet Hip Boot Jack. Jack, this is Ernie. From this day forward, the company thinks it's in the best industrial interest for you two to work together."

"My best work is done solo and in secret!" Uncle Jack shouted. "I was born with one shadow and I sure as hell don't need another one. It's not natural."

Ernie looked at Uncle Jack's boots. "I hope dat shadow of yours is not particular 'bout tromping 'round in dose tings all day. I tink if I vas dat shadow, I'd move damn fast in da opposite vay."

"You should both give it a shot, I think," the boss mustered in his best diplomatic voice. "Jack, you need someone to – how should I put it – to pick you out of mud a little when the going gets tough. Ernie's been here working on the docks ever since he got off of the passenger ferry. He's a damn fine worker and mechanic. He can fix anything, and he has an uncanny understanding of iron ore. He's wasting his talent loading freighters. It's exactly what the doctor, not to mention the mine stakeholders, ordered. You two will make a fine team."

"Absolutely not!" groused Uncle Jack. "I can't even understand half of what he's saying. I need to move fast and far, and he looks like he can't do either one. The sun is on the move and time's a wasting. I got a taconite train to catch. Good day to you, and good luck!" Uncle Jack tipped his hat to Ernie, spun his hip boots around, and began stalking off.

"I tink I vill take a cut in pay and stay verking on da docks and talk to da iron ore," said Ernie. "It is less noisy and more intelligent. Good day and good luck to your boots and your shadow!"

The mine boss shed all semblance of diplomacy. His face got red, and there was a glow in his eyes. He squared his shoulders, pointing one finger at Uncle Jack and one finger at Ernie. It looked like he was pulling pistols and pointing them in opposite directions. It looked like he lived for these moments of truth.

"You might as well tell the train to drop you back on the farm. I'm sure all those cattle stalls are just hollering out for a good cleaning" he said to Uncle Jack. "And you might as well get on that ore boat when you're done loading it and float it back to whatever school, or college, or wherever it is you came from," he said to Ernie. "That's where you're both going if you don't make this work. Good day and good luck – to both of you!" Pistols fired, the mine boss was gone into the sunset of his office.

Ernie and Uncle Jack were left standing together, staring at one another on the ore docks with red iron dust coming off the piles in whirlwinds and settling on the cold waves of Superior.

"Well, well," said Uncle Jack. "So you studied rocks? Or was the whole university built out of rock? I'm a little confused as to the wording – not to mention understanding your actual words."

"Vell, vell. You vill have plenty of time coming to figure dat vun for yourself."

Uncle Jack shook his head. "Well, well. I was afraid you'd say that."

Ernie had the rough bearded look of a farmer and the aura of a wizened grizzly bear. His talk was simple, his philosophy profound, and any doubts about his geological schooling were overshadowed by the fact that he was a mechanical genius. He spoke with the thick accent of his home country, and words changed when he spoke. They harvested into the English language from something more colorful and vibrant: Words like that, the, and those became dat, da, and dose. They became day, and there became dare. Thing was ting and will was vill. Complex sentences were not necessary when Ernie spoke. But if you listened closely, his thoughts came to life. You were never sure you were getting the whole story, but you always got it with a Finnish flair.

What exactly the Finlander Rock College was, or if it ever existed at all, *that* is a debatable matter. Ernie's home country was a tough place to attend a university. In fact, it was tough to simply eke out a living. The short season in Finland was said to be spring, summer, and fall blended into one blink of the eye. The rest of the year was devoted to winter. A large majority of its people were cold, hungry, and poor. Not exactly a conducive recipe for spires of higher learning.

What the country did possess were uncountable numbers of shimmering lakes and tributary streams springing through blankets of dense pine and birch forest. Ernie's home university was divided from Uncle Jack's wilderness ramparts by an ocean, but the two environments were hauntingly similar.

The iron was similar, too. In Finland, it was called bog ore. When Ernie floated into Ashland on a passenger boat, he landed at the iron ore docks. His past may have been lost in discreet shadows, but he knew about the iron. In the bogs and streams of Finland, an iron-rich rock sprung from beneath the waters themselves. Smelted down, it was pure iron ore with a grade so similar to taconite that the two could have been brothers save for a few chemical notations on the periodic table.

Maybe Ernie held an accredited degree from a foreign university. Uncle Jack knew more about Ernie's past than anyone, but he never said for certain, preferring to vocalize doubt every chance he got and keep everyone in earshot guessing about what he called "the hidden lies" of his partner's credentials.

I'd guess that Ernie made his start in the world reaping bog iron from the native wilds of his country. If he chose to call it a university, it would not be an unreasonable stretch. It wouldn't be any more unreasonable than the liberal fish-farm interpretation of Uncle Jack's iron-ore background. Bog ore or taconite; they were simply different paths to the same thing. What Ernie found in the bogs and streams of Finland was no different than what Uncle Jack found in the far reaches of Wisconsin. Fish lived along with the bog iron in Finland, just as they lived alongside Uncle Jack's taconite.

The sun set over Lake Superior and shone red on the stretching ore docks of the Ashland waterfront. The last rays held a glint of light from a twisted strand of fur and feather. It was tied around a sharpened hook, and it was stuck above Ernie's flannelled shirt pocket.

It caught Uncle Jack's eye as they walked from the shoreline. "What the heck you got tangled in your shirt?"

"Some-ting I been verking on. A fly, it is for catching fish."

"You don't say?"

"I been using dis one for catching big lake trout off da docks."

Uncle Jack smiled at Ernie for the first time. "You don't say? Have you hatched any other creations when you were supposed to be working?"

Ernie pointed at the map tucked in the breast pocket of Uncle Jack's own flannel. He snapped a thick finger at the compass around Uncle Jack's neck. "Vut are dose?"

"A map and compass, I guess they probably ain't invented them in Finland yet. They're for finding places."

Ernie's eyes widened in mock surprise: "Dat's amazing! How many places you find ven you vas supposed to be verking?"

"I've only found a couple."

"Good. I only make couple of flies, too."

They walked from the gloom of the ore docks and towards the open and waiting hills. If you didn't know that they had been born on separate sides of an ocean and that they really didn't care for one another, you could almost have sworn they were walking arm in arm.

I learned this on Taconite Creek, and that was a long time ago. Magnetic force separates iron from taconite rock. And it was magnetic force that drew Ernie and Uncle Jack together.

CHAPTER 6

Ernie came through. He did more – he steamrolled into the lore of Wisconsin's iron mining history with the sauna train. It was more than just a train. It was a gateway into the reaches of Taconite Creek.

Ernie conceived the idea one night in the sauna shack he'd built on a small rise overlooking the Ashland ore docks. The sauna itself was simple enough, nothing more than a wood-burning stove with rocks piled on top, a bench, and a barrel of water. Wood smoke rolled across the shore in the coming night breeze; the face of the sun poised to burn into the western horizon of the lake. There was something majestic in the simplicity.

Ernie's sauna had become a popular place for the mine workers to wash the ore dust and grime from their day's labors. In return, they hauled in birch, jack pine, and oak logs, splitting them and piling them until shavings and stacks of wood ringed the outside walls. Ernie's acquaintances trudged from the mines and docks to stoke the stove with pine and birch. Scented smoke rose across the docks like a dinner bell, wafting to the Ore Dock Saloon, a back-water eating and drinking establishment in Ashland sitting just downwind of Ernie's sauna shack. Barrels got tapped and tables wiped down as the men took their steam baths.

The men never touched the oak, as was agreed upon in the unwritten sauna-usage contract. They contented themselves with the quick-burning and more moderate heat of the softer wood. They'd wash up in the warming sauna, fill the water barrel from the lake shore below, and disappear, new and fresh, to fill their own barrels in the saloon. Ernie gave his friends first dibs on the sauna, partly due to his good nature, partly due to the fact that he wouldn't roll in until the last trout stopped biting, but mainly so the stove was burning just right when he got there.

He'd arrive after the nighthawks and bats were sounding along the shore, stuff the wood stove to the breaking point with oak, stow his fishing gear, and straighten up the wood pile for a few minutes, waiting till the time got right. Then he'd saunter into what he called "Da real sauna!"

On a given night, it was anybody's guess what heated merriment the swinging doors of the Ore Dock Saloon would reveal for Ernie's pals. But through the doors of "Da real sauna," after he got it going to his liking, the environment rivaled the gates of hell. Scalding water and steam washed away Ernie's sins, along with the taconite dust and trout scales. His sauna bath was a ritual cleansing, where, as he put it: "A man sweats out all da clutter in his head to make room for da mysteries of life."

Indeed, many a great thought was sweat out of Ernie's head in that simple sauna shack overlooking the peeling ore docks and piles of iron ore along the Superior shore. To hear him tell it, the sauna train was the pinnacle. "Vell, I sit on da bench sveating good. It vas a hot fire, and I pour darn near da whole barrel of vater over da rocks. Dat steam, it's really piling out. I'm sveating really good you bettcha, da oak logs vas crackling and popping and den it just popped out of my brain – why not make da engine run like da sauna?"

Ernie's sauna train was born in a steam-induced Eureka moment. He locked himself up in his shop for the better part of the winter, coming down to the docks occasionally for wheelbarrows full of cast-off taconite that hadn't made the final quality cut. There were special orders from the hardware store: bolts and rivets, sheets of steel and copper tubing. He made long forays into the farm country to talk to the farmers about their tractors. Pounding hammers and clanging steel rang over the Ashland shores till far into the night. It was a simple concept, but putting it together was something only the likes of Eli Whitney, Albert Einstein, or Ernie could accomplish.

When the banging and the clanging and the steam finally settled, iron-hard taconite rocks rested atop a wood burner with a large vat of water suspended above. Water fed from the vat and over the rocks. A steel case was hinged over the stove, trapping the steam and channeling it through ever-narrowing copper tubing until it was released in a hissing jet to turn the train pistons.

The train was compact, riding on big rubber wheels and burning any type of available wood. Hardwood was best, and the men who used Ernie's sauna were soon hard pressed to keep the oak woodpiles stocked. It reached a point where they started to think about taking their baths in the cold waters of Lake Superior rather than buck wood to keep the train running. Homesteaders of the back-country between Ashland and Superior soon learned to keep any lumber, or chairs and tables for that matter, safely out of sight when Ernie's train came chugging into view.

It was the talk of the Ore Dock Saloon on the day the sauna train was unveiled. Ernie rolled it out of his woodshed workshop, and all the iron miners piled out of the saloon to see the creation. Uncle Jack stalked out too, pacing around the train, stroking his chin with thumb and forefinger. Ernie followed, arms crossed, and looking every bit the part of an auto dealer ready to overcome a buyer's objections. Uncle Jack outpaced

Ernie, or maybe Ernie simply stopped to wait for him to circle around. They ended up facing each other with hands held at their sides like two duelers ready to have a go at it.

"Well, the steam engine's already been invented, so you're a little late there," said Uncle Jack. "But if there's ever a market opening for a steam bath on wheels, then I reckon you're going to be rich."

"Vell, maybe I get rich, but I know one ting for sure," Ernie said.

"What's that?" growled Uncle Jack.

"I vill not be cutting rail ties and hammering down track. I save dat for you. You picked rocks at da farming university – probably your back is used to dat kind of verk."

"I ain't doing all the hard stuff while you sit back and polish this here contraption," said Uncle Jack. "You got to pitch in. We're supposed to be a team, even though I ain't sure which side you're playing for."

Ernie kicked one of the train's tires, and it echoed like a bass drum. He waggled a finger at Uncle Jack like a schoolteacher making a point with a struggling student. "Ya, but see da veels for dis train are rubber, yust like dem big tractors. Dis here train don't need no tracks."

The mine executives had come out to the ore docks to see the unveiling, too. They huddled in tight circles of conspiracy, discussing the possibilities. A faraway look came into Uncle Jack's eyes. He was discussing the possibilities in a tight-circled conference room of his own.

The oversized, hard-knobbed wheels were grooved on the bottom. They could run on rails if they had to, and the train's engine had the power to pull a fully loaded car of iron ore. But as a reconnaissance vehicle, it was far above anything yet conceived in the taconite range country. The heavy wheels and the sauna engine were capable of carrying the train through the roughest terrain the North Country could set forth.

Wooden ties and steel rails weren't necessary, so the potential of time and money to be saved – at least on paper – really intrigued the mine executives. There were places the sauna train could roll into that a conventional train engine would find unreachable. Steep ridges and bog swamps hid pathways to untold mining possibilities. And once these remote taconite strikes were located, track beds didn't need to be graded and reinforced for the weight of a conventional locomotive. There would be no repeat performance of Uncle Jack's quicksand debacle. The mine heads doubtless brought up that point as they huddled in conference. The nods of approval among the suits and ties amounted to a majority.

Uncle Jack never glanced at the suit-clad men. As far as a majority was concerned, he was voting in the trout-filled boardroom of his own mind. With the power of a tank, the train could pull through a cedar swamp. Cedar swamps, along with deep running rivers of the rocky persuasion; those were what most intrigued Uncle Jack as he walked around, kicking at the wheels of Ernie's train. The unreachable places the train might discover along the seeping undercut banks of dark running trout streams.

"All right Ernie, you've sold me on it. You do the driving. I'll ride shotgun and navigate. But I tell you right now, if she starts on fire and tips over in the swamp, I'm bailing out like a rat off a sinking ship."

The train was accepted into their partnership, and the taconite rails switched into high gear. It's misted into the stream of time on how long exactly, just as a hard fought trout season can blend into the next year, or the next one after that, with only a winter's pause to remember. But one thing was certain. Taconite ore flew out of previously unreachable stretches and filled waiting freighters to the waterline along the Ashland docks.

Uncle Jack was a fine surveyor, clad in his boots, compass around his neck, map in one hand and a fly rod in the other. Ernie steamed the train around the thickest of trout-barring obstacles, tying flies as the sauna engine stoked, keeping her slow and steady. The two men developed sophisticated routes. They developed even more sophisticated reasons why all the taconite seemed to be found in the vicinity of trout.

The sauna train rolled, cobbling out a wealth of taconite rock along a network of hidden water. There were no checks and balances in place, so a collision was a matter of time. There were warning signs, and if they had been heeded by anyone save the working men of the far reaching iron mines, then the story may have unfolded differently. But the mine company was making money, and money is the ultimate blind spot to impending disaster. The other mine workers had a better nose for what was in the air. They smelled Taconite Creek coming in the wind. The bridge incident simply blew the rippling waters into a frothy torrent. It showed what two men and a train were really capable of as a team.

And after the Bad River Bridge, nobody much wanted any share of Uncle Jack and Ernie.

CHAPTER 7

Uncle Jack explained the story after it came out in the *Ashland Telegram* – the finest purveyor of northern news in those days.

"You know, technically, it wasn't even the Bad River we put the bridge over. It was below the forks in the river where the Bad flows into the White River. That's where the bridge went up on account of some high-priced, college-boy rock surveyor who was too lazy and too Finnish to walk above the forks where it was shallower. So the paper has it all wrong."

Ernie's take on the matter differed. "No, it *vas* da Bad River, I tink your memory is going bad as your casting. And if you had layed off da fishing and kept in on da verking, it vouldn't matter in da first place. None of dis vould have happened, and dare's no vay dat bridge vould have burned down. I didn't know you look at any more except da funny paper section of da newspaper besides."

Ernie and Uncle Jack tossed countless hooks at each other. But they were barbless hooks designed to slip free in an instant. I came to understand that it was all part of their greater plan. They were Yin and Yang. No one could ever figure who was Yin and who was Yang; who was light and who was dark. Their arguments were as arbitrary as calling out the name of a different fork on the same river, and depended substantially on who was fishing what fork and who was busy running up the other one and making excuses for his partner's absence.

Together, Uncle Jack and Ernie combined to produce a finely-tuned show, like one of those back-alley street games with a marble under a cup, the cups swirled around on the table by a magician, reversed and reversed again until it becomes so confusing that no one, especially the mine bosses, could ever keep it straight. The paper reported the facts as they knew them, but the problem was this: There were only two men who knew the whole story, and they preferred to remain anonymous and hidden beneath the ever-changing cups.

Ernie was chief engineer in charge of putting a bridge over the Bad River; that's what Uncle Jack said. Ernie, meanwhile, said Uncle Jack spouted off about being the crew chief to anyone in earshot, "so dat's what da hip-booted rascal must have been." It was quite convoluted. The only solid fact was that the river was a barrier along a necessary line of transport for the taconite track line. Ernie's train might have been the ultimate in bush-whacking transportation, but it was not a submarine. Mighty Lake

Superior tributaries could still pour enough water on the engine's rocks to stop it cold.

Anyone with sense enough to be in charge of building a bridge would have picked a shallow ford where a train could plod through with a minimum of effort. Instead, whoever was in charge – and truth be told, this one was a joint decision – opted for a deeper crossing, tossing in railroad ties along the banks and dumping in some two tons of railroad gravel to create a private spawning ground. Both men were well ahead of their time in that sort of trout-habitat management. They figured on hoarding the structure for Lake Superior browns that ran upriver in the fall. Some of the iron spots on those fish were the size of half-dollars.

The bridge was serious business, gracefully arched and shingled with cedar planking. Ernie thought it should be covered so he could park the train out of any inclement late-autumn weather; keeping the sauna stove burning for hand-warming breaks between the cold-weather landings of big trout. Uncle Jack kept the bridge construction crew occupied while the thieved rail ties and gravel were dumped in the river. He barked orders to pound foundations into the stream bed at the proper angles, sermonizing on how exactly to slope the covered roof to keep the winter snow from piling and caving it in. The air pulsated with profanity, and Uncle Jack gave off the general air that he knew details of bridge construction that the common man did not, even though he'd never built anything more technical than a wood shed. He kept the construction crew on edge, diverting attention from the real engineering taking place.

It would have painted a Norman Rockwell portrait: A fly fisherman holding a wicker creel and fighting a leaping fish; a rustic covered bridge highlighted in the background. If the picture was set in autumn when the big browns were running, with bright red leaves from the ash trees dotting the river valley and tamaracks turning golden – it would have been that more satisfying a scene.

But Hip Boot Jack couldn't quite wait until autumn. The closer the bridge got to completion, the itchier his line-stripping fingers became. He had to try a cast or two into the created fish factory. It was like grabbing a piece of an apple pie while it cooled on a window sill. It was too much to resist. He waited cagily till Ernie ran the sauna train back to Ashland one afternoon, bringing the early-shift workers home on a flatcar and picking up the late crew. It was late July with plenty of light hanging in the western sky and a full moon slated to rise. It would be a good night to work late. The bridge was almost done. Nobody remembered leaving a fly rod behind when the train left.

"No, I'll stay here and keep driving posts, Ernie. Take your time bringing the next set of men from Ashland. Go on and have a cool drink. Physical labor doesn't bother me like it bothers you. You got that fair skin, too – don't want you getting sun-burned. No Ernie, take your time. I'll keep working till you get back."

The second shift arrived in the flatcar to find a shovel stuck hastily in the ground, a post-hole pounder strewn down the bank, and Uncle Jack missing. On the surface, this was nothing out of the ordinary scope of affairs. The bridge workers might have been rough and tumble, but they were fully capable of reasoning matters out. They'd seen Hip Boot Jack swing down with a fly rod from a full moving train. Leaping off a standing bridge was nothing. Ernie was a little miffed. He figured Uncle Jack would come strolling in around quitting time, no sign of a fly rod on his person, but still managing a stringer full of trout in Ernie's face.

By ten o'clock, Uncle Jack had still not arrived. Some of the men worried a little, but Ernie could have cared less. He just wanted to be on his way, back to his sauna and his deep thoughts. The darker it got, with the moon coming full and the mist rising over the rushing water, the more nervous the men became, and the more Ernie began steaming like the wood burner on his train. Ernie was all for leaving him behind.

"I tink it vould serve him right to valk da ten miles home. I don't care if it is bear country. I don't feel sorry for him. I feels sorry for da bears, dat's who's I feels sorry for."

The men bent over the bridge railing and contemplated starting a search party. They marveled at how deep the river cut beneath the graveled beds below the bridge, peering intently over the side, looking for a hip-booted floating body or, at the very least, a floating map and compass.

Ernie, meanwhile, piled wood into the sauna engine and got her going red hot. He throttled the train forward, pulling the flat-car onto the nearly completed bridge. He let out one long blast from the steam engine, standing atop the train with arms folded in disgust while the rest of the men milled nervously like pacing deer. Then, with a smug grin, satisfied that he'd tried his best in a search party effort, he bade the men to climb on the flat car. His eyes and hands were intent on swinging the train around in an open clearing that sloped conveniently and dangerously down to the river bottom. It was the exact clearing, which until quite recently, had housed a load of fish-covering rail ties and about two tons of spawning gravel. He never quite made the turn.

Hip Boot Jack came around the upstream bend while Ernie was piling men onto the train. He was bent over at the waist and splashing after a monster brown. The fish was pulling him this way and that, running in tugboat bursts and really giving him the business. The brown was deep-bellied and looked like it might easily red-line a weighing scale.

Uncle Jack told it one way. "The big devil wanted to get back upstream in a hurry! There's thick brush up there at the shallows along the bank where he'd wallowed out of the roots to take my buck-tail streamer. But I wouldn't let him get back into that mess. He tried to dart between my legs, but I snubbed him. Then he decided to take off down to Lake Superior. I just went along for the ride."

Never heard the whistle, that's what he claimed. "Damned if I heard anything but that big trout snorting water. I was occupied. You know, concentrating. Why that crazy Finn wanted to go and blow that whistle and scare up all them deer is beyond me."

"Jack in dem hip boots, svearing big feesh dis and big feesh dat. Hollering and splashing. Dat's vut scared da deer." That was Ernie's take on the matter.

Somewhere between the two sides is where the truth lies. Somewhere between Uncle Jack's playing out of a big brown trout and Ernie blowing the whistle and ramming the train off the bridge. Somewhere in those tense moments, a herd of deer erupted from their stream-side browsing and scattered up the rail grade.

Ernie's attention was divided between swinging the train off the bridge and the spectacle of the fishing battle going on below. He didn't see the deer until the men on the flatcar started yelling. Then he saw them, alright, but not before he felt them first. They ran rampant behind the train in the moonlight as he turned the wheel sharp. He missed the majority by cranking the steering for all it was worth but, while power steering may have been invented, it was not a feature included on Ernie's prototype. Deer scattered and men hollered. Hooves and horns flashed across the grade. In the end, there was one deer Ernie didn't miss. It dropped with a *Whack* between the sauna train and the flatcar.

Uncle Jack worked below the bridge where railroad ties yawned over the current and gravel spread into the depths like a rockslide. The sauna train was unscathed, but the flatcar holding the men threw a tie rod, and one of its wheels careened down the side of the steep bank and into the river. Bridge workers spilled over the side with it.

The unfortunate deer wasn't going to make it anyway, but it likely died from shock right then and there. Hip Boot Jack went in over his boots as the train wheel and the men splashed into the river. Despite the chaos, he might have avoided a late-night swim, but he tripped on a rail tie that had been buried particularly deep by him and his partner. Uncle Jack bobbed through the run and under the bridge with rod upended like a periscope.

The only one making it clear of the carnage was the monster brown, leaping high into the air below the bridge, moonlight glistening along a majestic spotted body as it broke Uncle Jack's leader clean. It was calm and surreal as all after-battle scenes are. There were outgoing ripples fading in the water where the trout went under.

Uncle Jack crawled on hands and knees from the water to survey the wreckage as bridge workers milled about, shaking water from their clothes and looking at the dead deer and the cast-off train wheel. Some of the men levered the broken flatcar from its careened position with a pry pole cut from a cedar tree. Ernie unhooked his engine and chugged back onto the bridge and under the freshly-shingled roof.

One of the more intelligent and outspoken men summed up the situation. "Well, guess the damn thing's pretty much busted."

"How we gonna get home?" asked another, in a reserved manner and in the general direction of Uncle Jack and Ernie, whose authority and experience on situations such as this was well documented.

Most of the other crew put on a swaggering air, playing it off as just another challenge in the life of an iron-mine worker, which didn't change the fact that most of the men had wives and children who more-or-less expected them to roll in at some point that night

Uncle Jack and Ernie conferred on the bridge alongside the simmering sauna train. Uncle Jack was animated, gesturing in the air with flailing hands while Ernie slowly nodded. Pretty soon Ernie was nodding vigorously. He approached the men. He stared down at the hapless deer. "Going to be vun long valk home – might as vell have a full stomach to go on." Then he proceeded to skin out the deer beside the track bed, cutting tenderloins into long strips. Ernie fired more wood into his train, working it double-duty as a frying stove. He roasted venison on top of the piping-hot train engine, saving every bit of deer hair in a careful pile to the side. The deer hair was a minor detail lost on the men who where happily eating their fill. But when it came time to start the long walk home, it became clear that Ernie and Uncle Jack would not be making the trek with the others.

It was a buck-tailed fly that tempted the big brown out its root-bound hiding spot. Unfortunately, the fish had taken Uncle Jack's last one back to Lake Superior. There sat Ernie, cross-legged by the tracks, picking hair off the deer hide and tying up a fresh supply. He tied them on big hooks that had magically appeared.

None of the men even registered the fact that Uncle Jack and Ernie would have fly-tying equipment with them on a work site. None remembered, at the time, that Uncle Jack had a fly rod with him, or that Ernie had procured a similar fishing instrument from somewhere inside the sauna train. They didn't even recall until round about midnight. But at least the moon was full. There was good light for walking. When they finally remembered, they still had five miles of shining track in front of them to talk about it.

Uncle Jack told how it was. "There were browns splashing out from the banks and under the moonlight with reckless abandon. I threw flies at the gravel crib until my arms fell off. I never got a strike. It's too damn new, Ernie. These local fish are stubborn, and they have a problem changing with the times. I told you to put the bridge up at the shallows. Hell, I told you we didn't even need a bridge – too damn time consuming. But you got to go and over-engineer everything. Maybe in a couple of seasons our spawning bed might pan out. Don't take it too hard. You want to catch trout, sometimes you just got to wander and find them where they're comfortable."

Uncle Jack had found them feeding upstream above the shallows. They wouldn't come for anything but a buck tail. As it so happened, Ernie could tie a buck tail as soundly as Uncle Jack couldn't be trusted to build a bridge alone. Luckily, fate and the gods intervened and brought down deer hair from above (out of the stream bottom, really, if you want to be journalistically factual about such things). But the trifle workings of journalists and deities were not to be questioned by Uncle Jack and Ernie.

Under the full moon, they disappeared high into the Bad River shallows, or the White River shallows, or whatever shallows they were called. The browns put on a show, coming from beneath the shelter of overhung branches and smashing at Ernie's flies. Pines glistened like fragrant towers of light, boughs sighing beneath the moon as they watched the spectacle of two men fighting slabs of cold fire. It smelled and sounded like a poem.

It truly was a night for epic poems, beneath tall pine giants that also shielded a clear view of the almost-completed bridge. Along with the glare of the moonlit night and along with Uncle Jack and Ernie being soundly occupied with fishing poetry, it was no wonder that when the hot sauna train spit a belch of steam along with a spatter of venison grease onto the planks of the bridge...it was no wonder that they didn't see the fire until it was too late.

The fresh pine tar and cedar shingles went up like a funeral pyre. By the time Uncle Jack and Ernie saw the blaze and slogged through the river bottom to reach it, there was nothing to do but watch it burn. Ernie wrapped a wet wader sock around his face and crawled on hands and knees onto the crackling bridge. If he couldn't save the bridge from the fire, he was at least going to try and save the cause of it.

"I told Ernie not to try it. It was too dangerous," Uncle Jack related. "Told him I didn't give a rip about the train – told him we could just go and build ourselves another one. That foolhardy, thick-headed Finn just wouldn't listen. Then I remembered that the rest of our fishing gear was on the train, and I started cheering him on to beat all hell."

Ernie chugged off the bridge an instant before it fell into the river, piling up a whole lot more fish structure than either he or Uncle Jack had in mind. When it was all said and done, the mine company told Uncle Jack and Ernie to rebuild the bridge on their own time, which was no big deal, really, to two fishermen posing as bridge designers. After all, the Bad/White River was full of willing trout. But when their "own time" started cutting too much into the mine company's, the whole bridge plan was scrapped, and the sauna train simply crossed over the river in the shallows.

The *Ashland Telegram* reported the fire. It was big news in an area usually devoid of big news. Eventually, the whole story drifted off into the archives of remembrance, and everything was forgotten. More or less forgotten, that is. The mine workers still remembered. And from that day forward, they tended to shy away from any work involving Uncle Jack and Ernie.

It suited the two men just fine. It was, in fact, what they had been planning all along.

CHAPTER 8

Newspaper writings were of little concern to Uncle Jack. He was mostly preoccupied with the stacks of stories unfolding on his map. But he always found time to write the occasional letter to my mother, describing which backcountry hill he was currently digging up, and what news my mother's birth land in the Lake Superior region had to offer. Even though my mother had moved downstate to an area she called "more civilized," and where she thought it best to raise a family in a more advantageous state of education, she always looked forward to Uncle Jack's letters. Even when he chided her for her preoccupation with what he called "bookworm learning," she just smiled and shook her head, always going to the mailbox every day to look for the next letter.

My mother married a teacher, so I suppose you could say that higher education was indeed on her priority list. She moved south from the cold reaches of Lake Superior to the more accessible reaches of central Wisconsin. Downstate, the snow still piled up just as high in winter, but iron mining and railway expeditions took a backburner to political and current events. I was destined to be educated before I was even born.

I was ten years old when my education along the paths of the classical thinkers hit a seam in the current of life. My father died suddenly, and it was a wonder that I didn't drown, pulled down by the cold undercurrents that are always present in the human conditions of life but are so often hidden by a placid surface. You can read the great literature of the Greeks and Romans. You can ponder the mathematics of Newton, the philosophy of Aristotle, and you can read the poetry of William Shakespeare. Hell, I saw the pictures and pieced together the bitter play-by-play in the local newspaper – the very paper I ended up writing for later in my life. But there's nothing in any educational institution to tell a ten-year-old how to react when his father is killed by a night train on a bridge-road crossing.

It was nothing but a tragic accident, and no one could be blamed, because even if the train was moving too fast and had forgotten to whistle at the dark, river-bridge road, it still might not have been enough. My father was always deep in his own thoughts and might have failed to stop anyway. He was a great thinker. He gave me just enough of it before he was gone.

I could reason just fine, and I could have stayed out of the whole Taconite Creek business. But it was a lifeline that I needed, and it was a line that Uncle Jack offered up. I could have stayed out of Taconite Creek, but by doing so, chances are I would have sunk like a piece of slag iron. Instead, I found myself thrashing and flailing, making a hard effort through the waters of life to grab the other end.

Besides writing letters, Uncle Jack usually made it a point to show up unannounced after my father was gone. I see now that he was already winding the line in tight-looped coils, waiting till the time was right to make the perfect cast. My mother lit up at his visits, and she'd let him take care of anything that needed doing around the house: chopping kindling for the stove, patching a leak in the roof – anything that wasn't too involved like building a bridge. My mother had read of the Bad River incident but, growing up around him since birth, she knew about Uncle Jack's carpentry skills long before the taconite mine executives found out for themselves.

The best of Uncle Jack's visits were the stories. They were stories of the north, carrying me away from a reality too harsh for a young boy to have to face on his own. Uncle Jack could build a story if he couldn't build anything else. I'd listen from the outskirts at first, hearing whispers of iron mines and railroads and the names of who was living and who was dying.

After the general news segment was over, my mother repaired to the kitchen to fry trout. Uncle Jack always made sure we were well supplied when he showed up at our door. I'd come close and sit, hearing about the streams and rivers and about the deep places in the high hills and valleys. I was in awe of the exotic destinations that could only exist in the telling of such things by a passing traveler who has seen it and lived it.

Uncle Jack sized me up as he told his trout-haunt stories. He gazed far, fighting brook trout on a rod lighter than a feather duster, following the winding streams through nettle up to his eyeballs, playing a fish into slack water; or, maybe, wrapping his leader tight around a submerged log and leaping into the icy torrents like a diver, grabbing the fish by the gills and rising back up triumphant. There was always a trout darting to grab a fly from a dark pool. It was only water, north of nowhere on the point of a compass, but always it landed square and true in my young and restless mind.

The stories changed, but the setting never did. Uncle Jack watched from the corner of his eye as he stared out the window. He always kept me in sight, wanting to see my reaction – wanting to see if I was interested. Needless to say, I was so enthralled at the stories that I would have skipped breakfast, lunch, or dinner to listen. Even my favorite television shows took second billing – and for a kid, that's sometimes the ultimate test. He was sizing me up, and I was too caught up in his fish tales to notice.

Ernie floated into the stories. He was a teaser fly on the bottom end of a tandem rig. I never knew where it would lead when I grabbed it, but it was impossible to resist. Uncle Jack would be out with his compass, searching or working a mine site, which always meant another great fishing story – and Uncle Jack would swing Ernie in.

"We wound ourselves way up in the Marengo country – somewhere south of Ashland and somewhere north of the equator, mind you. It was barely a wriggle if it was even on a map at all, but I'd been hankering to scratch it on mine for quite a spell. I guess it don't really matter 'bout the specifics. Point is there was a hell of a lot of taconite rock just rising up out there in the middle of that nowhere."

Uncle Jack's narration rolled from his heart, his eyes glistening, watching me carefully.

"Ernie got his steam train back in there, jumping and crashing over boulders the size of small mountains, pulling a tiny boxcar behind and jarring every bone in our bodies the whole way. It was a hot day, and the Marengo river was just a stone's throw away, not that it actually mattered, 'cause it's what's flying above river that really counts. Marengo – it's a French-Canadian word that means mosquito. I don't get why them Canadian fellers couldn't just call it that – no reason to make something so miserable sound so fancy.

"Hotter than blazes and mosquitoes everywhere, so we decided to escape and cool off in the river a bit before excavating. I don't even know why we brought our rods. It was probably that crazy Finn's idea. Ernie's real smart about that book-worm stuff, but I don't think he's got a lick of common sense. I had my hip boots on, and Ernie was wearing his overalls, and, in the grass along the banks, we walked through the biggest, nastiest goddam..."

Uncle Jack looked cagily around for signs of my mother peeking out of the kitchen. He always pretended he didn't want to swear in front of me, but really, he just didn't want to swear in front of me where my mother could hear.

"Anyway, we walked into a big nest of wood ticks in the tall grass surrounding the river. I think they musta been having a territory war with the mosquitoes. I could just brush 'em off my hip boots, mind you, but they were crawling up through Ernie's trousers and all over his legs till he was covered with ticks near to his eyeballs. You would never think a big guy like that could scream like a school girl. He got half crazy with all that buggy crawling and jumped head first into the Marengo. He was stripped down to nothing, rolling around in the ripples like a big old steelhead trout that's darn near played out.

"By the time Ernie got done with all his splashing, I told him that now, not only was it too hot to fish, but he'd done gone and scared even the dumbest ones to an even more ungodly locale. Now, I'd have to go and search that spot out, too, and even if I did find some taconite deposit where I found the fish, there was no way I was going there with a big galloot of a Finlander who was scared of a couple of harmless crawling critters.

"I got to give Ernie *some* credit—he came up with a couple of small hooks out of his fly box. I don't know why they even invented a number for a hook that small. When they get that tiny, why bother keeping track. Anyway, he tied some little black gnat-looking things with thread from his overalls and some hackle from a big tuft of black bear's hair that he'd found someplace or another. He's always noticing and finding that junk when he's supposed to be helping me work, which is pretty bold and lazy if you ask me. Fortunately for us, his laziness paid dividends that day, because his little bugs seemed to imitate all them wood ticks we'd just stirred up on the banks, and I'll be damned if we didn't catch a nice mess of trout on them. In fact, I think the ones we caught that day are the ones we just finished eating for dinner."

"Did you get the taconite out of there on Ernie's train?" I asked.

"Sure did," said Uncle Jack. "Except that it took a lot more days than the company figured us for. We had to camp out on the river, with wood ticks crawling in our noses and ears and crawling into other places that I sure don't want to mention here at the dinner table. We found a little sand island in a wide stretch of the river where we pitched a piece of canvas for a tent. It was nice, with a little breeze blowing. It kept those French mosquitoes down, but the ticks were another story. Ernie didn't reckon that wood ticks could swim out to our island, and that goes to show you the limitations of his bookworm learning, because turns out they can swim just like the fish that we were catching on his cobbled together wood-tick flies."

Uncle Jack failed to add that it had taken more days than expected to chip the taconite rock out of the Marengo country because no one else on the mine company's roster of workers wanted to go with. Two men loading up a boxcar full of rock had quite a job set on their plates. I'm sure they might have finished it in half the time, but the clean-picked bones on my own fish plate after dinner, and the faraway look in Uncle Jack's eyes, said it was a momentous feat that the two backwoods bog miners even got out of there at all.

I'd heard about Ernie, but I'd never seen Ernie. Summer bled into fall and into winter. It bled into another year. The depression years were long forgotten in the archives of the newspapers as the Second World War broke across the globe. It seemed far removed from my small world, and it seemed further removed from the places in Uncle Jack's stories. Not only had my mother and I never met Ernie, but now we didn't see Uncle Jack at all, either. And we didn't get any letters for a long time.

I turned older in years, but without Uncle Jack to keep my mind wandering and alive, the loss of my father pulled and tugged me into deeper water. I struggled in school. My mother, it must be said, did a fantastic job. She was busy juggling her own loss with a job to support us. And all the while, she helped me walk a tightrope of denial and anger.

I wasn't the only one to deal with loss. The war took a toll everywhere. The newspapers wrote from the big cities about fighting overseas. Many men paid a heavy price. There were still no letters from Uncle Jack and, as the fighting escalated, my own emotional problems escalated too. I didn't advance with the other kids my age. Instead, I turned back 'round the rings of the stump and headed in the opposite direction. When the atomic bombs finally came, then, it was definitely over – except for picking up the pieces of lost and shattered lives. The papers reported those things. My life didn't seem any different.

The papers wrote that it was becoming too costly to keep digging the iron out of the northern hills. Scrap metal was plentiful, being recycled now from the surpluses of war, sometimes from the machines of war themselves. My mother worried. Uncle Jack wasn't writing. It was as if he'd dropped off the face of the earth. Iron mine after iron mine closed down along the Superior shores. Companies moved on to where the steel was cheaper to manufacture.

There was only one mine remaining that was still bringing in iron to the very end. That's what the newspapers said, though they were unsure of where it was coming from so far in the north. The papers speculated that a stockpile must exist somewhere. The last surviving company of the greatest generation had found some massive source of taconite iron, harnessing rock out of the land itself without leaving any telltale track.

Sometimes the papers get it right without understanding why. They were right about the telltale scar. It was cut in a place so deep that no one could have seen it until it boiled over.

They didn't know about Taconite Creek. How could they? The newspapers didn't have an inkling of what was going on in the vast Superior hills. Even most of the men who worked squarely in the network of ore docks and rail lines in Ashland didn't really understand what was going on. There are probably a whole lot of them who grew old and gray without ever knowing, but they were luckier than those who didn't have the chance: The countless who'd given their lives for the freedom of the papers to write what they wished.

Taconite came in for a surviving company to the last, until the sun rose on a day to find that one gone, too. The Gogebic retreated backwards across the rings, and the papers folded shut over the Superior iron ranges. It was no longer financially viable to keep the ore piling onto the Ashland docks. The network of rail lines into the back country fell silent. Maybe it had been a combination of circumstances, maybe it was a fire. Bridges had been known to go up in flames, sometimes even in the middle of a moonlit night. It was known and documented from the lumbering days of old, back before the captains of industry turned to mining, that when a lumber camp depleted the natural stores of the virgin forest, then they just moved on. Sometimes the whole operation, buildings and all, evaporated in flames for no apparent reason. Call it spontaneous combustion if you will. One day it was there, and then, overnight, it was gone.

The papers didn't know. They didn't send reporters up there, stumbling around in the birch and aspen slashing, climbing up the peaks and sliding into the shadowed valleys of the Lake Superior range to find out. The papers moved on like the mines.

I wasn't sure, either, but my mother must have known. Even before Uncle Jack showed up on our doorstep, she sensed the mining was over. Maybe it would be reborn someday, but she had to have figured that Hip Boot Jack had ridden his last ore train. In the back of her mind, I think she hoped and prayed for his visit.

But she was wrong about it being his last ride. His last ride was only getting started.

I don't think she expected him to bring Ernie. But after all, if it was going to be Uncle Jack's last ride, Ernie needed to be there. It was Ernie's sauna train, and Uncle Jack needed an anchor to lean on if he was going to throw me a line. He needed Ernie to conspire to haul me away.

CHAPTER 9

I was high in the branches of the front yard oak when I saw the red truck smoke into the drive. I was enjoying the smells and sights of spring and catching the wind from faraway places. The whole of life swept up out of the ground in damp glory, bringing new grass and flowers and thoughts of school ending and thoughts of endless summer rolling in. I was drowning the worries of my mind from forty feet in the air.

The rusted truck lumbered in with steam rolling from under the hood, chugging and wheezing like an old train. It stopped with a back-fire bang. Uncle Jack slid out of the driver's seat, popping the hood and shaking his head in disgust.

The biggest man I ever set eyes on got out of the other side of the truck. He looked like a grizzly bear pulling back on haunches and baring teeth. His face sprouted a silver-gray bushy beard and a wide smile. His teeth were worn and hardened from years spent cutting leaders and line with powerful jaws. His eyes shone in merry amusement like the buttons on a big stuffed animal. I knew right away he was not a vicious bear.

Uncle Jack's benediction cleared the smoking engine compartment and floated up to my perch. "Dammit, Ernie, I thought you said the radiator don't leak no more."

The giant bear bellowed back. "Ya, I say it don't leak no more. But I don't say it leak less, either!"

"Well don't just stand there gawking at it. There's a tap water spigot around back of the house with a bucket sitting under it – least there was the last time I was here."

Ernie strolled around the house in lumbering steps. He'd no sooner disappeared when out the front door came my mother. She hesitated a moment, trying her best to compose herself, before running to her brother and throwing her arms around his neck. She could have been choking him. She was crying a little, but she was laughing, too.

"Worried...didn't hear from you...the papers said..." I caught the shrapnel of my mother's words as she stood by the truck with the radiator blowing into the spring breeze.

"I'm awfully sorry, sis," said Uncle Jack. "We got a little bogged down and it got a little crazy up there. Well, we were a lot bogged down, actually – but that's a long story. The short version of it is – we're retired now."

"Will you stay? You can stay as long as you want. Your nephew certainly will be thrilled to see you. He's always just milling around the yard and off in the trees since his father, well, since the accident, and the last year or two has been rough, not a lot of bright news...I mean, you don't have to stay if you don't want."

Uncle Jack smiled at my mother. I don't know how he knew I was up in the oak tree, because I hadn't moved or said a word since I saw the truck come into the yard. But he looked up through the branches and winked at me.

"We're planning to stay a little. But just 'cause we're retired, it don't mean there isn't stuff that needs attending. We've got more important business now than when we were still bucking ore."

"Oh, of course, I know you do Jack," said my mother. "But you'll stay with us for a while?"

Uncle Jack answered with wet and shining eyes. "Yeah, we'll stay for as long as it takes. We'll help out with anything you need. You both mean the world to me. And as far as my nephew goes, I think this will be a summer he'll never forget. Of course, we'll need your blessing."

"Why do you keep saying we?" asked my mother.

Ernie came around the corner, bucket swinging loosely from a giant paw and sloshing water over the sides. Uncle Jack bristled and wiped his eyes, pretending he wasn't touched by my mother's emotions. He pretended he wasn't particularly concerned with anything but the smoking hood of the truck. He talked in a tone loud enough to be heard in the next county. I heard it clearly from my tree. And while my thoughts were intent on the matter of a summer I wouldn't forget, Ernie looked like he hadn't heard anything. He strolled slowly around the house from the back yard, intent on spilling as little water as possible over the top of the bucket.

Uncle Jack talked louder. "Of course I'll fix up anything that needs fixing around here. I might be retired, but I still know how to put in a hard day's work. I'll teach that nephew of mine about all sorts of things. I'm willing to bet that he'll get to be near as handy as me. I might even take him fishing if we get the chance and if he shows an aptitude for that sort of idleness."

Ernie set the bucket down by the truck and stuck out a big hand to my mother in greeting. "Hallo dare, I'm Ernie," he said with a sheepish smile. "I hope dare is no inconvenience for me to come visit."

My mother smiled at Ernie and shook his hand. "Why no, it is not an inconvenience at all." She was at total ease. Ernie had that effect on everyone he met. Everyone liked him instantly, except maybe Uncle Jack.

Uncle Jack quenched the fire in the truck's radiator while Ernie took my mother aside, speaking in a whisper just loud enough to make sure Uncle Jack heard. "I see dat vater spigot out back has leaking trouble. I found da bucket underneath da leak. But how is it dat Jack knew da bucket vould be dare?"

My mother glanced sheepishly over at Uncle Jack, who was slowly turning a shade of red to match the rusted truck paint. He slopped a little water over the side of the radiator, and it spilled down the side. He knocked the radiator cap from its resting place on the truck's bumper, and it rolled around in small circles in the gravel.

"Ah…well, I guess that's because Jack fixed the leak the last time he was here," my mother answered.

"Ya, yes sir, dat's vut I figured!" said Ernie, no longer whispering. "Good ting he retire, 'cause now he vill have plenty time to make more leaks. Now dat he ain't so busy mining da iron ore. Not dat I ever see him being too busy anyvays."

"Don't believe anything out of this here gorilla's mouth," said Uncle Jack. "It's a fact that they kicked him out of Finland for lying. But I'm not about to stoop down to that level and start spinning tall tales about his shortcomings. Not unless you got about a year's worth of time to here 'em all!"

The radiator drank in the bucket of water as everyone in the drive exchanged pleasantries. Or at least the two men were pleasant to my mother. Uncle Jack stared haughtily at Ernie. Ernie just laughed, ignoring Uncle Jack's stares while putting my mother slowly at ease about their sudden arrival.

Retiring towards the house, Uncle Jack broke from the group and came to stand below the branches of my perch. He searched the tree line of the yard as if for a sign. I think he'd seen me through the truck smoke the minute he pulled in. He spoke aloud, to no one in particular, and particularly to me hiding above. "Well, I'm sure he'll come scrambling in eventually. Guess I'll have to feed his share of trout to Ernie. Come to think of it, I better get inside myself if I don't want to miss out. That gol-dang Finlander can't carry his weight catching them, but he sure can eat a lot."

I was down the tree and sitting at the table before the fry pan started sizzling.

CHAPTER 10

Uncle Jack and Ernie stayed while my school year wound down. I speculated about summer school in my future. My grades were far from spectacular. Well, I guess they were kind of awful. I knew my mother was worried. I knew she expected more.

Uncle Jack and Ernie turned everything upside down. Even though my mother didn't know what was going on behind the scenes, she knew good teachers when she saw them. After all, she had married my dad. When Uncle Jack and Ernie were done with me, I'd discovered a whole new world. How it happened was as amazing to me as it was to my mother.

I had trouble remembering. I had trouble focusing. I had trouble studying. As a future career newspaper writer, it may seem hard to comprehend that I had trouble spelling and writing. Other kids memorized words for tests and, after the tests were over, the words hung around in their heads long enough to subsidize real learning. It seemed everyone was reading and spelling without even realizing how they knew the right letter combinations. For me, it was hard enough looking at words to begin with, not to mention memorizing them; and after the test, they simply vanished out of my head to be replaced by the fact that the sun was shining and it sure would be a good day to make a tree fort – maybe chase some cowboys and Indians across the prairie – shooting it up with one side or the other, depending on who I thought held the best chance for victory on a given afternoon.

I didn't realize that holding those visions in my mind: the sun and the wind through the leaves, or the way water sounds as it curls over moss-covered rocks, may have been as important as grammatically knowing how to write the visions down in the first place. For me, learning to write was like trying to cast a line to a waiting fish without being able to first strip the line off the reel. I could see the water for what it was, and I figured there might be trout, but reading the water and putting my mind into the proper current to give me a shot at catching the trout – when it came to school and me – that was like diving off a high platform into deep water before you learned to swim.

Uncle Jack figured the situation quickly. Maybe he quizzed my mom, but more likely he rifled through past homework assignments to find out where the problem lay. He caught on to my school dilemmas as quickly as he'd strike at a trout under a log pile. He had his own agenda, and I was part of that agenda. If getting my grades in order was what it took, he was going to have at it with a vengeance.

The routine started at the crack of dawn. Uncle Jack fried bacon first. Any and all subsequent fare would be sizzled in its grease. Uncle Jack and Ernie had brought a stockpile of eating-sized trout with them, and we ate them every morning until they ran out. After the trout supply was depleted, we ate a grease-fried variety including eggs, pancakes, and grease-fried oatmeal mixed with potatoes, which Uncle Jack called grits, but which tasted to me like half-cooked, greasy hash browns mixed with gravel.

Ernie vigorously agreed with me on the consistency of the stuff. "Dat's vut he call 'em, 'cause you has to grit teeth to chew 'em."

"I happen to know grits are brain food for a growing boy," Uncle Jack chastised, apron hung low across his waist in place of hip boots, a spatula and frying pan in his hands instead of map and compass. He pointed the spatula at me like a lawyer making a pertinent point to the jury. "School burns energy, and you need stamina to get through it. These here grits are nothing short of pure fried horsepower."

He waved the frying pan in his other hand at Ernie, spattering bits of smoking grease and potatoes and oatmeal like a lawyer spitting fire at a hostile witness. "And as far as you're concerned, you don't need to eat 'em if you don't care to. You've only been here a few weeks and already there's a basketball growing out of your belly. Skipping some breakfasts would do you good!"

I hoped we could get some more trout for breakfast, but Uncle Jack changed the subject every time I asked. He might not have been the best cook, but he was a darn good teacher. He didn't want me distracted.

Books were thrust into my arms as Uncle Jack wiped bacon grease out of the breakfast dishes and hollered me out the door to catch the bus. And there sat Ernie, tying his morning flies on the front steps, and then I would become distracted. He held a battered wooden cigar box on his lap, full to the top with hooks and thread and wire and pieces of fur and feathers. There were little flies with delicate, upturned wings, and medium ones wrapped tight with fur and looking like a bushy caterpillar. The biggest ones had clipped feathers wound onto the back of the hooks and you'd swear they were ready to take flight. He showed me how he twisted on the fur and clipped the wings. He recited names – Adams, Coachman, and Palmer. He said the best ones didn't have names yet because they were his original ideas. He said they had to earn their names.

The school bus honked me out of my reverie there on the front steps.

Uncle Jack poked his head out of the door and hollered at Ernie. "Quit filling his head with all those useless fly names! He needs to have his wits about him for school! You know damn well that you're just making names up, just like a little kid with imaginary friends. Furthermore, the whole school bus is staring at you. Nobody in their right mind wants to hang around a moping Finlander who sits on the steps all morning and builds little bugs."

I started every day filled with life when Uncle Jack and Ernie were around. They gave off a magic that made me believe anything was possible.

Uncle Jack took Ernie's place on the front steps when the bus dropped me off. He'd be drinking coffee and munching on a sandwich: fried bologna and bacon, or roast beef and bacon, or his favorite – a fried trout and bacon sandwich. Not only did he fry everything in its grease, but he'd also slap bacon on anything. It was one of his staples, along with onions, which he also put on every type of food known to exist. I didn't particularly care for onions. I also wasn't a coffee drinker. But by the time Uncle Jack was through teaching me, I'd hop off the bus, dunk raw onion slices in coffee, and swallow them whole like oysters on the half-shell. He was persuasive, and his habits naturally grew on a person.

We walked around the yard after our snack, looking at the general state of affairs that the rising spring season was offering. Uncle Jack never failed to ask about my day, listening and nodding the same whether my day was good, bad, or indifferent. It didn't matter what the day's victories or defeats had been. He just listened and nodded.

"Some days you wade slow and easy and the river's full of fish," he said. "Others, there ain't a fin in sight, and you trip over a rock and fill your waders to boot. It don't really matter either way. What matters is that you got the spirit to be out in the current in the first place, 'stead of standing and watching from the bridge."

I waited for the day's lessons to start, not realizing that they were already underway.

"What kind of tree is that?"

"It's an oak, Uncle Jack, you know that."

"Well, of course I do. I specialize in all sorts of growing things."

"How did you learn them all?"

"I don't rightly know. Near as I can figure, I saw so much when I was growing up and wandering around the woods that eventually I just started to put names to things. It sort of naturally happened."

"So you're naturally smart?" I asked

"Of course I am. Aren't you?"

"Heck no, I can't remember anything," I said, looking down at the ground.

"You knew that was an oak tree," said Uncle Jack.

"Everyone knows what an oak tree looks like," I said.

"Maybe they do, and maybe they don't. Let's go ask Ernie. He's goofing off somewhere around here. We just got to find where it is he's being lazy at."

Ernie was fixing the garden fence. Uncle Jack had patched it the last time he was here, but the rabbits had gotten in all the same. Ernie was reinforcing it with chicken wire and adding more fence posts, pounding them straight and true into an earth still soft with spring rain.

Uncle Jack just couldn't build or fix a thing like Ernie. My mother never came right out and said it, but she was glad Ernie showed up on our doorstep with Uncle Jack. The homestead was really taking shape. Uncle Jack could navigate through heavy swamp and timber without a second glance at his map and compass. But if he tried to put up a lean-to shelter at the end of the day, it would likely fall over in the night. Ernie, on the other hand, liked to stay put. He could get lost going to the outhouse, but he was smart enough to follow Uncle Jack's trail. And he could build a lean-to at the end of the day that would stand against a hurricane.

Uncle Jack was too proud to admit it, but he knew the facts of the matter just the same. Natural selection works in strange ways. Uncle Jack might have been proud, but he was smart enough not to mess with natural selection. Ernie might get lost going to the outhouse, but Uncle Jack was more than happy to let Ernie build the thing – else very bad things were bound to happen.

Uncle Jack greeted Ernie at his fence repairs in a fashion that I came to understand was also part of natural selection. There were not many that could see into the briars of their banter. But if you saw it as a whole, then you came to understand the importance of the individual trees that hid in the forest of their circular arguing.

"Christ Almighty Ernie, you're supposed to be putting up a fence, not an anti-tank bunker."

"Ya, I need to build the fence strong. It must keep out everyting, 'specially someone who smell like onion and bacon. It must protect new plants from dat kind of someone. And if dat someone fixed da fence correct from beginning, den I don't have to be doing anyting. I could be valking round da yard munching a sandvich, too."

"Take it easy Ernie, it's a fine fence," Uncle Jack said, kicking at a fence post and finding it solid, shaking his head with amazement and jealousy.

"It's the best fence ever," I said.

Ernie wiped sweat from his brow. "Tank you very much."

Uncle Jack kicked the fence again. "Anyways Ernie, we really came over to ask you about that tree standing in the front yard."

"Dat is an oak tree," said Ernie matter-of-factly.

"Very good, not only are you a good fence builder, but it seems you're a naturalist, too. What we really want to know – is what kind of oak."

"It look like a pretty beeg vun. Maybe 'bout tirty or forty feet."

I wasn't sure if he was serious or not. I didn't want to hurt his feeling, but I couldn't help it. I started giggling.

"What so funny 'bout da oak tree?" Ernie asked.

"The tree isn't funny," I laughed. "It's just how you said how high it was when Uncle Jack asked what kind of tree. I'm sorry, I can't help it."

"I think what he's trying to say, Ernie, is what species is that oak. Is it red, white, or is it something all together different?"

"Who da hell cares? It is da oak tree. Why do it make a difference da color?"

It was a good point. I stopped laughing and started thinking.

"I don't know, Ernie. I'm not sure why it makes a difference at all. It's a red oak because of the color and texture of the bark, and because the leaves are pointed and not round like a white oak, and because...well, because that's what it's called." I looked at Uncle Jack and shrugged my shoulders.

"It just makes a difference because it does," said Uncle Jack. "Some biologist thought it was a good idea to make up names somewhere along the line, just like Ernie does with his little bug friends every morning. Because we don't always know why some things are the way they are, it don't mean they're not important."

"Yeah, I guess so," I said.

"But you knew it was a red oak," said Uncle Jack. "That shows you're smarter than me, because to tell you the truth, I didn't know what type of oak it was, either. But I'm still smarter than that fence-making Finn over there. I bet that tree don't go an inch over twenty feet." Uncle Jack wagged a finger at Ernie. "You were thinking metric, Ernie. You know we don't measure stuff in that foreign mumbo-jumbo over here in America. I think you're still a little confused about it."

Ernie shook his head and kept building the fence. Uncle Jack wiped the remains of his onion sandwich on his pants and guided me towards the house; towards homework. He finished his afternoon lesson by saying, "And just 'cause you don't think spelling and writing is easy don't mean it ain't important. It don't mean you can't learn words and remember 'em either, just the way you knew what kind of oak that was without even knowing how you knew. There ain't no reason to think that remembering how to spell and write words won't come just as natural."

Those after-school affairs went on a lot that spring. I was spelling and writing with the best of my class before I even knew what had happened.

CHAPTER 11

I came home to find Ernie kneeling in the front yard and stringing line through guides on a long, drawn-out piece of bamboo. I had a lot of things swirling through my mind when I got off the school bus. School was drawing to a close for the year. We had tests coming, report cards would follow, and that was not something I was accustomed to looking forward to. Even with Uncle Jack's tutoring, I was still nervous about tests. I don't know if anyone actually enjoys taking one – but I dreaded it.

I was curious about the bamboo. I forgot my anxiety for a moment and walked from the bus, dropping my lunch pail into the grass. "What's that Ernie? Some kind of a fish pole? Where'd you find it?"

I knew we didn't have any kind of fishing equipment at home. My dad hadn't been a fisherman at all. My father had been a deep thinker. He had taken time out from his thinking to do many things with me, but fishing had never come up between us. He loved baseball, and we spent hours throwing the ball around. I remember cheering on the Milwaukee Braves, listening tensely with my dad in front of the radio, dancing wildly around the living room when Henry Aaron would sock another long ball. But we never went fishing. Maybe we would have if time had not been cut short. I don't know. I guess I'd never really thought about it.

We did take walks through the forest and over the farm fields. My dad liked nature, and he knew the names of plants and trees and flowers and shrubs. He even knew the Latin names for a lot of them. I suppose that's where I picked up some of my accidental knowledge – like the red oak. Dad probably knew the Latin names for a lot of different bugs, too.

Ernie didn't know any Latin, but he knew how to represent the bugs just the same. He held a bamboo fly rod that afternoon. It was the first time I'd seen one, and it was beautiful. It was one more step in the direction of Taconite Creek.

"Dis here is special kind of fishing pole," Ernie said. "I get it from da neighborhood. I go over to dat nice old woman next door, 'cause she catch me verking here, so she vant her garden fence fixed dare, too. I say, I am not too busy today, so okay, I vill fix her fence."

Miss Edna was a retired school teacher who lived down the road from us. She had never married. My dad used to help her out with odds-and-ends, and they always talked books and teaching and school stuff. It was pretty boring, but Miss Edna could bake some mean chocolate chip cookies, so I usually went with. I didn't know why she would have a fishing pole, or why Ernie had it now.

"Ya, so I fix da fence for da nice lady. Den she bring me some cookies. She make sure I eat so many dat I get a bellyache. Den she ask if I can help vit making a mouse trap in da garage, 'cause she have a problem vit too many mice getting into her garden seeds. I tell her to get a cat, but she says she don't 'specially like cats. She don't like mice neither – okay I help make some traps."

Ernie's storytelling was as entertaining as Uncle Jack's. He gave ordinary, daily occurrences a brighter life. With Ernie, you got a subtle version of the truth. With Uncle Jack, there was a lot more gray area.

"I make little cages from vire off da fence, vit little sliding doors dat I shave off some vood from da garden fence poles. I put a big piece of chocolate cookie in da traps. I couldn't eat no more cookies anyhow."

While Miss Edna didn't particularly care for cats or mice, she was squeamish about any animal, or rodent for that matter, coming to any physical harm. I spent a lot of time in the following days running over to Miss Edna's to check her traps, dumping mice far and wide over the fields and forest.

Ernie spied an old cane fly rod in Miss Edna's garage. It had been left there from days gone by; left to Miss Edna by her father, who had lived on the East Coast and was a fly fisherman of the tweed-jacket and pipe-smoking variety. Ernie lovingly admired the rod, and Miss Edna told him to keep it in return for his kind work on her garden fence and his handy solution to her pest control problem. He said he could never accept it, but he finally relented when Miss Edna threatened to keep stuffing cookies in him until he floated off like an oversized balloon.

Now, he sat in the front yard stringing up the bamboo fly rod, the likes of which might fetch an ungodly sum in collector's circles, and he'd acquired it by just doing what came naturally. Ernie had the line wound around a relic of a reel that Miss Edna had also given him. The reel wasn't fancy, but it had fine gears to prevent the line from back-lashing. Ernie said the gears were a little rusty at first, but he'd taken it all apart and cleaned, oiled, and polished it. The reel sung out like a well-timed clock.

Ernie had seen me get off the school bus. He could just as easily have been whipping the fly rod into shape in the back yard and out of sight. He knew I was coming. Uncle Jack was the set-up man in the Taconite Creek conspiracy, hurling stories like curveballs from thin air. But just as in baseball – just as I had learned from all the games I treasured listening to with my father – a set-up man is nothing if you don't have a closer to seal the victory. Ernie was the closer.

He began the final stages of my prepping by giving me a piece of gum to chew on. The gum was peppermint. Although I've chewed on countless pieces of gum through the course of my years on this planet, I can't rightly tell you the flavor of any of them. But I remember that peppermint piece of gum distinctly because, when I'd finished chewing it into a sticky ball, Ernie took the gum and stuck it on the end of the line, and I learned how to cast.

"See, you got to make dis rod a part of you to make it verk," Ernie started. "Den you don't remember vare your arm starts and da rod finishes, 'cause it is all vun ting." He demonstrated a back cast, hauling and stripping line with one hand while gently bringing the rod back. The line arched gracefully back in a loop, straightening out and landing flush with the ground behind him. It looked like the most natural action in the world. He did it several times and with the same result. The peppermint gum landed twenty feet behind him in a straight line on the ground. Even though his casting arm was huge, it seemed he didn't flex a single muscle.

"How are you going to catch a fish behind you?" I asked. You can't even see what's there unless you have eyes in the back of your head. I got some teachers with eyes like that – they see what you're doing all the time without looking – but I don't think even they could fish like that."

"Ya, but it is not da whole of it. It is only da half of it," answered Ernie. "Witout da half dat go backvards, you can't go forvards. Den you might as vell not go fish at all. Den you might as vell stay home and chew gum like a beeg fat cow."

He pointed to my wadded practice fly. "Now, you try to make da gum go backvards. I vill sit and vatch from underneath dat nice color oak – even though I know it is oak tree only, and da color don't make no difference."

Ernie played it out exactly. He sat beneath the oak while I tried to make the gum lay out flat behind me. It was a total failure. The line got tangled around my feet when I tried to strip it out. I almost stuck the gum in Ernie's beard several times, and once it caught up in one of the oak tree branches above him. The tree wasn't even behind me. It was twenty feet to my left. Ernie sat beneath the oak, coaching and smiling and enjoying the show.

I almost got the hang of it for a minute before I broke my fly off when it tangled in my own hair. We called a halt to the day's lesson and repaired inside. Mom cut the snarl out with a scissors while I sat red-faced at the dinner table.

After dinner, Uncle Jack went over my homework assignments with an especially demanding vigor. He knew my end-of-year tests were coming. He seemed determined to single-handily pass me with flying colors – though I was the one who would have to do the actual passing. Reading, writing, and arithmetic; my head spun around until I was certain I'd fail everything.

Uncle Jack was stubbornly ruthless. "Come on! I know you know all of it. Go through it one more time!"

I shouted in frustration. "I'm getting a headache with all this junk. I'm just going to screw it up anyway!" Even my mother looked alarmed, though she'd seen the steady improvement in my grades since Uncle Jack stepped into my schooling agenda. It was Ernie who waded in and bailed the sinking ship.

"Vut da hell you vorried 'bout da school questions for?" He rubbed his belly in contentment after eating a particularly solid helping of mom's meatloaf and mashed potatoes. Mom's cooking wasn't spectacular, but Ernie couldn't get enough of it. He always had seconds, or maybe thirds, every time he ate with us that spring. We never had anything left over when Ernie was around. I don't even think he remembered that we hadn't had any trout since the last of the bootleg stockpile ran dry.

"You learn all dat stuff from your Uncle Jack. You learn to cast backvards by learning dat stuff. Now's all you gotta do is goes forvard, den you get all good grades no problem. Once you figure da back cast, den, all your life, you vill know da vay forvard."

Ernie bade me follow him outside. Springtime twilight was waning soft, and the birds were settling down for the night. Faint stars and planets were coming out as Ernie picked up the fly rod where we'd left it lay in the grass after the gum-in-the-hair incident. This time, instead of gum, Ernie produced a fine strand of tapered leader from his front shirt pocket. He plucked a big, buggy creation out of the same pocket. The fly looked like it had just crawled out of a prehistoric swamp. It was wound with brown fur and had folded back wings made of rough feathers. A short, pokey tail made from the same type of feathers protruded from the end of the shank. The bug was both ugly and cunning. It looked real enough to scare the heck out of anyone coming upon it unawares. If my school tests turned sour, I knew a couple of teachers' desks where the fly might work creative magic.

Ernie tied the fly onto the leader and handed me the rod. "Now I go inside to help your ma vit dishes. You practice some more, and I vill keep dat crazy Uncle Jack fellow out of everybody's vay. In little vile, you vill know da vay forvard."

Something happened that early spring night. I don't know how to exactly explain it, but the fly rod became more than just an extension of my arm; it became meshed together with my mind. I didn't try to think about it. It came together; not thinking so much, and everything fell into place.

Stars were faint on the horizon. There were brighter beacons of planets popping up – Jupiter and Mars. Jupiter was the biggest of the planets, so naturally the large beacon in the east had to be Jupiter – it was so bright. And Mars was the red planet. I remembered without knowing that I knew. There it was, glowing like an ember above the red oak in the yard. The moon rose slowly. It wasn't full, but it would be in a few days. That meant the moon was waxing and not waning. I remembered that, too. Before I knew what was happening, the fly wasn't touching the ground. I wasn't even letting it get close.

I backed toward the oak without letting the fly tangle in the low-hanging branches. I felt the branches rustling behind me. I can't describe how I knew I was going to miss them. I just knew. I gave the line a little tug, flicking the rod forward with my wrist. The whole of the line, leader, and that ugly brown fly shot forward and sailed out across the yard and onto the driveway.

Wow, I thought. "Hot damn," I said aloud, repeating one of the finer phrases I'd picked up from Uncle Jack.

"You maybe can catch da big trout vit cast like dat."

Ernie and Uncle Jack had been studying me from the front steps. I wasn't sure how long they'd been watching. My face beamed with Ernie's approval.

"I see potential," said Uncle Jack. "Little rough around the edges, but nothing that a summer's worth of polishing can't shine up."

"What do you mean a summer's worth?" I asked, sensing something afoot, something grander than casting a line in the yard.

Uncle Jack deftly snapped the fly from the leader. He admired the rod. "I used to have a fine one just like it, but it got misplaced. It gnaws on me like a squirrel that hid a nut." He took a deep whiff of the night air. The earth was richly wet and soft. He gazed at the waxing moon and he gazed north. "When the wind comes in just right, I can almost remember where I stuck it. I'd sure like to get it back."

He shook his head, jarring himself back into the present. He tucked my rod under his arm and ushered me into the house. "Never mind that now.

First, you have to convince the school not to let them keep you for the summer. You've got some tests to take, and you can't let the rest of the team down by flubbing them. Watch your damn language, too," he smiled. "Can't have your mom thinking Ernie is being a bad influence. Just like your casting, he's a little rough around the edges, too, but I don't think a summer is near long enough to polish him up."

Ernie stood on the porch, and Uncle Jack handed him the rod. Uncle Jack made to go around, but Ernie blocked his way, clearing his throat and holding out his hand. Uncle Jack begrudgingly reached into his shirt pocket and handed Ernie's fly back to him.

"Tank you!" said Ernie, walking into the house.

I followed both of them. I didn't give a passing thought to test failures from the past. I found that I wasn't worried about what school might set in front of me, either. Uncle Jack and Ernie had seen to the back cast. The way forward would take care of itself.

CHAPTER 12

It turned out more than fine. The end of the semester brought my best grades ever. Uncle Jack and Ernie had worked their magic on me. Now, they focused their combined energy on my mother. Convincing her that I should disappear for a summer into the wilderness required both a set-up man and a closer. It was a double play of the highest order.

A mother's only son is her prize possession. There exists a tendency to hold close and protect from the big and cruel world. My mother was wise enough to know that I needed a chance to mold into something higher. It was a chance for a pupa to emerge into a mayfly on the rivers of the Superior iron range. Not that Uncle Jack and Ernie put it into that poetic of a scenario.

"Seeing as the boy don't have to go to summer school, I guess he's just going to lay around the house this summer and get fat and lazy," Uncle Jack said, as my mother was oohing and ahhing over my finely-honed report card.

"He has potential to be real good fisherman," added Ernie. "He's learning to cast real pretty. Too bad dare isn't many fish in da yard."

"Well, I'm certain you two can find time to take him fishing this summer," said my mother. "That is, if he helps out with the garden, and helps Ernie over at Miss Edna's place. I'm sure they'll be plenty of time to go around."

Uncle Jack ran his fingers through his bleached hair. Ernie shuffled his feet uncomfortably and shrugged his large shoulders. My mother was still under the impression that everyone was going to stay around eating her wonderful meatloaf and having a happy time. I wasn't sure what was going on, but I knew what Ernie said was true. No fish would be caught in the yard that summer, even under the covering shade of the big oak tree.

"Well, the thing is, the fact of the matter – I mean, the bottom line," Uncle Jack struggled to bring it out in the open. Then, deciding discretion was no longer the better part of valor, he simply blurted it out. "Ernie and I have a bit of unfinished business in the iron hills. It's pretty darn important; otherwise we sure as heck would stay. I reckon you'd probably get sick of Ernie and kick him out, but I'd stay right through the summer if I could."

"I thought you were retired," said my mother.

"Well…sort of," stammered Uncle Jack. "Retirement is a tricky business.

It takes serious thought and serious planning, not to mention we've got a portfolio of investments in a bank. I mean, sort of in a bank," Uncle Jack glanced a knowing eye at Ernie, who was staying closed faced as a poker player, so whether the investments amounted to a big pile of money or a small lump of change, or even where the "sort of a bank" was – it was impossible to read.

Uncle Jack rested a hand on my shoulder. "We have some cleaning up to do, but at least it's an outside cleaning. I'd warrant we might even be able to squeeze in a little fishing time. It'd be swell having an extra hand to help out."

Uncle Jack looked relieved to have finally laid it out on the table.

"Our final verk site is retiring, too, but it is little bit messy right now," added Ernie. "Ve clean it up, but mostly ve go fishing. Have a big fun time."

"How long exactly is this big fun time going to last?" asked my mother, arms crossed and eyes shooting a withering glare that even made the hulking figure of Ernie a little uncomfortable.

"We shouldn't be gone a month," said Uncle Jack. "It could be shorter – maybe a little longer depending on the weather and such. Why, if I had to guess, I'd say we'd be back easy by the Fourth of July. Then we can all go together to the fireworks. It'll be a fine show."

My head darted between my mother and Uncle Jack. I knew Mom wasn't going to let me go. My spirits were soaring at the possibilities, but reality kept my feet anchored right there in the yard. I was certain that's where they'd be anchored all summer.

"Well, I don't know. He's awfully young to be running around way up there."

I started to see faint hope. I could tell she was really thinking about it.

My mother went on, weighing the possibilities out loud. "Remember, I grew up there, too. There are bears and wolves, and what if he falls in the water? He can swim, but the currents in some of those rivers... They can bowl a grown man over."

"I was his age and ran wild all over the place," Uncle Jack said. "I was gone for days at a time. All them wild animals were more scared of me than I was of them. And I never drowned. I got in over my head a few times, but it built character, that's what it did. Look how I turned out."

"That's what I'm most afraid of," my mother answered. But she laughed when she said it. There was a faint glow of light at the end of the tunnel. I had kept quiet, but now I ventured my opinion on the matter.

"I better not go, it sounds like a great time and all, but Mom needs me around the house. We've got that wonderful fence around the garden now. I need to keep it weeded. And Miss Edna needs someone to dump the mice out of her traps. I should probably stay here."

I looked as forlorn as possible. I'd never been in a school play, except for once when I wore a turkey costume in the school Thanksgiving production. My only lines had been, "Gobble-Gobble," and I never invested a heck of a lot of emotion in the delivery. But standing there that day, amongst the cast of Ernie, Uncle Jack, and my mother, I emitted an Oscar-worthy performance of a depressed little kid.

Uncle Jack looked demoralized. "Well, I suppose that's as good a reason as any to skip a month of fishing," he said. "We're going to miss having you, though."

"He has good head on his shoulders," said Ernie, giving my mother a solemn nod before turning to me and winking. I was hoping to fool everyone with my performance. I think I fooled my mother, but you can never be sure about that. I wasn't positive about hoodwinking Uncle Jack, either. But Ernie, he saw right through my character study. He fired a fastball to close the game."

"I tell you vut, promise to help your ma 'round da house like you say, and you keep dat fly rod and practice hard. Ven ve come back, maybe ve find a place for you to catch da fish. Maybe, is pond or someting 'round here."

"Yeah, there's a river that flows through some farm fields about a mile back of the house," I said. "It's not too much, but there might be fish in there. That would be great. I promise to help Mom, if you promise to bring back some trout and stories. Be sure you bring back some stories too, Uncle Jack," I added as homely as possible.

"Stories and trout, count on it!" He stuck out his hand and we shook on it.

"Hold on a minute," said my mother, walking over to where Uncle Jack and I stood clasping hands. "Maybe it would be good for you to go. You certainly earned it with your grades. I don't see any use in you pulling up my vegetables and flowers in the garden, thinking they look like weeds. I can manage around here just fine for a month or so. And Miss Edna's just going to have to deal with a couple of mice. She taught first grade all those years. I'm sure she can dump some squirming rodents out of a trap if she sets her mind to it."

I shot into the air, poised for a victory dance, before remembering my act. "I guess it might be kind of fun," I stoically said.

"Well, you better ask them if they still want you," said my mother.

I looked over at the two of them and held out my hands in a "what do you think?" gesture.

"I'd be honored," Uncle Jack said.

"It vill be nice having someone 'long who don't complain so much," said Ernie.

"You can barely understand English. How do you even know it's complaining?" said Uncle Jack. "Let's get packing."

CHAPTER 13

All of my twelve years of existence got jammed into a Duluth packsack. The pack was resurrected from the depths of Uncle Jack's truck. He said I better take good care of it because technically it wasn't his.

The pack was oiled and leathered. There were pockets and compartments hiding in every angle of its roughened surface. There was even a special rod-case holder strung on the side. "A pack like this has been places and seen things. It's got enough character to darn near move around on its own," Uncle Jack said. It so happened that the pack's story was more overflowing than the pack itself after I was through loading it up.

"It rained for a week straight," started Uncle Jack as I stuffed in shirts, shorts, and pants. My mother kept feeding me enough clothes to complete a year's safari on the Dark Continent. You know how mothers can be, it was hectic. It was also an odd way to start a story about a pack.

"I learned my lesson about rain and mud long ago – quicksand is what it is – and it ain't pretty when a train gets stuck in it. We couldn't get to any of the mine sites, so we holed up and played cards in Eddie Barker's Ore Dock Saloon in Ashland. Eddie was a great bartender. But he was also a shady cribbage player."

Mom thrust a bulky sweater into my hand, and I stuffed it in. Uncle Jack fished the sweater out and threw it in a pile on the bed along with three pairs of shoes and five pairs of heavy-knit pants. I'm not kidding when I tell you Mom tried to make me throw in my snow pants. Uncle Jack just pulled them back out and threw them in the discard pile.

"For heaven's sake – the boy don't need to be dressed like an Eskimo. He doesn't need these nice Sunday clothes, and I don't see why he needs ten pair of underwear. One or two will do just fine. We're going to be running light, bouncing over some heavy terrain. All that stuff's just going to bog him down."

"Well it wouldn't kill you to take the boy to church a couple of times, Jack. I know there's as many churches up their as saloons, so there's no reason that he can't be dressed proper. And just because you don't believe in changing your underwear more than once a week, that's not a habit I want passed down to my son."

"Well, Sis," said Uncle Jack. "As a matter of fact, we have a private service every Sunday morning right on the stream bank. The dress code is real casual. We sing hymns, and it's real uplifting. Despite his other faults,

Ernie's a darn good preacher."

"That sounds wonderful. But he's still packing more than two pair of underwear."

"But that's the best part about our Sunday service," said Uncle Jack. "We hold it right in the river. We get right with the Maker, get a good bath, and wash our shorts all in one crack."

My mother shut her ears and stuffed more clothes into the pack.

"So how exactly did you get the pack, Uncle Jack?" I asked. "You were saying something about rain and cribbage." I wanted to know how he got the pack, but I *really* wanted off the subject of my underwear.

"Oh yeah, right, Well, it had been dumping rain like there was a darn hurricane coming off Lake Superior. By the third day, holed up in Eddie's, tempers were getting a little short. It was a big cribbage tournament we had going – nickel a game and a penny a point. That don't seem like much, but some of the boys got on a losing streak and the money kinda added up."

Uncle Jack chuckled. "Ernie tapped out right off the bat. I don't think cribbage is real big in Finland. He fired up his sauna train and sulked off through the mud. Nobody saw him for two days."

Uncle Jack cut the load of socks by half, throwing the extras on the floor. Mom promptly picked them up and stuffed them back in the pack. Every compartment of the pack groaned with more than enough to get me though a lifetime in the wild country. I tied my sleeping bag to the bottom. The leather rod case holder was still empty.

"It happened there was a little disagreement between me and Eddie Barker after he went and double-skunked me in the championship match. I accused him of cheating on his pegs. He said he would never do a thing like that. Maybe it was the cabin fever that got me, but I seen this here pack hanging behind Eddie's bar, seen it had a custom rod holder and everything. I asked Eddie why in the hell he needed something like that when everyone knew that he spent all his time inside the tavern, pouring beer and telling lies, and so a far-going pack was the last thing he needed. Furthermore, I told him he was a damn poor fisherman.

"It turned out that Eddie's brother-in-law worked at the Duluth Pack Company and had given him the pack as a gift. It ain't like the thing had any sentimental value 'cause Eddie couldn't stand his brother-in-law. But when I called him a poor fisherman, well, that sort of set Eddie off."

Uncle Jack hefted the pack, sizing it up for weight and balance, holding the straps up so I could get my arms through, bidding me to walk around in circles in the bedroom. "How does it feel?"

"A little heavy," I answered, stooping a bit. It was hard walking in circles in the hot bedroom.

"You'll get used to it. Let's take a walk over to Miss Edna's and check on her mousetraps, see how it feels to walk a little while in a straight line. If you got to walk in circles out in the back country, then you're likely lost as hell. Then you might as well unpack your stuff and wait for someone to find you."

He laughed at me as we turned down the drive and headed for Miss Edna's. "You look like a regular backpacking hobo. But don't worry, where we're headed, you're going to blend right in."

"Finish telling me about the pack."

"Where were we?"

"You called Eddie Barker a poor fisherman," I said.

"Yes I did. It's not something I'm proud of. It's okay to insult someone's family, and maybe even their good standing with the church, or chamber-of-commerce, or whatever. But you should never insult their fishing integrity.

"Eddie got a little agitated, and he said, 'I'll tell you what, you no-good cribbage-playing, backwoods-mining, train-riding, cheap-drink buying'... It went on like that for a while. The gist of it was that he bet me his pack against my favorite fly rod on going down to Onion Creek, right then and there, in the middle of the monsoon, and bringing back the biggest trout."

"It must have been awful fishing in the rain." I adjusted the pack a little to the left, where the lump from my two pairs of extra boots wouldn't bite into my back so much.

"I wouldn't say that. It felt good to get some fresh air after three days of sittin' on a barstool and playing cribbage. But it wasn't easy. The Onion River flows on the edge of Ashland and dumps into the bay right underneath the ore docks. After all the rain, it was near impossible to see where the river laundered out and Lake Superior started washing. It was one big slew of water. The pilings were under that red-stained mess all the way up to the dock planks."

Uncle Jack held his hands over his head to emphasize the high water, almost running into the barbed-wire fence that we needed to hop over to cut across a woodlot to Miss Edna's.

"I wasn't going to have any part of that kind of water along the lake shore. But when I left to head upstream, there was Eddie, out on top of that ore dock casting a deep-sea looking rig into the mouth of the Onion. I figured he was trying to hook a big lake trout. It's damn possible that a fish might have come up to the mouth to get out of all that seasick water. I couldn't see what Eddie was using for bait, maybe he was using one of them pickled eggs that he kept in that jar behind his bar. What I did see was that he had our big wooden cribbage board floating and rolling above his line on top of the water like a pegged-out bobber."

I pulled the pack off my back and stretched by removing a couple of mice out of Ernie's traps. Uncle Jack walked into the field with me to help set them loose. We didn't go very far, because Uncle Jack was in a hurry to get going. The mice would find their way back to Miss Edna's garage in no time flat. "Dump the critters here," he said. "If she don't want to get a cat, it's her own stubborn fault." I re-shouldered my burden, and the story continued.

"I was a little worried about Eddie landing a slab-sided lake trout. I knew I'd lose the bet for sure. Technically, I don't believe he was even fishing in the Onion at all, but it was impossible to say where the river ended and the lake began. And I felt kinda bad about accusing Eddie of cheating at cribbage like that, so's I wasn't going to bother getting him on a technicality.

"Me, I hightailed it to a spot I remembered, where a small feeder creek trickled into the Onion. It wasn't more than a drainage ditch when the weather got hot and the water got low. But it was spring-fed. I knew that brook trout congregated below there to cool off in the summer. I figured with all that rain there might be a nice brook trout or two trapped somewhere up that creek. And by the time I'd slogged way up that ditch, well, I guess then I wasn't technically fishing the Onion River any more than Eddie Barker was."

We turned into our yard. Ernie had just finished checking the innerworkings of the old red truck. We heard the hood slam before we even walked onto the drive and saw him walking to the back yard with the radiator drinking bucket. He was putting things back where he found them.

I pulled off the pack, and Uncle Jack heaved it in the truck bed. I sat on the grass in a nostalgic sort of way, looking around the yard. It was the yard where I had played catch with my dad, the yard where we had started so many walks together. It was the yard and the oak tree where I had learned so much about life without even knowing it.

Ernie came back around the house without the bucket. It seemed like only yesterday he'd gone to get it. It seemed like only yesterday when my dad was still alive and my world was not about to go off-center. Time flies fast, and only two things stuck in my mind as certainties: I was heading off into the unknown with a Duluth pack and, droning on oblivious and unconcerned to the turning of the spheres, Uncle Jack's stories sure took a long time to finish.

"I dug deep into my fishing vest and came up with a nymph that was wrapped tight with red yarn and hackled with a bit of tinsel off of last year's Christmas tree. It had a heavy bead tied to the hook eye, so I knew I could get it to wash deep. It didn't resemble anything I knew of, except maybe a big red worm, and that's what the brook trout seem to like most in that kind of water. The tinsel just added a little personal flash.

"I bounced it down the creek. It swirled in the mud coming off the banks until pretty soon I couldn't even tell where the dang fly was. I knew I had a lot of line out, and when I got snagged, I saw that the fly had tangled right into some scrubby chokecherry trees on the bank. The creek had shot its banks so high that the water was darn near up into the lower branches."

Ernie leaned up against the truck, listening. Uncle Jack was unmindful of the waiting truck and the waiting day. His mind was not even in the present moment. It was off somewhere on a rainy creek bottom. Present surroundings had lost meaning, swept away like the rain-choked creek. Uncle Jack kept fishing, and we were there with him.

"The water really got to swirling, and then the snag started to move further back into the chokecherries. Then I knew it wasn't a snag at all. It was either a drowning squirrel hanging on for dear life, or I was hooked into one hell of a fish.

"The rain came down harder. It was going sideways. My line tugged back into the bottoms and I didn't have a choice but to follow. My hip boots shipped creek water and filled to the tops, but I had to keep the line from getting tangled around the branches, so I mucked into the underbrush. I tripped on a sunken log or something and fell into the chokecherry thicket, and then I was on all fours in a ton of floating branches and water. That must have unnerved the trout, because it came up and jumped over a branch right in front of my eyes. It was a brook trout that went about four pounds, a real beauty.

"I would have lost it for sure, except the trout didn't quite clear the cherry branch. There was this big brookie, dangling from a chokecherry tree, flopping hard, spraying water, and slapping me with its square tail, trying for all it was worth to climb down the tree and back into the creek."

"Did the fish make it?" I asked.

"Not a chance. I was hell-bent on winning the bet. I tackled it – the tree and the trout – and there I sat in the driving rain with the water still rising, sitting on a branch with the biggest native brook trout I'd ever taken."

Ernie interjected with a snort, "And dat's vare I found dem. Jack and da big trout, hugging on da branch."

Uncle Jack came back to the present, looking around like he was surprised it wasn't raining, and surprised there wasn't water flowing in sheets over the driveway where we stood.

"I don't doubt that catching a trout like that in the middle of a flash flood might keep you young forever," he said. "That is, if it don't kill you first. My hip boots were so full of mud and water that it felt like I was mired in cement. I was as exhausted as the fish. I was in a pretty pickle, couldn't lift a boot, not to mention try to climb down the tree. No way to know if I would have drowned, but I'm sure glad I didn't have to find out."

"Ernie found you way back in there in a rainstorm," I said in amazement. "How did you know where he was?"

Ernie answered my question with one of his own. "Vut he tell about me playing cribbage at da tavern? Probably he saying I lose money. Den he saying I go off mad."

I shrugged my shoulders and looked at Uncle Jack.

"I hear dat story before. But vut really happen, vas after couple hours watching little pegs go 'round little wooden board… I say enough of dat – it vas not so exciting." Ernie pegged imaginary holes in the air with his index finger, spinning on his heels and shaking his head in dizzy circles.

"So I go to da big voodshed vare I keep da train, because vas couple pistons sticking little bit, and it vas good rainy time to verk inside. Dat engine can be temperamental like da veather and vun ting lead to another. Pretty soon is pieces all over da voodshed."

I pictured Ernie through the door of a tar-papered shed, cedar boards keeping out the driving rain. I saw him with pistons and gears scattered carefully on stacks of birch kindling. I smelled the wet, wonderful smell of split wood mingling with oiled machinery. Spending a rainy spell huddled over a cribbage board, shouts and laughter ringing into the muddy street – that image seemed right and pleasant. But so did Ernie's woodshed workshop.

"I have to slop true da mud to hardvare store. Den I have to go couple more times. Soon is couple days gone by before I am done. Big hassle – I don't know why I built da damn ting in da first place. Finally, I vipe off da grease and oil and go down to Eddie's tavern to see if da boys is still putting pegs in round holes and arguing 'bout how many da other vun is supposed to be counting."

"Well, Eddie Barker *was* counting too darn many," Uncle Jack interjected.

Ernie looked at Uncle Jack with dark, piercing eyes, fingering his beard thoughtfully. He looked like a mediating umpire who is only getting a one-sided view of an argument, knowing full well that both parties are in the wrong. My mother came out of the house to oversee the final preparations of our departure. She stood with a hand on my shoulder, listening as the story of Onion Creek and the Duluth pack finished up strong.

Ernie found the cribbage tournament halted, the men inside placing lusty wagers on who would come rolling in out of rain-choked water with the biggest fish. Gambling money was strewn on the bar, spilling around Uncle Jack's bamboo fly rod and the Duluth pack in the hazy smoke of the tavern.

The rod was the pride of Uncle Jack's collection. It could lay a silk line out straight and true with the merest flick of the wrist, popping a fly gently against the thickest brush piles that the taconite range streams could wash up. Eddie Barker had insisted Uncle Jack leave the rod behind as collateral, "Just in case you get skunked so bad that you turn tail and run out on the bet." But perhaps the main reason for insisting the rod stay behind, weighing in the back of Eddie Barker's mind and the minds of everyone in the saloon, was the possibility that Hip Boot Jack might wade his way into a mess of rising fish. Then he was liable go missing indefinitely, or at least until the trout stopped biting.

Ernie sized up the situation, cribbage players turned sport-fishing bookies, excitedly pointing from Uncle Jack's fly rod to the Duluth pack. There was a fevered pitch in the air, like the eye of a hurricane before the tailing storm moves through. It rolled in with cracking thunder through the open doors of the tavern, coming from the direction of Onion Creek. Men poured out of the bar and into the rain to see. Along the mouth of the creek, in a pile of splintered planks and floating debris, the dock pilings had given way beneath the rain-soaked waves of Lake Superior. The ore dock had collapsed.

The first thought the men had was to save as much of the dock as possible. It was their livelihood, and without a dock to load the freighters, there was no reason to go back on the taconite rails and bring any ore out. Ernie hooked his freshly-repaired sauna train to the dock pieces. With a considerable amount of effort and near-death experiences under the pounding waves and undercurrents, the men were able to haul most of the pieces onto shore.

Only after the debris was cleared did the soaked patrons remember that there was a fishing tournament going on. Then they started to wonder about the two fishing contestants. Ernie knew Uncle Jack's mind, and he also knew the unique ways of fishing the Lake Superior coast. He knew a spring creek was exactly where Uncle Jack would head in that kind of rain. "I had half mind to fish dare myself if da train vouldn't have busted."

"You would have still been sitting in the tavern playing cribbage if *you* hadn't got busted," countered Uncle Jack. "Good thing you didn't bet the train against them cribbage sharks, 'specially that Eddie Barker."

Ernie ran the train through the mud and rain. When he finally found him, Uncle Jack was in a bad way. "I vas not sure who vas da fish and who vas da fisherman," Ernie said. Water was up to his chest, and the chokecherry tree leaned precariously against the raging current. Uncle Jack still clung fiercely to his brook trout, and the trout was every bit alive as if it were still pounding its fins in search of rain-washed forage.

Ernie got his train into a position upstream of Uncle Jack. The train lurched precariously on the washed-out banks. There was a tense moment when it looked like the sauna burner might be extinguished by all the splashing water, but Ernie was able to float a line down to Uncle Jack, who hooked it around the tree. Then the sauna train pulled in the heavy catch. The roots of the chokecherry tree came loose from their moorings, and the whole thing was hauled upstream, with Uncle Jack and the trout riding on top like loggers coming home with a lumber payload.

"It vas a good ting I fix da pistons on da train before I take it fishing, oddervise I don't know if I could have hauled in such a ting," Ernie said. "Only 'bout four pounds was wert keeping," he added.

It was a nice rescue, but the jubilant mood turned to gloom when Uncle Jack rode up to the ruined ore dock on Ernie's train. "I seen the dock floating there in pieces," said Uncle Jack. "Then I seen Eddie Barker's tavern sitting up on the rise, and I seen all of Eddie's regulars milling around – but I didn't see no sign of Eddie. All that we ever found was a wooden cribbage board that washed up on the beach a few days later."

I looked at my pack, sitting in Uncle Jack's truck bed. I wasn't so happy about the pack anymore.

"That's horrible! How could you take the pack after all of that?" my mother chastised.

Uncle Jack stood in solemn silence. Ernie stood with him. They stared in a decidedly northern direction, and they stood that way for some time. They seemed to be meditating together. Finally, Uncle Jack broke the silence.

"I thought long and hard before taking the pack. I walked the Superior shores for a long time. I was searching for an answer. Hell, maybe I was searching for some sign of Eddie. But I never found either, so I did what Eddie would've wanted. I did what he would have done if the situations were reversed. I had that brook trout stuffed and mounted. I took the pack down off the wall behind Eddie's bar and hung that fish right in its place."

Ernie nodded his head in absolute agreement. "Now dare is people come from all over to see da fish and to hear da story."

"Yep, Eddie's wife and daughter run the place now," Uncle Jack added. "Business will be treating 'em good for as long as they care to stay at the Ore Dock Tavern."

Uncle Jack patted the Duluth pack. Turning to me, he said, "You got to take care special care of it because, like I said, it ain't technically mine. It's just borrowed. For all I know, Eddie Barker had hold of a lake trout that would have put that little fish of mine to shame. Maybe that laker pulled him into the water. Eddie was a good enough fisherman to hold on. Maybe Eddie won the bet. I'm sure going to ask him when I see him again." Ernie and Uncle Jack were still looking north. "Yep, I'll see him again someday, on top of that taconite range, way up there yonder somewhere."

Ernie took the fly rod, the one I'd learned to cast, the one I was still earning. He stuck it in the rod holder of the pack I was still earning as well. Then he handed me a small cigar box; a miniature version of the one he stowed his own flies in. I opened the box, and it held a dazzling and colorful array of flies along with coiled line and leaders. There was a small knife in the box, no bigger than a letter opener, and sheathed in a finely-tanned deer hide case. The knife was no letter opener. Its honed edge was sharp enough to slice a piece of stationary in two with the flick of a wrist.

"Everyting you need to live forever in da vild taconite country," he said with a huge bear grin.

I tucked the box into a folded side pocket, and we got into the truck.

That was how we left; pointing the truck north and heading somewhere I only knew through stories. My mom cried, but I held up pretty good. I hugged her and said I'd miss her. I told her to check on Miss Edna's mouse traps for me. Uncle Jack and Ernie wholeheartedly promised to take good care of me.

"Don't worry," I said. "It's not like I'm going to be gone forever. We'll all be back by the Fourth of July and go see the fireworks together. I'll still have the rest of the summer to spend with you; Uncle Jack and Ernie can stay, too. No summer school to worry about. Everything is going to turn out spectacular."

Mom wiped her eyes and smiled, nodding her head in agreement as we bounced out the drive.

It was going to be spectacular. Summer lay ahead, and I didn't have to worry about summer school. I was going to miss the fireworks, because Taconite Creek was waiting to take hold with grips of iron. I wish I wouldn't have lied to my mother – but how did I know that then?

CHAPTER 14

The trip didn't start out very eventfully. I guess I was prepared to see mountains or glaciers or something. I didn't understand what constitutes "north." In relative terms, you are always north of something, so maybe it's a state of mind. We just rolled on blacktop highway for a lot of hours, and nothing looked much different than the woods and grass right out my back door.

We stopped at a trucker's wayside to eat. We ate ham and eggs, washing them down with a white-enameled pot of coffee. The waitress brought three cups and didn't bother to look, or she didn't much care, that I was twelve years old. She was preoccupied, as if she had the weight of the world on her shoulders, as if there were any number of things she'd rather be doing. She set the cups and the pot down and went about whatever business she had, probably thinking about getting home at quitting time and going back to her own family.

I thought a lot about that waitress while I ate my ham and eggs. I wondered what people do, where they go after crossing paths so quickly with our lives and just as quickly fading out. I wondered what kind of lives they led and what constitutes north for them. I guess the world is a huge place.

I poured some coffee in my cup. It wasn't very good. It tasted like tar, not that I'd ever eaten tar, but it tasted like tar smelled. I managed a couple of swallows before we left the wayside, guessing it would grow on me and maybe taste better when we got further north. It did. It still does.

Uncle Jack had been driving first but, after lunch, Ernie took over the wheel. The two gulps of coffee kept me wide awake, searching the surrounding countryside with my eyes, seeing cattle grazing and farmers working their fields. Rows of fences with thickets of rock hedges piled dark and inviting. There were stretching hay fields, soybeans, and corn poking out in neat rows. The windows of the truck were open. I could smell the new crops growing, and it was a fresh green smell of flowers and lilacs; all of life, just waiting to grow into full-born summer.

"Keep an eye on that Finlander over there," Uncle Jack said, poking me in the ribs. "He gets a full belly and then he gets sleepy. We don't want to run off the road into a hayfield." Ernie shook his head and kept on driving. In another minute, Uncle Jack was snoring gently, head lolled back, and little bubbles blowing out of his bottom lip. A pot of coffee didn't faze him much.

Somewhere along the road the scenery changed. It was sort of like it is when you are driving south out of the snow regions. The snow banks get smaller and smaller. Bare spots melt in the fields and under the south-facing tree lines. You can't say exactly where it happened, but soon there is no snow at all. It's a gradual change.

That's how it was along the road to Taconite Creek. There were more pines, with maybe a few more lakes popping up off to the side. The water started to look bluer, reflecting the white clouds above a little brighter. The blacktop lanes got narrower, with not as many cars and trucks darting in a rush to get to wherever they were going.

The waitress at the truck stop crossed my mind again. It's a busy world. Everyone is in a hurry to reach around the next bend of the river. Though I was only one small part, I hoped that I would always take the time to stop and walk in the fields, crawling under the fences and into the hedgerows just to see what was there.

Uncle Jack came awake with a start, looking this way and that, taking it in with a sense of anticipation. No one said a word in the cab. Uncle Jack on one side, me in the middle, and Ernie steadily holding the wheel; no one said anything, but there was an impending wildness in the land, and the mood permeated into the truck. It swirled around our heads as we drove. There was no clock on the dashboard, and no one wore a wrist-watch. The sun was still high. I asked what time it was, but neither of my companions seemed to have any real idea. Or if they did, they didn't seem to really care. They just shrugged their shoulders. "I tink it is afternoon, or somevare 'round dare," said Ernie.

Uncle Jack nodded, as if Ernie had gotten the time exactly right.

Blacktop blended into the afternoon sun. It disappeared as quickly as a passing cloud casts a shadow. Just like that, we were bouncing along a graveled road. The trees weren't exactly up to the edges, but they were certainly creeping closer. There were fewer homesteads, front yards more sand than grass, leaning barns and pole-sheds with sun-faded cars and tractors rusting beneath them. Fire lanes twisted mysteriously back into pines. Trails wound up steep hills, disappearing over the tops with oaks and maples hanging low, like tunnels. Through openings in the trees, I caught glimpses of a railroad track that was shadowing our path.

We did not take any of the side lanes, continuing on the gravel until we reached a crossroad. It was not the conventional four-corner type. There were eight spurs coming out of the intersection, like the points of a compass with the half-directions thrown in at angles.

Clusters of ramshackle buildings were spread along the intersection. There were houses with clotheslines stretched taut between jack pines. A group of children sat on a set of porch steps, playing marbles, playing with well-washed rag dolls, or just sitting and dreaming about faraway, as children will often do. A Lazy dog sprawled in the dirt beneath the porch, tilting his head in half-interest as we stopped the truck.

There was a garage-front machine shop off to one side with the sounds and smells of cutting torches and clanging metal coming from inside. A small, white-washed church with stained-glass windows and neat beds of tulips sat on another corner.

In the center of the village was a low-lying building with rough board siding and smoky windows. It looked like a rail depot with tracks half hidden in the weeds, rusted steel reaching aged and tired in the direction of the intersecting roadways. Most of the rails ended abruptly where the roads took off from the town. The only track line that looked recently used was the one I'd seen following the road that we'd driven in on. If trains still came here, this was the end of the line. They'd have no choice but to circle around and go back the way they came. On a bench on the platform outside the depot, two men in faded canvas hats sat together with legs outstretched.

We got out and stretched our legs in front of a sagging and paint-peeled building. An aluminum sign hanging above said: Popcorn Corners Co-op Grocery.

"It's a little town, all the way back in here," I said, looking around. One of the children sitting on a porch front raised a hand to me in a half-wave. I waved back. The two men on the railroad bench watched our arrival with sharp, interested eyes.

"Popcorn Corners," said Uncle Jack. "Not much more than a collection of like-minded people who prefer to make a go of it out here rather than closer to civilization. It ain't much, but it fits me more comfortable than a bustling city street."

"And it is not so much in a hurry," added Ernie.

"Why is it called Popcorn Corners?"

"Well, if you look at the roads leading out of here, it kind of reminds you of a kernel of popcorn blasting out in every direction. This used to be a train station town, a hub for all kinds of folks: iron miners, loggers, trappers, hunters – anyone who came in to look the country over for a spell. That was back when trains were the only way to go, before the automobile kind of took over. In fact, I think Ernie came through this very place on his way into Ashland. I kind of miss those days – there weren't no leaky radiators on a train."

Uncle Jack gave Ernie a good-natured slap on the back.

"Now, the old track lines are just older roads. Some of 'em don't go anywhere in particular, but some of 'em do. It's like a piece of popcorn before its popped – can't tell from a small kernel what the popped corn is going to look like, so you just got to take one of them roads to see what's going to happen."

"Are we going to stay here for a while?" I asked.

"Not long," answered Uncle Jack. We need to make use of what daylight we have. The days are a little longer this far north, but it still ain't the land of the midnight sun. When it gets dark up here in the woods, it really gets dark. Then there isn't any use to go further. I don't want to sleep inside the truck with Ernie; he not only looks like a bear, he snores like one, too. We'll stay long enough to set in some supplies, just long enough to decide which of these popcorn kernel roads we need to take."

He reached into a side pocket of the truck cab and produced his folded parchment map. Ernie dug into his pack and took the cigar box full of flies that he had meticulously tied every morning on our front steps. I followed Uncle Jack and Ernie up the weather-stained steps of the grocery, craning my neck at the array of roads leading from the village. The group of children had disappeared down one of the roads with their dog in tow. But the two men on the railroad bench were still there. They watched intently as we went.

CHAPTER 15

A little bell jingled above. Light from the open door streamed through behind us and lit the floor in dusty waves. The floor was laid with rough wooden boards running long and parallel with the store. Sections of boards were warped and heaved with time, worn smooth and polished by the steps of countless years.

It was dark inside, but it was not a gloomy darkness. Floating from the shadowed corners were the scents of cinnamon and pipe tobacco. There were stacks of canned goods: beets and corn, peaches and pears. Piled in cardboard boxes were jars of dried apples and jelly. Bags of flour sat on barrels of nails and crates of garden seeds. I saw a shelf holding many spices – everything looking home grown and packaged.

A freezer stood against one wall with bacon, beef, and chicken, hand-labeled in white paper wrapping and looking fresh enough to have recently been delivered from a back-woods farm. Some of the wrappings were labeled "venison." Thanks to Uncle Jack, I could spell venison now, and thanks to Ernie, I smelled frying steaks along a lonely stretch of track.

A wooden counter stood in the front, and an old man sat on a high stool behind it, smoking a pipe and wearing a plaid sweater vest that was burned in places from pipe ash. On the counter was a fishing reel, disassembled into tiny rows of gears and windings. The old man peered and smoked over the reel's inner workings with the peaceful contemplation of a Buddhist monk. He nodded at our arrival without looking up from his meditations.

The counter had a glass display case underneath that was piled with wonders to rival the biggest city Christmas window display. Jars of bubble gum sat side-by-side with wooden boxes of triple-hook fishing lures. Hard candy wrapped in paraffin paper spilled onto fishing knives. Tightly woven coils of fishing line rested on fanned-out piles of old magazines and comic books. Fully assembled reels, much like the one the old man was working on, were polished and cared for; they lined the bottom of the display case along with a colorful collection of bamboo rods in a variety of lengths and weights.

Fishing flies were scattered in the case, too. The flies looked a bit like Ernie's, but I thought they lacked the life-like quality that Ernie could bring out. They were pinned to paper cards and leaning against cans of pipe tobacco. It seemed there weren't a lot of flies, and maybe they were spread out a little thin, but it was hard to tell in the vast display. I couldn't focus on one thing, because my eyes were constantly being pulled to another treasure.

The old man's eyes adjusted to the light from the open door. He looked up from his work, his face breaking into a grin of recognition. The broken reel was pushed aside.

"Whoever said that the dead can't come back to life sure ain't seeing what I'm seeing!"

"Halloo dare, Herbie," said Ernie, a sly smile breaking out on his rough bearded face. "I see dat business is still how you like it, nice and slow, plenty time to sit and smoke and tink da deep mysteries of life."

"That's about the size of it," answered the gray-headed man.

Uncle Jack shook hands with the proprietor. "It's nice to see you again, Herb. It's been a while since we passed through your neck of the woods."

Uncle Jack and Ernie eyed the fishing implements in the glass case. They looked at each other with a knowing, passing glance. Uncle Jack shook his head side to side, almost imperceptibly. Then the two men shrugged their shoulders and looked at me. It was as if they wanted to ask me something. Then the moment was gone. It happened so quickly that I wasn't even sure I had seen it at all.

Herb tamped new pipe tobacco over old, setting his pipe down on the scratched and worn counter. Ernie set his cigar box down next to the pipe, and Uncle Jack placed the map down on the counter, too. There was no cash register, only a yellowed notepad of paper with names and figures and annotated notes scratched up the sides of the columns.

Inquisitive and sharp eyes peered over the counter at me. One of Herb's hands rested on the map while the other rested on the cigar box. "What do we have here, a new traveler wandering through our humble crossroads?" He looked back and forth between me and my two companions. "You look pretty young and innocent to be running with the likes of this kind of iron-mining rabble."

"This here is my nephew," said Uncle Jack. "Ernie and I figure we can use a good strong back for this season's campaign, seeing as how we ain't as young as we used to be."

"No one's young as they used to be, only as young as they want to be," said Herb. "But I hear tell that it's all shut down now, even though you'd think that with the war being over, they could use all the iron that they could lay their hands on."

Ernie slapped the counter and breathed a mock sigh of relief. "Dat's vie ve come to see you, Herbie. You have da good information. Now dat ve know it's shut down, ve von't have to vaste time going back to verk! Vut else do you hear?"

"I heard you boys were the last crew. I heard the taconite ran dry, and I heard you lost your train somewhere back in them hills. But you know I deal strictly in rumors. Now that I see you passing back through, well, I say to myself, maybe the whole taconite campaign isn't quite as over as they say."

"It ain't that kind of campaign," said Uncle Jack. "This is different, like cleaning up after a battle."

Uncle Jack stopped for a moment. It got real quiet in the store, which was saying something, because the store had a small-town quiet feeling in the aisles to begin with. "Did you lose many boys?" His tone said he was genuinely concerned with the small population of Popcorn Corners, even though I knew from following the news that hundreds of thousands had lost their lives fighting for small towns like this all over the country.

Herb came from behind the counter and walked to the door. He opened it, and sunlight permeated the dark grocery store. He pointed across the intersection to the small church I'd seen when we drove into town. On a small hill behind the church was a fenced-in cemetery plot. It was as well tended as the tulips surrounding it, grass trimmed neat, the iron fencing polished and without a single spot of rust. There were new crosses of wood among the older granite and white stone markers in the plot.

Herb pointed out the new crosses. "We lost five – five that came back here to rest, anyway. There's still four missing, but I guess that don't mean they're gone. Maybe they got a taste of the world out there and decided they just didn't want to come back."

"If you lose yust vun, dat is vun too many," said Ernie, shaking his head. "And if dare are vuns who don't come back, I am grateful yust the same. Day gave part of dare soul so ve can come back here for dem."

Herb stared at the fresh crosses. He blew a final trail of smoke out of the corner of his mouth and contemplated the worn stem and bowl of his pipe. "I reckon there are things I'll never be able to figure out sitting behind this counter. I reckon there are even things that you can't sweat out in the sauna, huh Ernie? Some of those mysteries of life are buried in the ground with the deepest iron."

"Dat is da truth."

We started pulling items off the shelf and stacking them on the counter. Uncle Jack and I did, anyway. Ernie opened his box of flies and started going through them with Herb. We picked out dry goods: flour, oatmeal, and rice. We stocked up on canned vegetables – corn, beets and peas – but most importantly, we took two big crates of rutabagas that were sitting alone in a corner of the store like they were saved for someone special.

"Ernie can't get enough of these," Uncle Jack said. "But it's a good idea not to get too close to him after he's been eating 'em. He's downright combustible."

The somber mood of the cemetery passed. We picked out wrapped packages of bacon and canned ham. We took nothing more perishable than that. Uncle Jack added two bags of yellow onions to our rations. He took an onion out of a bag and started eating it the way most people would chomp an apple. We ended up with quite a pile of supplies on the counter.

Ernie and Herb were laughing like old friends. The wartime memories had left them, too. Ernie's flies were piled on Uncle Jack's folded map. Herb was going over the flies, twisting and pulling on the hackle and wings, peering at them the way a jeweler examines tiny diamonds.

As we came to the counter with the last of our supplies, Herb appraised Uncle Jack. "Ernie tells me you're both retired. I see the map, but I also see you aren't wearing your hip boots. I see that you're riding in an old truck instead of a train. Judging by how many flies he's been able to fit in his cigar box, I'd say he's had some idle time on his hands. So, putting two-and-two together, and if anyone should come asking, I'd have to say that the iron mining is retired, moved on, and the two of you retired with it. That's what I think I'd have to say."

"For the game of horseshoes we're playing, I'd say you're close enough on that throw to score the winning point," said Uncle Jack, piling groceries in a cardboard box. "But you're wrong about one thing. I'm not retired in the true sense of the word. I'm just getting into my prime."

Herb nodded knowingly, relit his battered pipe, and sat down behind the counter. He looked to be waiting for something. He smoked in silence. Maybe he was pondering the deep mysteries of life, like Ernie said. He smoked and waited. Then Uncle Jack unfolded the map.

It was hand-drawn with red and blue ink. The paper it was printed on may have once been white, but those days were long gone. There were smudged finger prints and stains streaking the contour lines and map symbols. The stains looked like bacon grease, and the smudged finger prints looked a lot like blood. The blood alarmed me at first, until I saw dried, flaking fish scales stuck around the edges; then I saw them for what they were.

The crackled parchment was covered in a fine ash-like resin, which turned out to be taconite-rock powder. Try as you might, through blowing or rubbing, the powder never seemed to come off the map. I think there was either an eternal layer on the paper, or the map and taconite dust were bound together in a static-charged force that made the two inseparable. I never figured it out. I just know it was dusted with powder whenever I saw it unfolded. And in the coming weeks, I would see it unfolded a lot.

Herb reached into a front pocket of his tattered sweater vest and came out with a pencil stub. As an afterthought, he tapped pipe ashes into the pocket. He flipped through the yellow notebook on the counter, looking through pages of scribbled names and figures. There were no completely blank pages, only interwoven gaps among the writings in the crammed ledger.

When he finally found a blank writing space, I assumed he was going to start adding up the groceries. But then everyone huddled over Uncle Jack's map and started placing flies onto strategic points of the dusted paper. I didn't quite get how this was going to help calculate the cost of our supplies. When the talk turned to fishing, then I was really confused. I contemplated piping up and voicing my question, but quickly forgot as I became caught up in the strategic game taking place on the map. And what a game it was.

Flies were placed on blue-smudged lakes, rivers, and streams that popped up on the map. Some of the flies were bigger, some smaller. Some had wings tied turned up, and some had wings turned down. There were sparse feathers and bushy tails. Others were nothing but a twist of brightly colored thread and yarn.

The biggest and buggiest flies were placed on lakes, the medium-sized ones were put on rivers, and the daintiest flies were put on faint blue creek lines. I had to stare to find some of the smallest creeks, hidden as they were by the dust and the grease. Soon, a good section of the map was circled by armies of flies. They converged from different angles and onto different marked waters; but all radiated towards a red dot on the map fold that was marked Popcorn Corners.

Uncle Jack rattled off directions and names of lakes, rivers, and creeks. Ernie recited the names of his flies, placing them on the map next to the corresponding waters. Herb diligently scratched all of this in his notepad.

Uncle Jack knew the waters better than Ernie. He could call out fishable places in the middle of a desert, but he never bothered with the technical names of flies. The christening of the bugs was Ernie's specialty. The two men's genres converged in the places where the trout dwelled, but Herb had to be patient. Specific days and months needed to be scribbled hand-in-hand with the fly names and the map waters. He had to be patient because, more often than not, Uncle Jack and Ernie haggled fiercely over these specifics.

"Take these here gray feathered flies," said Uncle Jack. "They're the ones Ernie put together after poaching those Canadian honkers from that pond last fall." He gave Ernie a smug look before continuing. "They will only work on one stretch of water within a half-day's hike of your store, Herb. That would be the Namakagon River. Don't bother trying 'em until late July or early August, because the trout will just laugh at you."

Uncle Jack proceeded to shove every fly tied with gray wings and wrapped with dull green winding over onto the heavy-lined swath that was marked Namakagon.

"Day are Blue-vinged Olives," Ernie replied tersely. "Some vill verk on da Namakagon, but day vill be best trout killers on Flume Creek and da Outback River." Ernie tapped his finger impatiently on the corresponding map waters, sorting Uncle Jack's pile into three separate ones.

"Da bigger vuns are for da river, and da tiny vuns are for da creek. Den vait till dark, or get a cloudy day, den use da vuns vit vings turned up. I almost guarantee you vill catch da big vun."

"Don't listen to this goose poacher, Herb! For one thing, there ain't no blue on his olives – they look gray and green to me. If you sell his fly knowledge to any paying customers and they try these green olives on anything but the Namakagon in late summer – then you will be the laughing stock of Popcorn Corners, and you'll go out of business to boot!"

"Day are Blue-vinged Olives!" Ernie shouted. He pounded his fist on the counter until the flies on the map bounced. "Day hatch all summer long and day look blue ven day are in da vater. Day vill verk damn fine anyvare!"

"Everything looks blue in the water, you Finnish goose murderer," laughed Uncle Jack.

Ernie glared. "I yust chase da geese off da pond. Day fly away – I vade out and collect da feathers. Da geese keep honking and fly to someplace else – day don't mind, day grow more feathers later."

It went on like that. Uncle Jack piled flies on rivers and lakes. He called them black-bear hackled critter, squirrel-furred drifter, and chipmunk-tailed streamer. He didn't have an entomological clue what the proper names were, but he shoved them around the map with authority. Ernie called them hare's ear, bi-visible, and muddler minnow. His water locales overlapped Uncle Jack's, but the specific trout-stream manipulations were a vicious and unending circle between them.

The only fly they agreed upon was a big, furry mouse replica. The mice imitations were quite realistic, sporting bushy gray bodies, life-like whiskers, and what appeared to be actual tails. The mouse flies reminded me of Miss Edna. And come to think of it, Ernie was a regular on the trap line on the nights when I had been too caught up in Uncle Jack's homework drills to go myself. Both Uncle Jack and Ernie agreed the mice would work on any bass lake or brown trout river, provided it was a sultry night and the moon was missing from the summer night sky.

When the game was finally finished, Ernie's flies had conquered the map's waters surrounding Popcorn Corners. The fly-hatch dates had been argued to death and stowed away in Herb's notebook. I wasn't certain who had won the game. Our grocery bill seemed paid, so I thought maybe Uncle Jack and Ernie were the winners. But then Herb took all of Ernie's flies and began pinning them on small paper cards. Ernie closed his cigar box, which was now empty, and Uncle Jack folded up his worn map. Then we picked up our box of supplies and said goodbye to Herb.

Herb took a scoop of lemon drops from his case and wrapped them in a paper sack. Uncle Jack and Ernie bent down and took one last, long, hard look at the rods and reels sitting in the case bottom. They stood quickly back up when Herb handed the candy to me. Herb smiled warmly. "Good luck, gentleman – wherever the wandering may take you. And if you happen to come across any new and buggy creations or promising wet spots in your travels, just remember: I'll be sittin' here waiting to hear about 'cm."

We shook hands with Herb. We walked over the worn and uneven floor of the grocery. The bell over the door jingled merrily as wc left. "Just pondering the mysteries of life, right Ernie," Herb called after us.

"You bettcha, Herbie," Ernie said. "Dem mysteries – you gonna find dem someday. Den you make sure to tell me. Den you make sure to tell all of us."

Herb was chuckling to himself as we left. The broken reel was pushed in a forgotten pile on his counter. He didn't seem to be pondering any mysteries. He seemed more intent on scrawling names and dates on the back of his newly-won fly cards, sticking them way up front in the glass display case. I guess the game ended in a tie.

"What are you going to fish with now, Ernie?" I said, as we piled groceries in the truck. "You traded away all your flies." I turned to Uncle Jack. "And you gave away all the secret spots on your map."

"Vell, I guess I have to find some stuff along da vay to make some more," said Ernie. He looked at the crate of rutabagas in the grocery pile with an admiring gaze. "It look like it ver a fair trade to me."

Uncle Jack unfolded his map again. He turned the map this-way-and-that while Ernie peered over his shoulder. "I ain't worried about giving away all my spots. The bacon-grease stains are hiding most of them. I'm more concerned about how to proceed from here."

"You don't know where we're going?" I asked.

"I know where were going. It's how to get there that I'm not totally sure of. I've never been there from this side before."

Ernie pointed an accusatory finger. "You is going down to da eternal fires – dat's vare you are going. I ain't gonna follow you dare dis time, either!"

"Don't mind him," said Uncle Jack. "He gets jumpy every time we head off the grid."

"Isn't it marked on your map?" I asked.

"Sort of, but the world is a damn big place. To answer your earlier question about giving away all my secret spots, well, I've got so many of them that I plum ran out of room on the map, and a bunch of 'em just crawled right off the edge. I'm going to have to rely on my keen sense of navigation, so, I say we go that way!"

He triumphantly folded the map and pointed past the railroad depot. I noticed the two men in the canvas hats were no longer sitting on the bench.

"Ya, nobody knows. Nobody ever going to find dem spots again," said Ernie, shaking his head. "Dat's vut I'm little afraid of. And da keen sense of navigation, dat's vut I'm big afraid of!"

"Get in the truck, sissy," said Uncle Jack. Then he turned to me. "Why don't you ride in back? We could use a good lookout, and you'll get to see the lay of the land from up there. We won't be going too fast, so you don't have to worry about falling out."

"Maybe going so slow dat you might be able to valk and keep up," said Ernie. "Maybe ve get going in circles, so den you can yust sit under a tree and vait till we run 'round to pick you up."

Uncle Jack jumped into the truck and fired the engine. Ernie followed, putting on a show of dragging his feet and shaking his head. I climbed into the truck bed and situated myself among the bags and packs and boxes of gear. I never could figure them out.

We headed down the one-lane track past the abandoned depot with weeds coming out of the boards. There was ivy climbing up the back wall, and it looked like the depot hadn't had any traffic for quite a while. I wondered what had become of Ernie's sauna train. I made it a point to remember to ask him about it.

The last thing I saw before we left Popcorn Corners were the two men in canvas hats from the depot bench. They walked hurriedly around the white church, being careful not to step in the planted rows of tulips. They held fly rods in their hands and were going at a good clip in the direction of the Popcorn Corners Co-op Grocery. It was a tackle shop and an information center, too. A darn good one, now that I thought about it.

The two fishermen stopped their hurried pace when they passed the well-tended cemetery where five crosses stood out from among the rest of the stones. They raised their fly rods in a half-salute at the markers. I wondered if the missing soldiers were still out there in the big world, somewhere, maybe not far from the edges of Uncle Jack's map. I wondered if they were still alive, still making their way back home. I was thinking those thoughts and eating lemon drops from a paper sack as we rolled out of the old railroad juncture that was Popcorn Corners.

CHAPTER 16

I bounced around the bed of the pickup, over a back-woods maze of dirt roads that led to more dirt roads. Soon we were bumping through thick brush trails that even a deer might shy from. We weren't going very fast, as Uncle Jack had foretold, but it was hard to get comfortable amongst the gear stowed in the bed.

I squirreled around the boxes and packs, finally finding myself a nest between two boxes of braided rope. I sat on a suspicious bundle that rattled and clanked as we bounced along. My backside soon felt like there were spikes sticking into it, and I wormed my way further down in the nest of gear until my back rested on the bundle. That was okay for a while, until my back started feeling like there were spikes sticking into it.

Untying the drawstring of the bundle, I saw the problem. The large sack actually *was* filled with railroad spikes. There were hundreds of them. Some were rusted and bent, but many looked like they'd never been driven into the ground. I didn't know what fare the spikes would bring to the table of our journey. I wondered for a moment if I had been given the whole story about the purpose of this northern venture, before remembering that I hadn't even been let in on the real purpose to begin with. I'd wonder about that a lot in the coming days, but for now, all I knew for sure was that it was impossible to get comfortable situated on the clanking bag.

The front cab must have sensed my discomfort. The back window slid open, and a red canoe seat cushion flew out to me. I don't know why they had it. I never once saw either of them in a canoe. I guess both of them had spent a lifetime accumulating those types of things. With the cushion resting atop the bag, I was able to ride in comfort. I was able to really look around at the rolling thickness of the passing forest.

Pine and hardwood forest blended into miles. We went up high, round hills and through deep-cut valleys. Small lakes cropped up from nowhere, ringed with tamarack and spruce. There was a sharp pine smell in the air, and it seemed the whole world was breathing the boughs as they swayed. There was no sound of civilization besides the steady chug of the truck. The chugging got steadily louder, and we were finally forced to stop at one of the small lakes while Ernie got out and went down to the lake with a bucket. He came back and poured the bucket down the throat of the thirsty truck radiator.

As the truck cooled, Uncle Jack and Ernie leaned over the map and debated with animated gestures. I walked down to the water to stretch my legs. It was quiet compared to the noises I was used to: cars rolling and doors slamming, telephones ringing and Miss Edna yelling at the mice to get the hell out of her garage. But as I stood by the shore and listened more closely, what I had thought was noiseless was really a symphony.

I heard the low croaking of frogs. The unseen songs of birds came from the thickets. Even the wind made a sound, like a whisper in the high pine branches, trying to tell me something that I almost – but couldn't quite – make out.

What I had thought was silence was really a whole new world of sounds. All I had to do was stand and listen, and the sounds came like waves into my ears. Even the low murmuring of Uncle Jack and Ernie arguing over the map was lost in the new life I heard coming from the shores of that small wilderness lake.

I took off my shoes and waded in. It was surprisingly cold for a small lake. Soft muck squished between my toes, and minnows darted away in frantic schools. One group shot over a weed bed where a rotted tamarack lay out across the water. There was a quick, loud plop, and a bass wallowed out of the deadfall hole and inhaled a minnow. I wasn't even sure I saw it surface, it went that quick. All that was left were ripples where bass and minnow had collided.

It was one of those moments when you know you've seen something and been somewhere, and you know it will stay locked in your memory to be resurrected on duller occasions – maybe school, for instance – but I wasn't thinking of school just then. I was locked away in a moment of time and space that nothing from the outside world could penetrate. I looked up the sloping hills that rose from the lake edges to where birch and maple overtook the pines and showed the silvery-green underside of their leaves. I couldn't imagine that a finer place might exist. I was soon to find that I was mistaken.

I walked back up to the truck to discover that our back-country navigation had gotten scientific. My two companions were orienting the map. Uncle Jack's compass had made an appearance and lay open on the crusted paper. There was a heated discussion going on about the difference between true and magnetic north.

"Dare are magnetic lines across da globe, I tell you," lectured Ernie. "Liquid iron deep in da earth, so's ven you say ve are heading north, ve are really going along vun of dose magnetic lines. If you refuse to take dat in account, ve may end up in California."

"That is the biggest load of manure I've ever heard," countered Uncle Jack, implying and phrasing something more specific than manure. "I don't know what kind of compasses you had in Finland, but this compass don't care about no imaginary lines. And the fact of the matter is, once we're in iron country, the compass is going to point to the biggest ore deposit around and you know full well that's where we're headed. Furthermore, you wouldn't know liquid iron from a chunk of taconite, even if the chunk fell out of the sky and cracked you on your thick head. We're going the right way, like it or lump it."

Ernie threw up his hands in disgust, slammed the hood of the truck, and flung the bucket into the back where it clanked noisily against the bag of rail spikes. Uncle Jack got into the driver's seat and stubbornly folded his arms. On the surface, it seemed to be a tense moment, except it seemed both of them were trying to hide smiles.

I began to suspect that neither of them cared in the least about being lost. And after standing on the shores of that small lake, seeing through the curtain of silence and into the true nature of what was really out there, I found that I really didn't care, either. I assumed my cushion perch on the bag of spikes. The radiator had drunk its fill. All was right with the world as we continued our journey over the northern-cut trails, along whatever magnetic-bound line Uncle Jack and Ernie had decided to follow.

We were high on an outcropped hill when we stopped again. There was no mechanical trouble this time, but once more the map was unfolded, and the compass turned circles in Uncle Jack's hands.

I stood up in the truck bed. Far below, I saw a cold shimmer that was bright and intense in the falling afternoon sun. The wooded lake on our last stop was a shaving mirror compared to the full-length refection of pounding waves in the distance.

Smells of sand and driftwood floated on a cool breeze. It's nearly impossible to describe those smells to someone who has never stood in a truck bed on a high, iron-range knoll and seen Lake Superior shining below. It was a smell peculiar to a large body of water, not unlike an ocean when you smell it because of the salt, and you know it is an ocean even with your eyes closed; but when I closed my eyes in the back of the truck, I could smell that iron-packed sand and sun-bleached wood washed on the shore. There were red clay banks climbing up the shores into the hills, and I swear I could smell that clay, too.

Contrasting with the cold lake in the distance, heated debate came once again from the front of the truck. The back window slid open, and Ernie's bearded face filled the opening. "I ask, 'cause you are part of da team and should have equal say. If ve follow your uncle's directions, den ve vill end up down in da big lake. Me, I say da compass says go dat vay." He pointed in the direction we had just come from. "So's if ve listen to him, I yust vant to make sure you can swim."

"Don't listen to him," Uncle Jack shot back. "That's Chequamagon Bay. You can see the Apostle Islands out there if you look close. And if you could see around that point, then you could see clear to Ashland. We're close. We just gotta get a little closer."

Uncle Jack was talking in riddles. But if I shaded my eyes just right to cut the glare of the setting sun, I could make out some distinct shapes riding far out in the lake. They might have been low-lying clouds. But maybe, just maybe, they were islands.

"What do you say?" asked Uncle Jack. "You're our navigator, so we'll leave it up to you. Do we go down this hill, or do we sit here and let Ernie play with the compass?"

I had no idea. One direction seemed the same as another. But if we were going to end up spending the night in the truck, I thought that waves pounding against the sandy shore would make fine bedtime music.

"Sorry, Ernie," I said. "It's not that I doubt your compass readings, but I think we should head for the lake."

Uncle Jack crowed. "That's my boy! It's good to have someone on these kinds of trips, besides myself of course, who's got an ingrained sense of direction."

Ernie shook his head and threw the compass out the window. Rolling laughter erupted as Ernie tried to push Uncle Jack out of the truck. A bellowed Finnish curse shot off the high hill and floated over Lake Superior. I didn't understand the language, but I could tell a good swear when I heard one. As he crawled into the bushes to retrieve the compass, his bearded face glared at me in mock disgust. Then we rolled down the hill towards the lake, with nothing more to go on than my fascination with the distant water.

It was a good thing that the brakes on the truck worked better than the radiator or we just might have ended up swimming in the cold waters of Lake Superior. We inched down the range toward the lake along a grade that would warrant signs for truckers to test their brakes. Every time Uncle Jack let out the clutch, we started moving fast. We actually slid sideways a few times. It was steep and bumpy, tires bouncing over jagged rocks, and quarter panels scraping the brush.

Scrub-oak branches sounded like fingers down a chalkboard against the truck. It was a little agonizing. We hit a big rock, and the whole truck lurched. I buried myself in the back and hid my eyes in the folds of the railroad spike sack. Uncle Jack whooped and hollered up front, having a grand time by the sound of it. We hit another reddish hump, and rock and clay rained over the windshield. We actually left the ground. I think kids nowadays call it "catching air." I buried my head deeper in the sack.

"WHOO-EE!" Uncle Jack hollered out the window. "That's pure-grade taconite rock we just rolled over. Ain't it a fine sight!"

"Whooo...eee," Ernie replied in a much more subdued manner. It looked like he wished he had a sack to hide in, too.

Just when it seemed we would careen over the clay banks and crash down to the shore, Uncle Jack turned the wheel hard to the right, and we funneled into a shallow depression through the rocks and underbrush. It was almost imperceptible at first; just a low swale, not even big enough to be called a ditch. I caught one last glimpse of the lake before the funnel deepened. Then the growing banks swallowed our truck, and I lost sight of the water altogether.

What had started out as nothing more than a cut soon become a valley through the guarding hills. The stunted scrub oaks gave way to their full-grown brothers. The trees towered above in a sheltered canopy. Stream beds angled from deep within the hills, water trickling over mossy rocks. Our tires sent sheets of water into the air as we bounced over the rivulets. Many of the small streams dropped into cave-like openings on the lake side of the valley. The openings were ringed with high ferns and lichen, looking green and inviting, but a little dark and scary. They weren't big, hardly big enough for a full grown man to squeeze into. Cool air flowed from the caves and into the warmth of the main valley. Along with the cool currents, the hidden sound of the Lake Superior surf echoed up through the chasms.

"Lake caves," Uncle Jack said, as we stopped to look at one of the bigger openings. "They go clean through. Twisting and turning and dropping right into the lake. Ernie claims that the glaciers from the ice age ran off through theses valleys and made the caves. He says the glaciers made all these here valleys, too. He should know – he's probably old enough to remember the ice age."

Uncle Jack walked to the rocky hole. A small stream ran across the valley floor, emptying with a final rush down into the cave. He looked at the stream, and he looked at the opening it poured into. He bent down and stuck his hand in the water, splashing it into the valley air. The sun was falling due west down the valley, and the rays turned the drops into prisms of gold. He squirmed into the cave up to his waist, rooting around like a badger.

Ernie watched Uncle Jack hanging vertical down the shaft with his knees wrapped around a root. "I don't quite remember da glaciers, but I am old enough to know better dan to crawl 'round in caves dat drop hundred yards straight down into da lake."

Uncle Jack's voice echoed out of the darkness. "If a man were to use a little dynamite and blast down here, I'd be willing to bet the whole thing is lined with taconite ore." He pulled himself back out of the hole and brushed watery moss from his hair. "The hills are alive with it. No reason not to imagine the water from the hills has been bringing down iron and dropping it into these caves since the beginning of time. Maybe even for a million years!"

"I tink da beginning of time is more dan a million, and it don't matter how long da caves have been here. I still vould not crawl 'round in dare," said Ernie.

"Quit splitting hairs; you're a geologist, not an archeologist. I'm just thinking out loud, anyways, thinking about some of those mysteries of life that you and Herb are always going on about. I'm just saying that it wouldn't be anything at all to blast that iron out of there, bring a barge up to the shore, and throw all that taconite right in the boat. Not that I'd have a mind to mess with Mother Nature to that extent."

"Ya, Mother Nature vould bring in her own boat for sailing you to da funeral," said Ernie.

Uncle Jack gave Ernie a sly look. "I bet if there were trout swimming down below them caves, it would be a different story," he said.

Ernie wrinkled his forehead and looked at the yawing opening in the green hillside. "Maybe Mother Nature vould sail us both to da grave," he replied.

Uncle Jack nodded. We got back into the truck and drove further into the deep valley, leaving the lake caves behind. Soon, we were traveling in a land that looked lost in time, like nobody had gone before. Except that wasn't quite right. Uncle Jack and Ernie had gone before. They had gone to beat the mining companies at their own game, to beat Mother

Nature at her own game. They had gone to fight the trout in a place far removed from the eyes of the common world. I didn't know it, but it was a match they were still finishing. We were headed for the game field on Taconite Creek.

CHAPTER 17

The valley leveled out after several miles, disappearing into birch and poplar slashing. We might have been following a faint track, or it may have just been a heavy deer trail. I couldn't tell from my truck-bed vantage. We stopped once to refuel from several containers of gas that sloshed alongside the gear in the back. We got going again right away, because now it was getting late. The sun cast long shadows through the white of the birch trees. For the first time that day, Uncle Jack and Ernie seemed in a hurry.

The truck arrowed through some of the thickest brush we'd yet gone through. It looked like the trail might close up and swallow us. Alder twigs scratched the side panels. Tires bogged through pits of mud that swam up to grab at us, turning into full-blown swamp. Overhung vines with large, evil thorns hung low enough for me to grab at from my perch. With gloves to ward off the thorns, I might have easily jumped out of the truck and gone hand-over-hand through the forest tunnel.

Logs angled from the underbrush like giant spears set against an advancing army. They were everywhere in the brush alongside the faint trail. I leaned over for a closer look and saw they were railroad ties, buried in the swamp, weathered and waiting. I realized we were driving on an abandoned railroad grade that had all but surrendered to the evergrowing jungle.

Uncle Jack and Ernie were at ease as the truck slid and lurched in the wet-bottomed ground. They seemed to have found what they were looking for, though I didn't know how they'd ever found it to begin with. I didn't realize that taconite meant money, and no wilderness is deep enough to hide that truth.

We broke free of the brush and in sight of a clearing when, with a final gasp like a runner collapsing scant meters from the finish line, the truck slid sideways into a fern- covered mud hole and sunk to the fenders. The engine sputtered and died. The sun sank over a high hill across the clearing. Boulders sloped up before us, and the last rays split into rainbows, turning the rocks into glowing iron. It was more a mountain than a hill, rising above the scrub brush and giving birth to large stands of pine. A gaping chunk the size of a football field was cut out of the tree-clad slopes. It was a man-made quarry, no doubt, but with a look of abandonment and disrepair. The rising hills and setting sun were the only life in the midst of the swampy forest.

Blown-out rocks split the sides of the pit down the steep incline. The shadows of the hills brought a cool breeze, and a fine mist came down from the dark spruce and balsam trees over the top of the hole. The source of the refracted sunlight on the rocks and the falling mist became evident, first to my ears, as I heard the sound of fast flowing water, then to my eyes, as I picked out a tumbling stream rushing on a switchback course alongside the opening.

The stream came out of the ridges above the pit, skirting the top like a tightrope walker, somehow managing to stay on top before turning sharply down a freestone rocky run and crashing into the clearing. The clearing stopped the torrent, widening it and deepening it, turning it into a dark snake that disappeared into tendrils of tag-alder swamp. They were the very same tendrils that had welcomed us in, and in which we were currently half-buried.

I wasn't quite sure how the rushing stream could make it across the top of the pit without spilling down the ridge in a waterfall plunge. The break in the side of the rising hills was big enough to drive a train into. The question of the tightrope-walking stream quickly went on the back-burner of my young mind, because, tight to the bottom of the ridge there actually was a train. As a matter of fact, there were two of them.

The first was a peeling wooden boxcar, half-buried in the rock-slide rubble, its paint stripped away, and its slat siding warped. The iron wheels were rusted and the lower frame was twisted. It looked as if a giant had tired of playing with his toy and discarded it down the grade.

And right at the ridge bottom, jack-knifed and looking like it was in-grained in the ridge itself, was the high stack and stove-box cab of Ernie's sauna train. It was buried in rock shadows and looked like it was a natural order of the whole wild place.

Uncle Jack proudly climbed out the driver's seat window, as the door itself was firmly wedged in mud. "Welcome to Taconite Creek!"

"Velcome to da Taconite Creek train wreck," Ernie climbed out the other window and squished through the muck. "It vas perhaps your Uncle's finest hour in da employ of da Ashland iron mines."

Uncle Jack hunched his shoulders and squished alongside Ernie. "Maybe it was and maybe it wasn't, but you were in on it from the get-go, so you're just as guilty. It wasn't just me who decided to start pulling taconite out the side of this God-forsaken hill. It was a joint venture, and you know it."

"Ya, but ven I first came, da creek ran forward. After you vas done vipping and lashing it vit your fly rod – now it don't know vut direction it vants to go."

"I'll be damned if all I was trying to do was save a click or two of time and money. Furthermore, you two-bit Finnish rock hound, you were the one who designed the wing dam and the pump house. And you were fishing them pools right alongside me, too!"

Volleys of argument shot forth, regarding who was fishing instead of doing *something*, whatever it was that *something* was supposed to be. As accusations flew, Uncle Jack and Ernie carried boxes and packs from the back of the truck, tracking muddy footprints across the gravel and sand in front of the half-buried boxcar. I leapt from the back of the truck bed, avoiding the worst of the swamp and trying to stay out of the way, trying to figure in my mind what that *something* was.

Ernie slid back the rusted side-door and pulled himself into the dark opening. The smells of creosote, tar, and old timbers floated down. Uncle Jack and I handed up gear, and Ernie stowed it in the car. Through the falling shadows, I made out the shapes of boxes and barrels stacked along the walls. There were coils of rope resting on rail ties. Pick axes and shovels leaned in the corners. There were plenty other tools of construction and destruction lining the walls, too. And there were crates and crates of railroad spikes.

Uncle Jack hefted my nemesis bag of spikes onto the ledge opening, and Ernie wrestled it to the side and plopped it with the other boxes of spikes. "Make sure to look careful in them dark corners, Ernie," Uncle Jack shouted into the depths. "Hope there ain't no big black bear hiding in one of 'em, 'cause I heard them bears are mighty partial to Finnish food."

"It is true dat da bear is a fine dining expert," said Ernie, examining the contents of a steel-banded barrel. "But I have da bear repellant a-right here, so's I'm not vorried."

"What kind of bear perfume are you gonna find in a rusted bucket?"

"It is da finest essence of da axel grease," Ernie proclaimed, reaching a slow hand into the barrel, turning just as quickly around, and plopping a handful on Uncle Jack's head. "And it verk yust as vell on an old-fool train wrecker!"

Laughter howled over the taconite mine clearing. The glow of the fallen sun slanted through the pines on the high ridges and caught fire in the mist rising from the rushing creek. Uncle Jack's curses echoed through the pines as he chased Ernie up the slopes and through the creek.

I was getting comfortable with the chaos. I hopped up into the train car and began stowing my gear. Three folding cots had made the trip with us. I unfolded mine, spreading my sleeping bag on its taut, canvas surface. I stowed my pack underneath, resurrecting a sweatshirt from inside the folded depths. It was growing chilly with the sun hidden behind the ridges. I was glad my mom insisted on doing the packing, because the sweatshirt was folded neatly right at the top. Moms have a sixth sense about those kinds of things.

The commotion in the clearing died slowly. The two men walked side-by-side along the banks to where the water curled deep into the swamp, Uncle Jack pointing and Ernie nodding agreement. Uncle Jack looked like a tracking bloodhound. Ernie still resembled a big bear, but he wasn't plodding along – now he was dancing. His head turned light and quick. Both men studied the water gliding through the undergrowth. They paid special attention to the places where the water cut beneath the banks, tailing through the alders to form dark, mysterious pools.

They were deep in conversation. It came to me that this was how they found this place. They worked together with the familiarity of a team who had been together for many years. When they finally broke their huddle, they cut across the clearing to the swamp-bound truck.

Fly rods were assembled from a battered case behind the seat. There had been a light in their eyes when they jogged from the creek banks, but now, oddly enough, neither man looked too happy. Uncle Jack looked wistfully at the cracked joints of his rod. The handle, once cork, now consisted of faded wrappings of duct tape. Ernie's wasn't much better. It was bamboo, but the bamboo that had spawned the rod had either grown at a curved angle from the time it sprouted, or time itself had withered the piece into a spanning arc.

Their reels were pitted and battered, with a distinct grinding noise coming from Uncle Jack's as he peeled line to string through the bent rod guides. I'd heard enough stories from Uncle Jack to know that back-country fishing is hard on gear, especially taking into consideration carrying it on countless trains, jumping off those trains while at a questionable speed, and tramping about on taconite-rubble explorations of the roughest order. Uncle Jack had been known to hide rods and reels the way a squirrel stores nuts, with a haphazard way of chasing his tail to remember all the hiding places. Who knew what kind of storage facility those hiding places entailed? But judging from their sour demeanor as they rigged up, something was amiss above and beyond the normal wear and tear that such adventures inflict.

Ernie confirmed my suspicions. "Fishing vit such as dis, I only vant for a satchel to tie on da end of my rod, and I could be railvay hobo."

"Quit griping, Ernie. At least your reel don't sound like a caboose with a squeaky bearing."

Uncle Jack glanced up the ridge, looking hard at where the creek rushed across the pit. Water sprayed across the jumbled rocks of the mine opening. He shaded his eyes with a hand towards the last shafts of falling sunlight.

"Besides, we got plenty of time to get the good stuff back."

A back eddy of water swirled in the creek above, spilling in tiny waterfalls down the slope. "I vould not say plenty," said Ernie, shading is own eyes and looking up at the rushing course of Taconite Creek.

"It's time enough for our purposes," Uncle Jack said. "You forget we got a third hand to our game of cards now. That means we got triple the time."

Uncle Jack pointed his duct-taped rod in my direction. "He's small, but that's an asset hard to come by in these parts. After all, we hand-picked him, didn't we?"

Ernie nodded. "I betcha he got da iron in his blood, too. I tink he might even learn to drive da train pretty quick."

"We'll see about that," said Uncle Jack. "You got to get that sauna-bath piece of junk out of the rock slide first. I do know it will be nice having someone else around here who can talk English – that much I'm sure of!"

Ernie's eyes gleamed. "I tink it vill be nice having someone 'round who don't talk so much in any language – someone who can catch a share of fish for da camp, 'stead of scaring 'em down vit all da talking!"

I had a million questions, but Ernie and Uncle Jack turned away, huddling together over a small fly box that had appeared in the midst of all the faulty fishing gear and the traded insults. The two men peered into the box with supreme concentration. There was business at hand.

"It's a damn good thing I saved this box of flies," Uncle Jack trumpeted. "I never dreamed you were going to trade all of yours in on a crate of rutabagas."

"Maybe da mayflies are starting to hatch?" questioned Ernie. He never took his eyes off the fly box.

"They'll be dropping close to the banks, right underneath them overhanging willows." Uncle Jack said, sporting a devilish grin. "Make sure you keep that bent tree staff you're using pointed towards the water so you don't crash the brush and scare all the bugs away."

"I vill make deal vit you. I vill forget dose are my flies to begin vit and only ask for half. But you stay far avay from my spots. Dose vailing noises from your reel sound like a buzzard and vill scare every trout in da swamp."

"Don't hardly seem fair, but I guess you got a deal," said Uncle Jack, handing over half the mayfly imitations that had been tied by Ernie in the first place.

Uncle Jack and Ernie didn't seem to give our mud-buried truck a passing thought. It crossed my mind, though, as I glanced over and saw it slowly settling into a more comfortable position in the bog. Like I said, there were a million questions dancing in my head, but I found that the proprietary rights of whose fishing flies belonged to who was not the least bit confusing. I was slowly learning.

The two iron miners started towards the stream. Ernie knelt in the brush and snagged a hatching bug, twisting it in his forefingers and peering intently before pulling a fly from his pocket and tying it on the end of his line. He gave the line a testing pull, and his bamboo rod groaned menacingly under the strain.

Uncle Jack was similarly occupied, comparing a winged insect he'd snagged from the air to the remaining flies in his box. He heard the groan of his partner's rod, but he never looked up from his careful study. "Don't worry, Ernie; we'll have the good stuff back soon enough," he said.

Uncle Jack quickly tied on his own fly and cast under the willows with a sandblasted racket issuing from his reel. It didn't seem to scare the fish any, because a fat brown trout darted out from beneath the overhang, and his own worn-out rod was soon dancing. He glanced back over his shoulder and shouted as he fought the fish.

"Rustle up some firewood before it gets too dark! There's some fallen pine up the slope a ways. It'll be seasoned just about right for Ernie to burn a trout dinner with. His damn train should still be good for that, anyway!"

I stood in the clearing, with the tumbling sound of Taconite Creek above and the faint whish-whish searching of fly lines coming from the bottoms. I'd forgotten all about my own fly rod stowed in its holder beneath my train-car bunk. Uncle Jack and Ernie seemed to have forgotten it, too. How many pounds of taconite steel had they had gone through to get to this point? How many years spent honing their relationship to a fine edge?

I left my fly rod beneath my cot. I needed to earn my fishing right-of-passage. I climbed the ridges of Taconite Creek ridge to carry out my orders.

CHAPTER 18

A taconite mine met a trout stream above the swamp. A stone and mortar wing dam twisted the flowing water back from the gash in the earth. In some stretches, the water gave the illusion of running uphill. I lay on the top of the raceway, dipping my hand deep in the spring-fed ice that slapped and worked steadily against the mortar.

Rising in the air along the stream was a ghostly mist. I reasoned that, when the sun rose over the clearing, it must shine a good portion of the day on the rock field. Now that it had slipped over the high ridge to the west, the temperature of the air, rocks, and water created the perfect ambient temperature. It was like pouring cold water over the rocks in a hot sauna. Rainbows of setting-sun steam fell gently down the ridge and shrouded the clearing. Ernie's sauna train lay buried in the broken rocks below, falling steam curling around its tarnished frame – a train designed to run like a sauna, resting in a natural sauna of its own. It was the perfect blend of nature and man; the purest of waters falling across blasted taconite rock and down upon the very conveyance that had gotten Uncle Jack and Ernie in here to begin with.

Trout dimpled the water above the dam. They tailed in slow and easy rises, taking in winged bugs that floated down with the falling mist. I guessed the floating bugs to be the mayflies that Ernie and Uncle Jack had spoken of in hushed tones. The bugs seemed so small upon the water, but some of the feeding trout looked to be downright huge.

I started to gather the knotty branches that were shattered across the ridge from fallen pine giants. They were victims of the same blasting and hammering that had opened the side of the earth. I knew the pine knots would burn down into glowing coals. Gathering more fallen timber down from the dam, I stumbled upon the ruins of a pump house. It sank into the damp earth. Rotted rubber hose ends and rusted nozzles poked from the boulders surrounding it. The nozzles looked to have been used as a hydraulic force to wash the slopes. Now, the broken machinery looked like ancient serpents peering from their holes, craning and twisting, hoping for a glimpse at the swirling brown trout in the water behind the dam.

The pump house foundation itself was a wreck. Not much was left of the collapsed doorway leading into the stone building. It was less of a door and more of a crawl space. In the darkness beyond, I saw rough-hewn planks, splintered and broken. Water seeped out of fissures in the stone floor, dripping in places, coming in spurts from some of the bigger cracks. A winding stream of water trickled out of the collapsed door itself like an artesian spring. I faintly made out a large pump in the center of the trashed room. Smaller pumps were sunken below the floorboards, the cracked dials reflecting the rising water.

Through the fading gloom, I made out the outlines of several bundles in the back of the pump house. They were rolled on a plank shelf that tilted precariously. I thought I might be able to squeeze through the collapsed opening for a closer look, but it was a little too scary in the growing darkness.

I stepped back and took an overall view – the crumbling dam, the silent and rusted pumps, and nobody home to supervise the whole of it. What it really looked like to me was a creek reclaiming its right-of-way.

As I walked down the rushing creek bed with an armload of gathered wood, I saw the shadowy figures of Uncle Jack and Ernie below. Uncle Jack was huddled over the sauna train, starting a kindling fire in the burner. Ernie was cleaning three glistening brown trout with his knife. He wiped the knife on his pants before using it to pry open a crate of rutabagas. I could see from my vantage point that we would not be going hungry tonight.

They seemed a fine outdoorsman team, alright. I was in good hands. Mom had nothing to worry about. Uncle Jack and Ernie were just waiting for me to stoke the cooking fire, and then we would have a fine dinner.

Maybe tomorrow I'd ask both of them about the ruined pump house. Maybe tomorrow I'd get a chance to try out my fly rod, see if I could entice some of those browns. I looked over the valley of Taconite Creek, and it was all like a dream, stunning and clear, and I was awake for it all.

CHAPTER 19

The coals burned down in the open grate of the train stove. We sat on the ledge of the boxcar and, when the pine knots popped in the stove, they cast shadows that looked like dancing trout.

My stomach was full of rutabaga on the half-shell and trout fried to crisp perfection. I even ate the tails, crunching them in my mouth like potato chips. "I could eat trout every night for the rest of my life," I said to no one in particular, my eyes watching trout-tailed shadows dancing on the boulders, my ears listening to the rushing flow of Taconite Creek coming down from above.

"Trout and rutabaga – day don't eat dat good in heaven, I betcha," sighed Ernie, rubbing his belly in contentment, basking in the claimed spoils that went along with catching the biggest trout of the evening.

Uncle Jack tried stealing the honor, but I was the final judge. I measured the fish myself, deeming that Ernie had won by a good half-inch. It didn't sit well with Uncle Jack. "One of you's got no grammar to speak of, and the other one can't read a ruler. It's a fine lot I've got myself in with."

Ernie just kept rubbing his belly and grinning like a cat. We'd eaten every inch of trout, and there was no evidence left. I imagined that by tomorrow morning, Uncle Jack would be clamoring that his had been the biggest after all, and it was just the campfire darkness that had fooled with my sense of measurement.

"How did all of this get here?" I asked. "It's the greatest thing I've ever seen."

Ernie chuckled quietly. The light of the dying fire illuminated his eyes and his shaggy hair. His cheeks were sunburned red. He could have been a Viking marauder sitting over his spoils. Even his beard still had some flaking trout from dinner hanging in it.

"What's so funny?" I asked.

Ernie spoke to me in his home language. "*Kauneus on katsojan silmissä*. It means dat beauty is in da eyes of da watcher. It means it is a good place now. I am glad dat you like it here, but is good ting you never werked for da mining company – 'cause I think day fail to see da beauty like you do."

Uncle Jack's eyes perked up. He got that far-off look that meant he was about to start reliving the past like he was in it. I lay back and watched the cold stars above. Ernie's chuckling subsided, and he swung his legs back and forth from the ledge of the boxcar. I thought I might be in for a good bedtime story but, as it turned out, it stretched much longer than that.

"It's a story," started Uncle Jack, "that you won't fully understand just by hearing it. It's a story that's not even done writing itself yet. We'll have to see how it shakes out. I'd warrant that there's even a place in it for you now."

"Start at da beginning. Seems like da best," Ernie said.

Uncle Jack grunted an approval. Then he started at the beginning. It was a story, like he said, that was still writing itself. And all the main characters were gathered around the sauna train's glowing stove.

"It was a rumor that got tossed around since the old logging days. The old-timers marked their routes by name – every mile of 'em. One-Mile Water Station, Two-Mile Bridge, Three-Mile Camp – every mile was named for some landmark. Those loggers came up with plenty of names, but they weren't none too original, either. It was mile this, and mile that. All the way from the Ashland saw mills to back here in the willy-wags. Twenty-Mile Creek they called it; I don't know if anyone but the native Indians had ever bothered to name it before. Maybe they didn't bother, neither – but I bet the Indians knew about it – 'cause they were pretty fine fishermen. I'd wager that they used fishing gear that was a far cry better than the rigs me and Ernie are toting right now, too. Tavern rumors had it that the stream running down from the hills was full of trout. Brook trout as long as a man's forearm was the story I heard."

"You maybe never seen a brook trout dat big, but you should know 'bout da stories from da Ashland saloons," Ernie said. "All da time you spent in da taverns researching for da big taconite business."

"I *was* researching, you Finnish fraud. I had my ears open. I knew that if the stories were true, then these ridges had big potential. I remember the look on your weather-beaten face, the first time I brought you back in here. Your eyes got big as saucers when you saw the water rushing down and tailing off into the alder swamp."

Ernie belched. He rubbed his stomach. "It is true. And my eyes got even bigger ven I see all da trout."

"Yeah, my eyes got pretty big when I saw them, too," Uncle Jack said.

Uncle Jack gestured up towards the tumbling water. "Some of the hardiest woodsmen supposedly got back in here with horses in the winter and took some of the best red pine ever seen in this country. I plied one old lumberjack feller with beer and, after a pint or two, he started to reminisce that that the ridges were so red with iron that it was impossible to tell the pines from the rock. He said in the end, they had to pull out with what lumber they could get – said the rest of the ridge was too damn much work. They couldn't get to it from one direction because of the swamp, and there's no way they were going to come down from the top – too steep, and too rocky. They'd have stripped it clean if they could have run a rail track in here, but there was no way to do it.

"I asked the old guy about the iron. He finished his beer in one mighty swallow and told me that a bunch of red rocks weren't none of a logging man's concern. He said if I wanted to make them my business, that was fine with him, said he'd give me a nudge in the right direction if I'd be kind enough to buy him another round. As it turned out, after the logging camps moved on, all of this was left untouched and mostly undiscovered, rolling down from the ridges and through the timber just like it does today."

"Day maybe should have called it Nineteen-Mile Creek, 'cause day only get about dat far. Too many bad spots, too many big rocks, and too much sinking vet," Ernie said, with a rumble starting low in his stomach, quickly escaping into something more.

Uncle Jack made to go on but stopped and pointed an accusing finger at Ernie. "You're going to blow us all sky-high someday by eating like that. It's a wonder that we're even going to try and shovel out your sauna engine. You might as well just keep eating and blow it out of the rocks yourself!"

Uncle Jack threw a night log on the stove. Ernie and I laughed until tears streamed out of our eyes. We'd regain our composure and then start right back up. I couldn't see Uncle Jack's face while he stoked the fire, but I could tell from the shaking of his shoulders that he was laughing right along with us.

Uncle Jack brushed a hand at the dark shadows cast from the towering rock slide above the train car. "Those ridges stretch. There ain't many people living in this whole part of the country that's ever been way up there."

"Except for vun person sitting here who has," Ernie said. "Way up dare is ven all hell start to break loose."

"Yeah, I've been up there," said Uncle Jack. He didn't rebuff Ernie's accusation. His mind was elsewhere. He just kept on, like a witness at a jury trial, relating the facts as he saw them. "It was darn near a whole hill of taconite rock. It started in the swamp and went up along the creek. I renamed it Taconite Creek on the spot, and then I went and fetched Ernie. We fished the swamp below the ridge for a week, lost our way more than once, and never did get to the end of it. It dumps into Superior somewhere, but hell if I know where that happens. We didn't even know what kind of insect hatch was going on. There were always multiple ones that whole first week. We caught big fish and lost bigger ones. The stories that I'd heard from the old lumberjacks were pretty much dead-on, except they was all browns – never hooked a brook trout in the whole first round at Taconite Creek.

"It sure looked to be brook trout water, too," continued Uncle Jack, shaking his head. All that fast-flowing water coming from up above."

"If it vould have remained so – only looking like, and not becoming – den tings may have been different and not so out of hand," said Ernie.

"If you would have stayed home in Finland instead of shadowing me through the hills with your rock hammer – then things wouldn't have got so out of hand, either," railed Uncle Jack. "You were in on it right from the start, taking rock samples, tapping them out with your hammer, studying the results late into the night. I remember you in the swamp pools, hooking browns from those mucky, upturned roots. You forgot your samples entirely for hours and days at a time, only coming back to them at intervals to see if the quality had changed or, more specifically, to tie new flies to replace the ones you lost in the brush. I happen to know you kept your tying material in your sample kit!"

"I do not deny it," said Ernie. "Dare are yust days I vish I hadn't."

"I know, Ernie. And to tell the truth, I'm glad you had those flies in your sample kit – I've always been meaning to tell you that I may have borrowed one or two from it. Truth is also that we both had ample time to discuss approaching the mine company at all. It ain't your fault any more than it's mine. I know there are some days you wish you never took those first rock samples but, if it means anything, there are some days I'm almost glad you didn't stay in Finland."

That was as sentimental an apology as I'd ever heard from Uncle Jack. I guess Ernie must have thought so, too. He smiled briefly, continuing to speak on in the glow of the burning stove.

"It is true dare vas much discussion. Da moral discussions, ve can debate who is responsible till ve are blue in da face, but along da technical lines, dat vun vas my fault. Conventional mining methods vould not cut it. Da terrain vas too rough."

"But you had something that would cut it!" I exclaimed. "You had Ernie's train."

"That we did," said Uncle Jack. "When we made it back to Ashland after the first expedition and met with the board, it should be said that the mining officials were apprehensive about the remoteness of the operation. It was so far removed that no one with any real authority – meaning no one who held the purse strings – even knew what county the ridge was located in. Some of 'em didn't even know if it was still in Wisconsin. But the ore samples we brought back were of a premium grade that was unheard of, and suddenly it didn't seem to matter if the rock was locked up in Siberia. Everyone got excited, and the name Taconite Creek bantered around the coffee stains and cigar smoke of the boardroom like wildfire. There was some heated debate. A lot of land got leased, bartered, and maybe outright stolen. This was uncharted territory. But finally, on the boardroom walls and in the stuffy land offices, great swaths got marked on maps and, in the end, the company gave us free rein to fire up the sauna train and start up excavation operations at the quickest possible convenience."

"But ve had to be extra sneaky in putting together da crew," Ernie said.

Uncle Jack nodded vigorously. "It had to be done right. We couldn't have everyone in Ashland, especially those who knew enough to tie a piece of string and a hook on a stick, finding out that we were pulling taconite from underneath the nose of the best trout fishing spot in northern Wisconsin. We thought the problem would be keeping the trout hawks out of Taconite Creek; turned out the real problem was getting anybody at all to come along on the operation. It seemed we had developed a bad luck reputation ever since burning down the Bad River Bridge. It sort of grew proportionally after the ill-fated cribbage and fishing tournament."

Ernie looked around cagily, silhouetted big and dark in the dying embers of the fire. "But ve didn't take no chances – it vas maximum security all da vay."

Uncle Jack had made the rounds to all the miner-haunted taverns he could think of. He had started giving directions to all the trout-fishing spots he knew throughout the northern reaches of taconite country. And he knew a lot. He knew so many trout holes, had been so concealing of them over the years, that he had developed a war chest of information. He prudently cashed in his trout-water stock portfolios and sent trout-fishing mine workers happily on their way, all the while concealing the true gem of Taconite Creek.

A rumor, circulated as a final form of trout-stream insurance, said that there were dens along the rock slopes harboring black bears in excess of five hundred pounds. Ernie cemented the bear story when he misjudged an angle beneath his train one day. The wrench he was using to tighten a brake line slipped, popping free of the fitting, and delivering a nasty cut along his cheek as well as a black eye.

Uncle Jack told everyone that Ernie got his beat-up face by chasing a particularly ornery she-bear out of a cave near the potential mine. And in that way, a crew of workers was garnered, one by one, interviewed carefully by Uncle Jack and Ernie. The Taconite Creek mine workers ran the gamut from young to old, married to single, nationalities and heritages diverse as they come, but they all held a common bond. They were hard-working, loyal, and looking to scrape together a living from the wild and remote reaches of the Lake Superior hills. And to a man, not one of them cared a whit for trout fishing.

"It vas open business at da Taconite Creek Mine, and business vas good," Ernie said.

"It was too goddamn good," confessed Uncle Jack. "Day in and day out, busting rock onto flat cars and laying rails and timbers to get over the real wet spots of the swamp. It was pure back-country mining, and the taconite started rolling in. The mine company was elated, high-grade taconite free and clear, out of sight and out of mind as long as the money rolled in. We were left to our own devices. Nobody even knew where we were."

There was a minute of silence in the clearing. The fire in the sauna train stove shot a final umbrella of sparks. Three sets of eyes sat watching as the embers died. I yawned; it had been a long day, and the bedtime story had come to an impasse. It mirrored the iron-hard problem that faced Uncle Jack and Ernie along the rocky slopes of the Taconite Creek mine.

Ernie finally proclaimed the obstacle. "Da trouble vas, dare vas so much ore and ve had so few people vit us, dare vasn't 'nuff time left to fish."

Uncle Jack belched a punctuation of approval. "And there was no point in living like that."

The waning smell of fried trout and rutabaga floated one last time through the air. It smelled like sleep. With an unspoken agreement of stories yet to be told and stories yet to be written, we crawled upon our cots inside an old boxcar. We fell asleep with stories of taconite and trout left unfulfilled. But for a night, mindless of unfinished business, three train hoboes couldn't have had it any finer.

CHAPTER 20

It started in the opening of a speeding train. The car was not faded like the storage car I had bunked down in. It was shining steel and glowed like freshly-polished chrome. The walls hurt my eyes to look straight at them. It was like staring into the sun.

It seemed impossible for any physical thing to look so polished and bright. The glow was scary, but I found myself drawn close, the way a moth can't resist investigating a burning flame. I ran my hands down the sides of the car walls, and there was the smooth sense of touching air. The walls were transparent in their existence.

It was raining gray pellets out the open door of the careening train. It made the bright walls stand out even more. There was no sign of a sun. If it existed at all, it was buried behind a rolling mass of clouds.

The pace of the train over the rails warranted thunder. It should have been deafening, an earthquake vibration. I should have been hearing rain pounding on the roof. I'd stood before at many a railroad crossing, watching as close as I dared, wondering what it was like at the end for my father, feeling the rails pounding and resonating through my very soul. That was when I still denied him being gone. That was another world ago. I'd moved on, leaving my thoughts of denial tracked far behind. They crept back upon me in that silent and transparent speeding train. Maybe they weren't gone. Maybe they were only hiding deep.

At the very least, there should have been a rushing wind as I stood in the entrance. But the only sound was a steady *click, click, click*, like a child's toy train as it paced round an imaginary landscape. I was a plastic figurine, helplessly caught in the diorama of a constructed landscape while an unseen engineer cheered the train around and around.

The unseen engineer seemed to hear my thoughts, and the rain drove into the car opening like a punishment, whipping my face and stinging like burning nettle. I stumbled backward into the steel-lined car, but it followed my every step. I wondered how that could be, before finding that the rain was also penetrating right through the smooth steel walls.

The rain hit the car floor in rivulets and pools, turning the darkest shade of red. It was the shade of blood that had died on dead leaves. It was red turning into brown iron. It ran in tracks on the floor like the scrawling on Uncle Jack's broken map. Every line was drawn with a rusty marker. Hesitating, I reached down to touch the flowing lines, and my hands came away clean. I touched nothing at all, like touching the walls of the speeding boxcar. It was not blood in the same way the walls weren't tangible steel. It was a phantom nothing.

The thought of blood scared me initially, until I satisfied myself that it was really nothing at all. Then it didn't bother me. The first heart-pounding shock that I might be standing in flowing pools of an unseen pumping artery wore off, and my mind relaxed. Then the rain stopped stinging. The phantom world seemed to hinge on my mindset.

Holding on, I leaned far out of the car opening, craning my neck to see what kind of locomotive could be pulling the iron-pooled boxcar so fast. The air outside was fog-whipped and dark. I could just make out the shape of a steam-fired engine hooked to my car. And there sat Ernie, riding high on the wooden bench of his sauna train.

"Slow this thing down before we jump the tracks and crash!" I yelled through the storm. I remembered how white Ernie looked, rolling down that rock-studded grade above Lake Superior, Uncle Jack whooping and hollering, and him holding onto the dashboard for dear life. Now, Ernie was mercilessly gunning his train at a harrowing pace.

He must have heard me, because he waved merrily, turning back to his controls and revving it up another notch. His hairy and muscled arm swung forward and pointed up the tracks into the rain. The *click, click, click* of the train sounded faster. It bled together into a roar. Ernie pointed ahead up a steep grade. He pumped a fist into the air, and I realized we were fixing to shoot the high ridge in one fell swoop.

Boulders popped from the landscape as we rose. The rocks blended into fantastic shapes in the mist, for mist was what it had become. The rain had abated without me noticing. I began to hear the blowing and rushing of water and found myself standing in pools of iron-stained water that had overtaken the shining steel floor of the boxcar. The rushing of water grew steadily. It overran the noise of the train as we rolled to the top of the hill, losing speed like an elevator coming to a stop on top of the misty ridge. I felt the ascension in the pit of my stomach. One minute we were speeding higher. The next we were stopped.

We rested at the threshold of a plank bridge spanning a roaring river far below. Rough hewn boards splintered across the gorge, sitting atop round pine pilings driven deep into the river bed. The pilings were moss-covered and slick, and the smells of old tar and river mist hung beneath the bridge in a thick air. By the looks of it, the bridge had stood in place for many years. The stack from the sauna train coughed curling puffs of steam and added to the river fog. It was impossible to say where the steam ended and the rising mist took over.

I careened down from the train, getting my bearings, staring down at feet that should have been wet and tarnished from standing in a pool of red-stained water. I was getting used to all the crazy, and it didn't surprise me that my feet were bone dry. I stomped along the tracks towards the head of the bridge. I'd had enough, and I headed with purpose towards the sauna train to give Ernie a serious piece of my mind. The rail tracks ended at the bridge. I thought for a moment that the lack of bridge tracks was the reason we had stopped...till I remembered that Ernie's train didn't need any.

Maybe the boxcar couldn't make it, I thought, heading deeper into the steam and mist, cursing Ernie all the while. It blended thick around me, and I got turned around. Thinking to regain my bearings, I retraced my steps back to the steel boxcar, but found that it had vanished from sight. "What the hell is this?" I shouted through the dense air, my own voice startling me in the silent gloom. I guess it must have startled the mist too, because it curled open for a moment, and I saw the sauna train sitting upon the old wooden bridge. Not hesitating, I ran up to the steaming contraption, and I was going to jump right up on there with Ernie and get in his face – and I didn't give a damn how closely he resembled a grizzly bear.

But Ernie was gone now too, vanished like the boxcar. Now, there was only the sauna train with steam rolling in gentle spurts as the engine cooled, smelling of the smoky burnt-wood embers mixing with tar from the bridge pilings. There was still the bridge, too, and the river flowing over the rocks below it, with the rocks now looking more and more like ragged tombstones in the fog.

Taking a deep breath, smelling those smells of burnt wood and river water, it came slowly that I was having one of those rare dreams that allow control of your actions. Maybe there had been too big a whirlwind of traveling going on. I'd stuffed a pack till it overflowed, but I didn't realize that my heart and mind had already been packed before I left. It finally became too much, leaping out of my subconscious and showing itself to my rational mind, like a trout that has lain in wait, finally splashing to the surface where before there was nothing but hidden darkness. My body was ready to awake, but my soul still slept.

Dreams are said to jumble together thoughts and remembrances, breaking them down and digesting them for the mind to handle. I remember a psychologist once telling me that dreams don't tell the future as much as they try and make sense of the past. I can't tell you even today if it was a load of bullshit that he was making up, or if there was some scientific and psychological basis to it. I only know that train dreams are certainly adept at overriding the laws of physics.

Now that I sort of knew what was happening, I looked harder, trying to remember if I could. So many of our dreams are lost forever and left behind in the night, with no way of recollecting except in fragments. It's like vaguely remembering the glories of a faded past that can never be put back together. Fragments are all that are left. I wanted to hold this dream together as long as possible, staring beneath the bridge at the river rocks, etching them into my mind. They seemed important. They danced in the rushing water like swaying crosses, reminding me of the small cemetery in Popcorn Corners, but these river tombs existed in a graveyard not so neatly tended by humankind. The river was caretaker here. The tombs were worn down by the power of ageless flowing water. It was a graveyard gone unchecked, leaning hard against a cold rush.

Figures took shape slowly in the rocky yard of river. I saw the last soldiers come, the ones from Popcorn Corners who had been lost, unable to make their way back. Now I knew that they never would. They were ghosts now, drifting in and out of the river-bank boulders. Battalion helmets were replaced on the warriors' heads, replaced with fishermen's hats like the ones upon the heads of two men sitting expectantly on a bench outside an abandoned rail corner station.

I thought about the two men waiting patiently for Uncle Jack and Ernie to divulge their secrets, piling the grocery counter high with spent wings and tied hackle. Two old men waiting patiently, disappearing into a crossroad village store, coming back down the warped board steps at an eager trot, heading for points known only in the strange dreamscape that existed between the old fishermen's minds and the scribbled directions on an iron-stained map.

Only yesterday, I'd seen the slanted and dark light of the grocery, hearing of hidden waters, and peering through dusted glass at the hatbands bristling with flies. Not enough time had elapsed to turn the cosmic spheres through a single revolution. But it seemed like forever, and that thought jolted me higher from my slumbering and tangled dream. I was now somewhere lost in the state of consciousness where reality and dreams collide.

Like the hats of the two bench sitters, scarred and ringed by years of fishing with the fly, the slanting hats atop the heads of the ghost soldiers were ringed with flies, too; and the ghost flies shone cold along the ribbed hackle, and the high dancing wings were layered and shot through with iron-melting fire. The rifles of war were as absent as the soldier's helmets. Instead, the spirits advanced on the river with fly rods held high, wading into the river below the rail bridge upon which Ernie's train sat idly steaming.

It was too many stories and too far a road traveled; maybe it was too many rutabagas and trout. Sleeping on a cot in an old railcar prolonged it, but as the dream faded like the mists of the ghostly river, the soldiers broke apart, some going upstream and others wading around the bend below the bridge, each in turn saluting with their rods the bridge and the waiting train.

The bridge meant nothing, really. There was no symbolism in it to portray a shadowed crossing into the eternal. It was beneath the bridge that really mattered to the spirits, crouching along the banks in never-ending pursuit of what I knew in my heart must lurk in the river. Trout there were, no doubt, but I knew that was only a small part of the whole. The soldiers were walking the misty banks for an eternal peace.

Only one figure remained at the end, wavering in and out of my dream as I tried hard to hold onto the remnants. I tried with every shred of slumber I had left in me, because the remaining spirit was my father. I called to him, tried to run to him, but my dream legs were gone, spinning uselessly like dream legs so often do. I didn't know that I even missed him so much. I desperately wanted him to come and get me, but he shook his head sadly, and I knew it was not yet my time. The last thing I remembered was the sauna train still sitting alone on the bridge. It had cooled, and there was no steam remaining along the outskirts of its wood-burning engine.

It was hidden down deep. It took a dream to bring the emotion to the surface. My father raised one hand in recognition beneath the bridge. Twin rivers of tears ran down my face.

Sacred waters like Taconite Creek can pull you in until your dreams get all crazy. Sometimes you don't even know what is real anymore. I didn't understand that fully back then, but I have had years to think about it, and I've come to know that it is true.

CHAPTER 21

I awoke to gray fog and a summer morning rainstorm, slow leaks coming through the roof of the boxcar and dripping on my head. The source of my water-torn dreams became evident, but I still felt the emotional strain tugging deep within the pit of my stomach. I lay there, with a steady drip, drip, drip, sounding like the clicking of the dream train, so that started to make sense, too. The dream emotion went slowly out of me. A dream only carries you so far.

I was on my cot, in a damp sleeping bag, under the leaky roof of a boxcar. I shrugged my hand through damp hair. An early morning blend of light fell through the cracks, and it was musty as an old barn in the boxcar. There was the rumble of thunder in the distance. It was still raining at a steady pace outside, but I felt in the air that the storm was passing.

Both Uncle Jack's and Ernie's cots were unoccupied. Their fishing gear was gone, too. I rose to the day, because only an idiot would lie under a leaky roof, but I guessed it to be something more compelling, something approaching fanaticism, to be out at this early hour in the rain storm.

I poked around in the crates and barrels along the boxcar's walls. There were piles of rail-tie lumber and rolls of tarpaper, hammers, and nails. There was enough building material to construct a good-sized dwelling, along with bags and boxes and barrels of rail spikes. My butt still felt bruised from sitting on a bag full of the iron devils.

It was hard to believe that I could be hungry after the dinner I'd consumed last night, but my stomach grumbled. It's a wonder what living outdoors will do to your appetite. I pawed deeper in the crates and found a small tin of canned ham (Spam, I guess it would be called nowadays). I opened it and squatted down on the floor, eating the preserved meat with my fingers. Granted, it was Spam, but to me it tasted like a fine-cut steak

The rain stopped as I licked the grease from my fingers. A single, long ray of brightness rolled through the doorway and over the cracked, wooden floor. The sun's rays split over the trees and through the fog, the boxcar reflecting golden warmth, the receding drips of the rain sparkling. Ancient cobwebs in the corners took the sunlight and held it. It was not only one of the best breakfasts I'd ever had, it was one of the best sunrises I'd ever seen.

It takes a spell of time for a whopper-sized dream to pass into the coming day. But as the fog-shrouded night lifted into the morning, I sat easy and cross-legged on the splintered floor. A morning like that puts to rest any twisted night tangles that the subconscious, not to mention ample portions of trout and rutabaga, can throw at you. My stomach settled from the Spam, which in itself seemed something of a miracle.

The sun was on the move into a northern summer sky, and it stretched before me in a single line of clarity. There were endless days ahead. The whole of my life was ahead. Floodwaters of war and death and childhood dreams couldn't stand up to that. I eased the fly rod out of my pack and pocketed the cigar box of flies. I hopped down off the boxcar ledge, bending forward to climb the ore-stained ridge. I aimed to find out what exactly this game of fly fishing had to offer up.

Looking at the waters of Taconite Creek was like studying a complex problem. Not just quickly memorizing something to be forgotten later; not just a passing glimpse like the one I'd had on yesterday's walk-through. I came to realize finally and fully what Uncle Jack had been trying to teach me. What he had been trying to teach me about keeping my mind open to learning and knowing.

He said that to know something for the sake of knowledge itself was far more important than what you actually did with that knowledge, though he hadn't been so articulate when he told me: "God gave you ten fingers to count with, and if you don't really care to count anything bigger, then you're pretty damn much set up for life."

There is satisfaction in the comprehension of a greater whole. Ten fingers are only a physical stepping stone for a much greater number. I couldn't put my thoughts into those exact words that morning on Taconite Creek. I was only twelve, for God's sake, but I've since found that sentiment echoed in classical writings and in the majority of the great religions of the world. There is only so much we can physically see. It boils down to setting your mind loose after that. If you don't have the curiosity and the love of the big problem, then you might as well stop at a number you can understand.

I don't think Uncle Jack even knew he was being philosophical. He was straightforward, and he just wanted me to pass my tests, wanted to set me loose from an ordinary life: "If the number ten is too hard for you to remember, then you might as well start cutting off a finger at a time until you get to familiar surroundings. Glue the other fingers back on later." It was shouted in a moment of exasperation, during a particularly hard study session. I think he was kidding, but I'm not positive.

Taconite Creek was the start of something. It was my first study-course on the workings of rivers and the workings of the environment. It was the first inkling of what lurks below the current in places too deep to see; a grasping of what happens when you run out of fingers to count with and begin to decipher the scrawling bend of numbers too large for physical description. It was the beginning of how trout water works and how to manipulate that water into working for a purpose and an objective. I couldn't see the big picture yet. I started with one finger and worked from there.

The creek cut deep. It cut seamless into the foundations of the ridge. The winding rush was broken by the dam, edged back at odd angles by concrete and rock that had been placed to bind the water into a proper course of taconite excavation. There were also natural obstacles in the river. Logs and brush and sand spits, and pockets and runs in the stream bottom created by those things. I walked the boulder-blasted shore, peering beneath logs, getting down on my belly to stare through stunted alder brush and into the rolling water. I studied what I could see. And what I saw in those dark places were moving phantoms. I saw trout.

The water sprayed my face as I peered over the dam. The stone and mortar jigsaw puzzle was built with small rocks and big rocks, piled in crazy fashion one upon another, pushing aside the flow with a tenacious hold. The dam was only a short cast from the pump house; rusted pipes and hose-clamped ends jutting deep under the water, running beneath the rock to the abandoned building. The hoses and pipes were bent and kinked. It seemed the watershed was struggling to get into equilibrium, struggling against the piled stones, struggling to get to where it wanted to be.

That a dam was not exactly a natural part in the order of a wild trout stream didn't cross my mind. Maybe it was because moss had slowly started to creep up the piled rocks and small sprigs of green weeds, and delicate flowers seeped from its cracks. The dam wasn't natural, but the wildness of Taconite Creek was doing its best to make it so. The sunken hoses and the pipes didn't seem to bother the fish. It certainly didn't stop the heart-racing excitement I felt as I caught watery glimpses of the dark-spotted trout. I decided that the shelter of a created pool was a good enough place to start my fishing. It seemed a simple enough thing to comprehend. It was math, one by one on my fingers. It was an easy and fine place to attempt my first fish.

Sitting on the rise of the crumbling rock, the sun peeking over the ridge warming my neck, I laid the bamboo rod on the rain-damp earth, twisting the joints together slowly, and leaning the rod against the rocks. Flashes of gold and brown drifted below the pump-intake tangle, becoming invisible, becoming one with the designs of modern advancement and using the man-made brush to full advantage. The golden flashes made my heart roll as I tried to go about everything in a well-organized manner. I seated the reel in the cork grip of the rod handle, assembling it with glowing pride and anticipation. It got more difficult after that.

It was fussy work stringing the heavy line through the guides. The line kept slipping back and coiling like a snake at my feet. The morning birds were in the trees, chirping merrily and whistling happy tunes. They mocked me. Finally I pulled the end through, stripping slack out of the reel with an easy clicking sound that reminded me of the train wheels in my dream. I opened the cigar box and fingered one of Ernie's buggy creations, and that led to the next bit of trouble.

I jammed the heavy fly line in needled bursts, but the eyelet of the hook was far too small to accept the fly line. I didn't understand. The sunlight made rainbows through the spray of the creek. The birds kept up their incessant racket. Taking a deep breath, I crumbled off a piece of mortar from the dam and contemplated throwing a rock at a particularly happily singing sparrow on a branch across the stream from me. I caught myself in time and took another deep breath, staring into the morning sun through the dripping brush.

I was making it too difficult. I knew it. It was a panicky and pointless arrangement, like studying for school all over again. I tried to remember the lessons that Uncle Jack and Ernie had so patiently (Ernie, at least, patiently) given me back home. I dropped the ballistic bird-killing rock. I smacked the side of my head, muttering in amazement at my stupidity.

Of course I needed to attach a leader to the end of the fly line; I'd seen Uncle Jack tie on the transparent and lightly-coiled end a dozen times. I'd seen him do it just last night, quick and easy in a flash of time. He'd tied it as he was walking, rather quickly, too, if I remembered, trying to outrace Ernie into the tall grass and brush where the creek leveled out. Trying to beat him to the best fishing hole – not that there weren't plenty of them but, after all, that hadn't exactly been the point. The point had been simply getting there first.

It looked easy enough and, peering into Ernie's cigar box, I saw that it held several wound and tapered lines of different thicknesses. My fingers found the heaviest one, supposing in an ill-prepared but rational sort of way that a heavier leader would lead to the best and strongest tug-of-war connection between me and the shadowy shapes that swam in the pool. Connecting the leader to the fly line proved to be more difficult in reality than I'd pictured in my mind. When I'd seen Uncle Jack do it, it was a twist of the line and a quick loop. When it was complete, it was strong enough to dangle a sack of rail spikes without breaking.

My first attempts ended in snarled bird's nests, which urged the morning sparrow across the creek to sing stronger. The smaller nests pulled quickly apart and, while the bigger tangles held firm, they were easily twice as big as my rod guides. They stuck in the guides tighter than glue. I may as well have connected the leader to the line with the piece of peppermint gum that Ernie had taught me to cast with.

Finally, more through luck than any kind of logical-knot deduction, I connected the two lines in some type of granny knot, splitting the difference between strength and fluid line dynamics. It was a first step, but it was a step nonetheless. I have since learned and forgotten more fishing knots than you could fit in a dictionary-sized volume. But I've never been able to replicate that first one from that first morning on Taconite Creek.

Tying the fly onto the leader proved easier. The thinner line was much more forgiving to work with. The hook's eye provided solid, twisting purchase that I could really wrap a hum-dinger knot around. I chose a black-feathered creation – unlike any kind of fly or bug I'd ever seen. But, like the heavy leader, I figured the bigger the better.

I was ready for the moment of truth, stripping line like Ernie had shown me, making a careful back cast, imagining how I'd done it back home under the oak tree; backwards to go forwards. Except I couldn't go forward, because my back cast got caught ten feet up in a balsam tree. Turned out there was a whole stand of them. But if I wasn't yet an accomplished fly fisher, at least I could climb a tree like nobody's business. I shinnied up the balsam and unhooked my fly.

I tried a couple more casts, and I ended up climbing a couple more trees. My hands were sticky with sap, and my clothes smelled liked fresh balsam. I'd have to wash my hands eventually, but my clothes became scented enough that I wouldn't have to worry about taking a clothes-washing bath with Uncle Jack and Ernie later.

I finally managed to float the fly on top of the water for a few moments before the current pulled it under. No big trout thrashed from the depths, and the fly ended up swirling in a back eddy of shallow water. I tried it several times with the same fishless results, but at least I developed a nice rhythm. I found that I didn't need to put a lot of muscle power behind my casts to land them where I wished, which for the time being, was basically anywhere that didn't involve climbing a tree.

I began to get a feel for the creek currents as they sloshed angrily at the wing dam. Every cast, before the fly was pulled into the shallows, floated over the submerged structure of pipes and hoses. It floated right over the tops of the dark, wavering shadows in the pool bottom. Whatever kinds of feathers and fur the fly was made of – they looked like a raven or a crow and the hair from a black cat to me, but whatever they were – the weight and flotation of the fly kept it from sinking an inch. And not sinking an inch was a measurement that these trout cared nothing about.

It was like the knots in a way. I didn't yet understand about insects or the designs to imitate them. I didn't know that some insects hatched on the stream bottom, rising upwards to the surface, and sometimes just below the surface, before making it all the way to full-born floating on top. I didn't know that you weighted fishing flies differently, achieving nymphs and emergers and floating duns; these were terms and concepts beyond my years, still locked away in volumes of books and fly patterns.

I did realize that the fish weren't seeing my floating offering, and thus I made a big step in the logical progression of fly-fishing wisdom that morning. I made a step forward – not a brilliant breakthrough on par with the invention of the wheel – but it was a breakthrough nonetheless, and it was my very own breakthrough. I concluded that I had to get the fly deeper. Picking up some pebbles, I debated how to tie them onto my line in order to sink the fly before remembering the pinched pieces of lead that rolled around in the bottom of my cigar box tackle supply. I wondered why Ernie had put them in there. The lead was grooved along one edge. Then I knew what they were for.

Pinching a piece onto my line above the fly, throwing the weighted rig above the dam, watching it pull down into the current, slowly circling and twirling – the whole of the fly looked so real, and the slanting rays of the morning sun caught it just right. The slightest breeze rippled through the balsams behind me, and I shivered. If I hadn't just cast it above the stone dam myself, I would have thought the fly was part of the natural order of the morning. It was alive.

There was a pause in time that I still feel all these long years later. It was only a heart beat, but it still reverberates in my chest to this day. The fly disappeared in a flash of gold from the depths of the pool. Then, like the fly, my rod sprang to life. Line spun from the reel, and a heavy weight shot upwards and broke the surface in a cascade of water. It was a brown trout, perhaps not the monster that you see on a magazine cover, but it was plenty big enough, and it was my first trout, and that's a fact that all the magazine photos in the world could never capture.

The trout didn't break my knots or throw the hook on the first leap. The line held firm on the second and third jump, too. After the air show was over, the trout shot away from the dam and headed upstream through a riffled stairway. It headed up Taconite Creek, and I did my best to follow, chasing with my bamboo rod in the lead and the extra line twisting in the breeze behind me.

The fish knew I was in pursuit, sensing me behind through the vibration of my pounding feet. It turned around all too quickly and headed back to the shelter of the deep pool. I reeled as fast as I could, the line coming onto the reel in snarled and knotted loops. A tug-of-war ensued for what seemed an hour but couldn't have been more than a minute. The fish lost ground onto my reel, then shot back into the deep, my twisted line grudgingly ratcheting through the water. The trout flashed through the sun and into the shadows.

I wanted that fish. I wanted him for Ernie and Uncle Jack. I wanted him for myself. I wanted him for every dream and for every fisherman who would never again haunt the steps of Popcorn Corners. I didn't fully understand those thoughts then – in the heat of battle, I couldn't have articulated them properly if I did. There have been years since spent dwelling on it, and maybe now I'm just an old man who is putting too much sentiment into something as basic as hooking a fish on the end of a line. But back then, on that rain-soaked morning above the dam on Taconite Creek, I simply wanted the fish and wanted it badly. It was an emotional battle that I didn't fully comprehend. And all these years later, I'm still trying to comprehend.

The tangled mess of reel and line and bad knots finally brought the whole thing to a stalemate. The trout wrapped around one of the jagged pipes on the bottom of the pool. The line stuck firm, and I gave a mighty pull, feeling certain the whole rig would come undone. The circled end of the line rose up the pipe like a slip knot, the noose tightening at the top. It was close, but the knot made it. The fish flopped into the shallows across the creek. He rolled and shook his head, trying to spit the hook from his jaws. I couldn't reel line in, and he couldn't take any more out. I hesitated, the wheels of my young mind rolling full tilt. I felt the tangled line straining, the trout rolling in the sand of the shallows, silt washing downstream in mushroom clouds. Logical reasoning went out the open window and a torrent of panicky emotions came through to take its place. I plunged waist deep into the cold spring water.

In no time flat, I was chest deep. A moment later, I was swimming. I knew it was deep, but there was no real judge of measure to know how deep. Dark water is deceiving, and I quickly found that the pool was at least as deep as I was tall. I held my rod above my head and paddled like a lop-sided dog, rod tip twitching in my upheld hand, drinking in mouthfuls of the stained water, and tasting copper and iron with every swallow.

It felt like a lifetime, looking through the reflecting glass of youth, like that mirror in a funhouse where everything appears out of proportion, or maybe a small dog chasing and nipping your heels and taking on the characteristics of a wolf. But it seems now, with every passing year, that the stream crossing was over in the blink of an eye. I was still vertical in the water when I realized that I was in the shallows on the far bank and in no more than a half-foot of water. Bottom sand sucked at my ankles and spilled into my soaked shoes. I leveraged a fist into the sand to prop myself up, holding the rod in the other hand and wiping wet hair out of my eyes. Then I pounced on the flopping trout like a tiger.

I knelt like I was praying, holding the shining fish up against a backdrop of pines that were now burned clear of morning rain and fog. Spots the size of tarnished dimes ran along the sides of the fish. The spots flashed from dark red to brown in the sun. The head narrowed into a delicate arch above a hooked jaw. Its tail slapped back and forth and cold against my arm. It was my first trout. I've caught many since, but I've never held a better one.

CHAPTER 22

"Christ Almighty – didn't I tell you the boy had potential!" Uncle Jack's voice echoed from the boulders and across the dam.

I rolled over in the sand of the shallows, clutching my wet prize, and there stood Uncle Jack and Ernie on the far bank, rods propped against the stone dam. Their prickly wool and heavy-set trousers were still damp from their foray into the early rain. Clothes steamed in the rising morning. Both men were arm-in-arm and grinning brighter than the sun-reflected water.

"You should have seen it, Ernie! You should have seen it, Uncle Jack! It was a battle – it was a wonderful battle!" I babbled and beamed, holding my trout and shouting across the creek the ordeals of the fight.

"You bettcha, big and vet and vild!" Ernie's voice boomed over the rocky ridges. Uncle Jack was jumping up and down and slapping his knee like he'd bet on a long-shot horse to win the race and was holding the winning ticket as the horse crossed the line. The horse was wet to the bone, and it had been a photo finish – but it had come through just the same.

"Your mother would be proud as a peacock to know that you haven't even been up here more than a day and are already bathing and washing your clothes," Uncle Jack said. "Come on over here across the creek with your fish. It will be a sparse breakfast, but it's better than nothing. I'll tell you, Ernie's flies didn't come through one damn bit for us this morning. We got skunked. I want to see with my own eyes what you enticed that trout to eat – 'cause it sure as hell wasn't one of this here Finlander's creations. Might as well as left him back at camp for all the good he amounted to!"

I slogged upstream to the rocky and shallow water. I crossed over to my waiting companions and showed them the fish. "That's a fine native specimen," said Uncle Jack, turning the fish this way and that, hefting it to feel its weight like he had a built-in scale of measurements. With quick up-and-down jerks of the fish in his hands, he did the calculations in his head. "It will run two pounds, with about two ounces change. He ain't exactly a Granddaddy, but I warrant he's decent enough. Now, if this here was a brook trout, why, then you would have yourself a trophy."

"And if dat vas a brook trout" added Ernie, "den you vould have caught something down here below dat might have saved lot of vare and tear, maybe even saved us from wrecking da whole place."

"What do mean wrecked?" I asked. "This is perfect! The rockslide and the pines, the water and the dam, your train in the rubble down below added to it all. So what if it doesn't run anymore? The burner still works real fine to cook on. And besides the leaks in the roof, the boxcar is wonderful to sleep in. We can patch the roof up with all the supplies stored in there. It's so perfect that I can't believe it's real."

A look passed between Uncle Jack and Ernie. There was a gleam in both of their eyes. It was a gleam as hot as the fire in the sauna train's stove.

"It is quite suitable as it stands this moment," said Uncle Jack. "If it would stay this way, stay in this moment of time with the trout in the deep holes and the creek running and steaming over the hot rocks, no sounds to be heard but crickets and the rain at night, why, yes sir, then it might be more than suitable. Then it might be perfect."

"Why can't it stay this way? What's to stop it?" I pointed at the stream and the crumbled stone dam and the deep running pool where I'd landed my first trout. "You said yourself last night that hardly anybody knows where this. There's no way that anybody could ever find us here."

"Maybe not today – but someday, maybe sooner than later," said Uncle Jack, sweeping an arm across the rock-strewn ridge. "There's money involved in all of this. When they get a mind to, and they will eventually, they'll come back for it."

"Who are *they*?" I asked.

"The mining companies, and I reckon the people behind the mining companies – people like me and Ernie – people who know what to look for. People who make it their business to cut through miles of swamp. They'll climb their way out of the mud and onto the surface of this ridge someday, when the economics and politics come full circle. What lies beneath that surface is money and power. And there ain't no wilderness deep enough, no swamp wet enough, no ridge high enough, and no stream fast enough to stop that."

"So what are you going to do? You and Ernie were here first. That should stand for something, right?"

"Well, technically we got no claim on any of this. Technically speaking, I don't even know who has a claim on it. It's all on paper somewhere in some lawyer's file cabinet or on some boardroom wall in a big city somewhere, and I don't even know if that stands up against the native people who got here long before that. To tell you the truth, it's something me and Ernie never thought of when we were wandering around and finding the rock, mining the ore, and carrying on like there was no tomorrow."

Ernie saw the confusion in my eyes. He looked sort of guilt-stricken, pawing the pebbled ground in slow circles with the toes of his boots. "Vell, maybe it is time for da whole truth to come out. It is time for da whole chapter to be set in stone before da whole ting collapses. Maybe only den can ve move on."

Uncle Jack walked down from the dam to where the pump house was sunk like a tilted ship along the rocky shores. I followed with my thoughts, carrying my snarled rod. Ernie stayed behind for a moment, cleaning my fish with quick and expert slices of his knife. He plucked the black fly from where it still stuck imbedded in the trout's jaw, examining it carefully in the palm of his hand. "It vas a big vooly bugger – dat's vut day vanted." Ernie spoke aloud and to no one in particular. But Uncle Jack heard him clearly as we walked towards the fallen entrance of the pump house.

"You wouldn't know a wooly bugger from a wooly mammoth. You just tied that thing up off the top of your head with no rhyme or reason – just some extra thread and probably the hair off of a skunk that you ran over with your damned train. It's a testament to my nephew – likely a testament to the great tradition of fishing prowess in our family – that that miserable piece of skunk fur caught anything at all."

Ernie followed us to the pump house, holding my trout in one hand and his wooly bugger in the other. "I suppose you know da skunk ven you see vun. Day sure seem fond and happy 'round your company."

Uncle Jack held his silence, lost in thought outside the collapsed entrance. I stooped down like the night before, peering through the fallen timbers that held the rock walls akimbo. Light pierced the holes where some of the smaller rocks had abandoned the puzzled construction, falling inward or outward with no logic as to how they tumbled. The wrapped bundles still sat on the shelf, on the far side of a maze of busted valves, pipes, and bubbling water.

I felt their eyes watching me. Uncle Jack held the suspect fishing rods, still attached to reels that groaned and whined. Ernie held my prized first trout. I turned from the caved opening and watched them both. Now my two friends weren't arguing, weren't jabbing each other with barbs; they were solemn and they looked at me and they looked at each other with questioning eyes.

Uncle Jack shrugged. "I guess there ain't but one course of action left."

Ernie shook his head at Uncle Jack, who was looking at the rods in his hand with a wild and fiery look. Ernie gently set my rod off to the side, easing my fish down beside it. He crossed his arms and shook his head.

He kicked the pebbled ground and looked at Uncle Jack. "I don't know, maybe dare is something else, maybe someting in da air, something bigger den us telling us to leave everyting alone now."

"Maybe you're right, Ernie. Maybe I'm a fool."

I swiveled my head between Ernie and Uncle Jack, wondering what was transpiring. I'd fallen into the routine of the unexpected, slowly and unconsciously, but I'd fallen to expect such crazy things, such wonderful and crazy things in this wild and broken trout land. I didn't think I'd be surprised by anything that might pop up out of the weeds now. But what Uncle Jack did next caught me off guard.

"I'm a fool, but I was born that way, and I can't do nothing 'bout it now," he said with a calculating demeanor. He took the fly rods in his hands and snapped both of them over his knee. Then he took the reels from the broken rods and threw them in a long and sinking arc into the deep hole below the dam.

Ernie winced. "Vell den, I guess dat is dat."

Uncle Jack discarded the broken rods off to the side like he was clearing away brush. "Now, there's only one thing to do in a situation like this," he said, kneeling next to me in the pebble-strewn dirt, my eyes wide at the broken rods, my mouth open in a circle of amazement, cringing at the crack the rods made, like the crack of a broken bone you have just seen played out before your eyes.

"What's that, Uncle Jack?" I stammered.

"We can't go backwards. We've done run out of room for the back cast. We gotta go forward and hope to hell that we don't end up wrapped around a deadfall stump." He looked at the fallen entrance, looking at me at the same time; staring at me with that far-off look and those glazed, wandering eyes, all the while continuing to peer into a smashed-up opening so small that I didn't know if you could even squeeze a stunted deadfall stump in there, not to mention there was no way a grown man could wrestle through.

I wasn't a grown man. I was very young. But I figured it all out pretty quick. I sensed what was coming with that far-off look. I knew then where that forward cast was aiming to land.

CHAPTER 23

"Uh,uh – no way. I'm not crawling in there." I was adamant, and I meant it. Uncle Jack hunched beside me. He squinted through the angled timbers and the broken rock, cupping his hands over his eyes to cut the glare of the sun that was now fully over the high ridge and bouncing off the rocky slopes. It would be hot today. The cool rain of morning had passed. It would be the real start of summer.

Uncle Jack got down lower to the ground. "I'd go in there if I was even half your age or had half your jumping agility. I've seen you climb trees, squirming around on them branches like a monkey who misplaced a banana. Squirmy and flexible, that's what you are. Not like me. I'd blow a gasket somewhere deep down inside, and not a doctor anywhere hereabouts could fix it."

He twisted his neck and a joint cracked. It was fine dramatic effect. He gestured at Ernie, who was still pacing in the gravel, my trout stretched at his feet and not looking near as fresh as it had a few minutes ago. It looked like it might start baking in the sun.

"Ernie would go in there except he's too fat from eating all them rutabagas."

"No vun vould need to go in dare at all if you had your head screwed on bit more. A man who put stuff in dare in da first place is crazy. A man is not right in da head who goes off crazy up da ridge instead of minding da vater pumps like you vas supposed to. It is no different dan a squirrel dropping nuts in a hole too small to get dem back out. A squirrel, or a man like dat, is crazy, and he deserves to go hungry. I don't know vie da verd crazy keeps coming out my mouth – but ven I look at you dare on your belly, looking into dat hole – den dat verd keeps coming!"

It was a long speech for Ernie. I figured that whatever was in the pump house must be important for him to string that many words together. "What's so valuable that anybody needs to crawl in and get it?" I asked. That was really the million-dollar question. But I'd been taught by Uncle Jack for quite a while now. I'd been groomed by Ernie, too. I'd begun to learn, not just school learning, but how to asses a situation and figure on my feet (or I guess on my belly, too), because that's where I found myself, looking into the ruined rubble.

I already knew the answer: Canvas-covered cases and pack-sized bundles on the fallen shelf, wedged between tangles of busted valves, wooden floorboards underwater and covering up a ten-foot-deep bottom basement with more sunken pumps. I looked at the broken rods that Uncle Jack had created, looked at the deep pool below the dam, the pipes and hoses and a pair of battered fly reels that had sunk into the bottom. I looked at my single rod resting at Ernie's feet, which was now the only rod we had among us, and at my trout, which was the only one we had among us.

"All of your fishing stuff is in there, isn't it? I mean the good stuff, the good rods and the good reels. That's what those bundles are." I thought about it, added it up in my mind, and I asked another question. "Is that why you brought me here? Just to crawl in and get your stuff?"

"Hell no, that's not why I brought you up here," said Uncle Jack. "We brought you up here… I mean, I brought you up here, because I'm the one responsible, being you're my nephew. But Ernie agreed with me, so he's kind of responsible, too. We brought you up here because we seen something in your eyes – something that you can't learn in books, something that isn't really… What's the word I'm looking for?"

"It is in here," said Ernie, beating his fist against his heart. "Da Finns call it *Sisu*. It is someting connecting vut you see wit da eyes, to vut you feel in da chest." He made grand gestures, pointing to his eyes and beating his broad chest, pointing every which way – to the tall red pines stretching far up as you could look, to the oak and birch leaning on the high end of the stream; pointing to the rocks where the water jumped and splashed and turned to steam like a sauna.

"It's called spirit—that's the word I wanted!" exclaimed Uncle Jack, who had been mulling it over with fingers scratching through his bleached hair. "What the hell's got into you, Ernie?"

Ernie pointed wildly across the ridge, at flowers dotting the hills and song birds winging onto the forest floor to scavenge for grubs. The world came down in such a heady mix that it was too much for Ernie to point out all at once.

"Ernie! The boy knows a damn bird and a bunch of flowers when he sees them. He probably knows the names of them better than either of us, so take it easy with the nature lessons." Uncle Jack rested a hand on my shoulder. "You got a certain type of spirit. You just swam a pool of water to go after a single trout. I've watched you since you were no bigger than a sprig of grass. There was always something about you that wanted to grow tall. You listened to my stories. When you lost your dad, no one would have blamed you if you had crawled into a shell and hunkered down, but still you sat and listened to me rambling on about trains and mines and trout."

Uncle Jack glanced up at Ernie. "Why, I know a lot of people who could not care less about my stories. People older than me and younger than me – even people from a different country, where the sun don't know better than to stay away all winter and then thinks it can make up for its laziness by shining all night in the summer. Even people like that would glaze over in the eyes at half the tales I spun in front of you."

"Da eyes glaze over yust to tink of such tings," Ernie muttered.

Uncle Jack squirmed right to the entrance of the pump house door with me. His voice echoed into the watery gloom. "The point is that I believe you see as much with your heart as you do with your eyes. You're able to feel more than what's just sitting on the surface. You feel what lies beneath it all."

Water continued seeping out of the door in rivulets. I wasn't sure if Uncle Jack was feeding me a line of propaganda just to get me to crawl through before it collapsed, but it sounded good, what he was saying about me. It felt good, too. It felt good around about the area of my chest that Ernie was talking about.

"Alright, I'll do it. But on one condition." I'd decided that if I was going to be a full part of this, then I couldn't simply lie in the gravel and let Uncle Jack and Ernie roll over me unabated. In fact, I had a feeling that they didn't want me to give in too easily.

"What might that be?" asked Uncle Jack.

Ernie smiled a knowing look, like he knew that I had mastered the back cast and was about to swing the line forward.

"I'll crawl in and retrieve it, but then both of you are going to tell me how two so-called master trout fishermen managed to lose their gear in a fallen down pump house. Not just lose it, but lock it in so deep that you needed to drive out of the wilderness to find a young kid to help unlock it, and then not even remember how to get back without the help of a beat-up map that looks like it might be the only thing right at home and comfortable in this crumbling shack. Then you go and trade fishing flies for rutabagas so we have something to eat when we get here, because we sure can't eat any fish without rods and reels to catch them with!"

I took a deep breath while Uncle Jack and Ernie danced around like two giddy school girls. "That's my boy!" said Uncle Jack. "I don't tink no vun coulda said it better." said Ernie.

Water spurted harder from the foundation.

"We gotta hurry," said Uncle Jack.

"I tink da end is near," said Ernie.

Then I was on my belly and wiggling into the wreckage.

I got stuck for a moment, but Ernie gave me a push, and I squished through. The water was bone-chilling. Granted, I'd just floated across a whole creek of the stuff, but that was fishing. There was a big difference between swimming in it and crawling on your belly through it. The stone foundation ran squarely around the edges of the house with wooden planking covering the center. I got to my knees and slowly crawled over the floorboards. There were sections missing, and the water was clear enough below to show pumps sunken in the flooded sub-basement like abandoned shipwrecks. The boards still in place bowed and sunk with every crawling inch. My knee broke through, and I sprawled on my belly, hugging the rotted floorboards like a thin sheet of ice. Water swelled up angrily. I was in for a deep and dangerous plunge if the ice broke.

"Go careful, you almost reach da udder side," Ernie coached. The far ledge was almost within reach.

"My sister would strangle me if she saw this," Uncle Jack strained. "I would deserve every throttle of it, too."

There was an audible crack as I stood up on the last of the boards and grabbed at the shelf. The rest of the boards began cracking in unison, and the water level rose quickly as I teetered. Two curses echoed from the doorway, one I can't repeat, and one I didn't even know for sure to be a curse as it was belted out in Finnish, but uttered with enough venom behind it as to leave little doubt what it meant in any language.

My balance held in a heartbeat as I grabbed at a rod case. It rolled with me, and I went down, one knee on the ledge, and my trailing leg strung down into the water. I made a last grab for the shelf and caught purchase on something firm. It constricted in my hand, and I grabbed just enough of a fistful to regain my balance. I pulled myself onto the ledge and found I was holding onto one of Uncle Jack's hip boots that had caught on an upturned nail.

"Uff da," croaked Ernie.

"Hells bells," squeaked Uncle Jack.

Water began flowing rapidly as I hefted two waterproof rod cases off the shelf and set them down. They floated like wet-noodle life preservers. I grabbed two other canvas gear cases, stuffing Uncle Jack's boots in one of them and throwing them down with a splash next to the rod cases. I straddled the rod cases and held one of the canvas bags under each arm.

The water was flowing rapidly up from the depths. Small whirlpools formed as the current came to grips with the new level it was trying to achieve above the foundation. Planks broke free and swung round in circling eddies over the sunken cistern. Without thinking, I kicked off the back wall like a swimmer going off at the start of race. The shelf fell behind me with the crack of a starting gun as I skimmed with my bundles over the fallen boards and the rising water, heading for the sunlit world of the doorway.

Ernie and Uncle Jack grabbed me at the doorway, pulling me through and scraping skin from my elbows. There was truth in their firm grips about why they had brought me to Taconite Creek. Both men were far more concerned for my welfare than their fishing gear: looking me over, alternating hugs, and patting me on the head like a champion. It was only when they were sure that I was okay, and when a tumbling crunch of wood and concrete stone heralded the far wall collapsing, that they remembered my life-preserver bundles.

Ernie reached through the doorway and snagged the rod cases. Uncle Jack managed to grab one of the gear bags. But the bag with his hip boots floated just out of reach on a back-current that unleashed itself through the collapsing floor. I shook water out of my hair and rolled out of reach of Ernie and Uncle Jack. They lay breathless and sprawled on the ground, watching the walls of the pump house disintegrate. I dove once again through the doorway.

"Stop! Stop! Stop! It ain't worth going back for 'em!" hollered Uncle Jack.

But I was already in the bubbling water and swimming for the last floating bag. I had it in my clutches once, but it snagged on a submerged pipe and sucked under. I reached further, my head and shoulders fully below, grasping for the sinking gear. I was in danger of getting snagged myself, and it wouldn't be a snag easily rectified by breaking off the leader. This snag would be final and forever.

Ernie reached a long arm through and grabbed my ankle, but he didn't try and pull me back right away. He knew what I was after. He realized that the fishing gear in the bag wasn't nearly as important as my attempt to reach it. The attempt was something above and beyond. It signified the boy trapped within me. It signified a deeper and older spirit trying to break free. He knew about the spirit, he knew about *Sisu* – so he let me have a go at it.

The underwater world of the pump house was garbled and fuzzy. The sounds of boards hitting metal were amplified in slow waves. A board rushed by and struck my forehead with a cornered edge. The sound waves got slower, and the underwater scene spun into dizzying clangs. There was the taste of iron in the water, filling my lungs and penetrating into the pit of my belly. I started to sink into the darkness of the pump house, into the foundations of Taconite Creek itself.

The bag was in my hand before I passed out. I don't know to this day how it got there. The next thing I remembered was the hot sun glaring down, Uncle Jack pounding on my back, and about a gallon of Taconite Creek coming out of my stomach and into a retching mess on the gravel. Ernie was jumping up and down like he'd been stung by bees. He was talking all garbled, and I thought there might be something really wrong with my ears, because I couldn't understand a word.

Ernie noticed my eyes were open. He still kept jumping, but garbled Finnish started mixing with some words I could make out. "I tink you vas a goner. I tink how stupid in da head I vas to let you stay in dare for da stupid bag of junk. Even if dare are whole dozens and bunches of flies in dat bag – you should have let dose smelly boots drown! Dammit but dat vas vun heck of da rescue job. Boy Oh Boy! I should not have let you stay in dare! Jack, you can quit pounding da boy on da back now! "

Uncle Jack was pale. He stopped the rhythmic slapping of his palm between my shoulder blades. His face slowly regained color, and he looked in shock and amazement down at his hand, as if seeing for the first time the stinging palm that had been pounding water out of my lungs. He looked up at Ernie.

"How the hell am I supposed to concentrate on stopping anything with you going off like a Finnish jumping bean? It's a damn marvel that you ain't brought the whole side of the ridge tumbling in on us. My God, you should really think about laying off those rutabagas. I don't think an earthquake could create such a ruckus!"

The pump house was a pile of rubble. The dam above had held, but now a secondary stream flowed at our feet, winding and splashing down the ridge and through the collapsed building. The cold water hit the hot rocks. Jets of steam and spray clashed with the tall pines. On the sloping realm of Taconite Creek, the collapsed building was nothing more than a deep hole in the bottom of a new creek branch.

I sat up next to Uncle Jack. Ernie sat down, too. We sat in a living fog of condensing water. The wet canvas smell of the fishing bags swam in the air around us. Then we slowly smiled at each other, sitting in the mist and the hot sun and feeling like something amazing had just happened. Something foolhardy, no doubt, but amazing.

It wasn't just Uncle Jack and Ernie anymore, sitting on the blasted iron ridge. Now there were three of us. It was bright daylight, and it wasn't a dream, and there were no ghosts. There were only the three of us, and it was as real as could be.

CHAPTER 24

The steam rising from the rocks dissipated as the sun and the icy water reached a mutual agreement. Ernie fried my trout while Uncle Jack simmered a pot of hot water, adding fistfuls of potatoes and peas. Nobody spoke as we ate. We were that hungry. But as we slowly filled up, I noticed Uncle Jack and Ernie's eyes lustily wander to the rod case and canvas totes. They were ready to start in on them for dessert.

Uncle Jack reached for a bag. Ernie reached for a rod case. I stood up and tossed the bones from the trout into the dirt between both of them. They looked at me with sheepish eyes. I kicked the rod case away and stepped down hard on the bag to keep Uncle Jack from opening it. He made a half-hearted attempt to pull it away. I knew that he remembered the promise, but the lure of lost gear was strong. I stepped down harder and wagged my finger in his face before he let go. I didn't have it when I woke up, but somehow I had found something along the way, and I amazed myself with my new-found authority.

"You guys owe me. No one touches anything until you tell me."

"Or else what?" asked Uncle Jack with a half-kidding smile.

"Or else I'll take everything sitting here and toss it right into that new big hole up on the creek. The pump-house hole I think we should call it, or else the lost-tackle hole. I don't think any of the trout will mind sharing the place with an old rod case and a couple of canvas bags full of junk."

Ernie's eyes said he thought I was kidding. I stared him down, and his eyes lost some of their shine. He realized I wasn't.

"And I'll take every rutabaga I can lay my hands on and toss them in the hole with the tackle. I don't expect the fish will mind them, either."

"Mercy, "cried Ernie. "I tink ve vill come clean!"

"I'm coming to the same conclusion, Ernie," added Uncle Jack. "Why don't you pick up the story where we left it last night? After all, it was mostly your fault that it happened."

"I vill pick it up. But my only fault only vas to get hooked up vit a train-valking, hip-boot-varing scoundrel like you."

"I'll take that as a compliment. But remember, without me it's ten-to-one odds you'd still be scraping bog ore in whatever third-world country you crawled in here from."

"You're both stalling," I said. I was right, too. This was the same diversionary tactic that both men had been using to their advantage for years.

"I've got nowhere else to go, so you two just work it out. I'm kind of worn out from all the excitement. I'll take a nap right here and use these canvas bags for a pillow. Wake me up when you guys are ready to tell."

Ernie waved a hairy forearm in my direction. "He's leetle too smart for comfort."

"I taught him everything he knows," said Uncle Jack.

"Dat is vut I am afraid of," Ernie answered. He sat down against the sauna train; Uncle Jack rested back on his elbows, one arm lovingly on the hip-boot bag. Both men stared up the torn ridge at the creek, two creeks now, really, coming down through the rocks.

"Good night," I said, settling down comfortably and crossing my arms behind my head. "Wake me if the fish start biting – not that you'll have anything to catch them with if they do."

"Vell... Dis vut happened," started Ernie.

I sat up, maybe a little too quickly. Ernie smiled knowingly. He knew he had a captive audience.

"Ve mined ore, verking our tails into da ground. Ven da first autumn came, somevare between da last flowers and da first snow, ve had da ridge busted up pretty good."

"There were times we were sorry we started the whole mess," Uncle Jack chimed in. "The men were complaining that they didn't get enough time to rest between shifts. Ernie and I were there constantly, watching the ridge open up, sending the early loads of rock back to Ashland for testing. There wasn't time to breathe."

"Sampling and mining, mining and sampling," said Ernie. "And da rock came out so pure, da company vas yumping to get it processed. Day vas itching mad to see vinter come. Day couldn't vait for da snow to melt in da spring so ve could get back to verk."

"We had the company begging us to keep working the rock beds till the first snow flew and the ground iced over. They never figured that we had them right where we wanted 'em. All of the past escapades – those were the company's exact words, 'past escapades' – of Ernie and me were forgotten and swept right under the rug. The hook was set good." Uncle Jack said.

"It vent on for da next year and da year after dat. Den came da vor, and lots of da young and strong men enlisted. Many of our crew vent over to fight. Ve stayed here and did vut ve could to help. Ve kept da iron coming in."

Uncle Jack sighed. "Ernie and I were too old to go over and fight, but

I reckon we weren't too old to stay behind and hump rock. It got tougher to pick through the men that stayed behind, too – this life sure ain't for everybody. Ernie and I did our part for the cause. We put fishing on the back-burner. We were strictly on the straight and narrow for a good long stretch."

"But finally dare come a day ven da var vas over...," Ernie started.

"And that's when it really started," finished Uncle Jack. "The autumn winds swept back the brush along the swamp. There were brown trout spawning on the gravel bottoms below the ridge. They were golden in those rocky pools. We figured – me and Ernie – that it would be decent enough to catch a few and put on a fish fry for the men. You know, as kind of a victory celebration and a reward for working so hard."

"It vas a happy time and, by golly, it vas a lot of fun."

"Yep, that's the ticket, Ernie. It was a happy lot of fun. We'd hook up with those big browns, and it was a lot of fun indeed. They'd jump out of the riffles below the mine, and there were enough big boulders piled below to make the footing a bit treacherous. When the fish shot off down for the swamp, you'd have to scramble over the boulders, jumping from one rock to another like the fish themselves. You always ended up far below – sometimes waist deep in the swamp with the line still tugging as you tried to reel in all the line you lost on the downward scramble."

"Day vas nice fish and it vas good times."

"Yes, sir," said Uncle Jack.

"Den you seen da brook trout."

"Yes I did."

"Da brook trout started it."

"Yep."

"And den you finished it."

"We finished it together, Ernie. Just like always."

"Ya. I guess dat is da truth."

The sunken well of the pump house gave an audible spurt above, and a small slide of rocks came down the ridge. We watched a split board saunter down the creek, rotating through the summer day and into the swamp. We moved into the shade of the boxcar. There was a warm breeze blowing, and the pines on the ridge were swaying softly. Ernie warmed a pot of coffee on the stove while Uncle Jack peeled an onion. Through bites of onion and sips of coffee, stretched out in train-car shade, Uncle Jack and Ernie kept talking. I kept listening, storing it away in my memory for a distant time.

"Ernie engineered the dam and the pump house," Uncle Jack said. "The dam shifted back the creek so we could keep pounding at the big rocks without caving the sides of the pit. But the water backed up something fierce and started spilling over. It builds up a hell of a flow from where it starts way back up in the hills. So we built the pump house to check the flow and hooked it up to hydraulic hoses to wash the mine deeper. More rock, less men, and more money for the company, and would you believe after all that time, they still hadn't bothered traipsing back in here to check on us. Maybe it was because everyone was concentrated on the fighting overseas. But I really think that as long as the taconite kept coming, it was out of sight, out of mind."

Uncle Jack took another chomp at his onion, breathing out a sharp aroma.

"There was an autumn breeze blowing on the day that Ernie took the sauna train into Ashland. He took in the last flat of ore for the year, and he was going to bring back a boxcar. We were going to haul out the mining equipment for the winter. The plan, and if I remember right, it was Ernie's plan, was to load the gear and the men and call it quits for the season. It was as dry as could be, so I know he didn't get stuck coming or going. Why it took three days to get back is beyond me. He won't admit it, but I think he sat in his sauna by the lake for at least half the time – not that I could blame him, 'cause we hadn't had a proper bath all summer."

"Da pumps needed to be fired every so often to keep da vater level down." Ernie was pointedly looking at Uncle Jack. "Ve had discussed it much before I left. Ve needed to keep dem running until da ground froze."

"I seem to vaguely remember those discussions," Uncle Jack admitted, "but winter was a distant notion. It was Indian summer. Brown trout were spawning bright in the pools, and the sun slanted down through colors of red and orange on the hills. By God, the water level in the pump house wasn't rising an inch, steel blue above, and not a cloud in the sky. It was dry, I tell you! "

Uncle Jack admitted to fishing a little harder and working a little less. The company would get their iron. No one would be the wiser. The brown trout were putting on an autumn show, the pump house water level was stagnant, and there was fresh trout for dinner every night. The men didn't seem to mind Uncle Jack's lack of diligence. Days were crisp and fine and, at night, the rocks were ringed with only the slightest hint of frost. There was light at the end of the tunnel. They were in high spirits, slated to head home upon Ernie's return with the storage car. They even laid down a few rails over the worst of the swamp to give the convoy a head start for home.

So when Uncle Jack disappeared, they didn't even notice. Not for the first day, anyway. But by the end of the second, with Ernie still not back and Uncle Jack nowhere to be seen, they started to get a little nervous.

"I was sitting on the ridge with my fly rod in my hand and the morning sun just peeking over the hills. It was a fresh morning, and I could see my breath. I was contemplating the browns below. They were fanned out on the gravel bottom, and I was planning a sneak attack from above. That's when I heard the splash in the pool. It was right behind me, upstream from the dam. It made me jump. My breath frosted like a smoking plume. It was a big splash."

Shining silver in the morning sun was a brook trout the size of a football. It was spawning in the pool above and was the first brook trout Uncle Jack had seen since coming to Taconite Creek. "It made me a little crazy inside to see a fish like that," Uncle Jack admitted. "I cast over the top with a feather minnow, twitching it right over her nose. She must have seen it. Maybe I got a little nervous – it was the biggest brookie I'd ever laid eyes on – or maybe I twitched too hard. I crawled on my belly up to the pool and peeked over the bank. She was gone. I'd put her down."

"I tink you is not so sneaky a fisherman. Dat's vut I tink," added Ernie.

"That feathered fly of yours looked like it was still attached to the damn bird. I was scared of it myself. That's what I think." Uncle Jack countered.

However it happened, the trout was gone. Not below. Uncle Jack would have seen it slide by into the cascading riffles. It went back up. Grabbing a pack and shouldering his fly rod, Uncle Jack followed. He ranged far up into the high country, through the pines and moss and over rocks and logs to where the creek narrowed and ran through cut-bank valleys. He lost track of everything, getting caught in a dark squall of late-autumn rainstorms that flew in high off Lake Superior and raised the creek level above. He forded on, and it didn't cross his mind that it was raining and that the creek ran downhill. The trout wasn't going downstream, anyway. It was headed up. It didn't matter anymore about the big brook trout. It could have been a little one, and Uncle Jack would have followed. The sizes of the fish were immaterial. The places they called home were what beckoned.

"I'd never been up the ridge to where the creek started. It was some place. There are hills up there that shine a view all the way to Lake Superior. I found more brook trout up there, too. I couldn't catch a single one, but it wasn't for lack of trying. I stayed two days and three nights exploring the reaches. Those rain squalls kept flying, but I slept under an old pine deadfall and covered myself with fallen leaves in the night for warmth. In the morning, my leaf bed was covered with frozen rain and frost."

"And let it be said, da fact dat it vas raining never bothered him," said Ernie.

"Hell no, it didn't bother me. But the fact that the brook trout were mocking me did. They were thumbing their fins at me. I was waiting for the rain to let up. With all the weather moving in from Lake Superior, I figured they weren't hungry."

In his rush to follow the trout up into the hills, Uncle Jack forgot to bring anything to eat. His was a one-track mind, and that's what made him such a fine trout fisherman. Maybe that's why the trout didn't want to eat, either. Uncle Jack was so attuned to the trout that he started acting like them, or else they became like him. Either way, it amounted to the same thing.

"I tried chewing watercress, but it was brown and half-frozen. I threw in some likely-looking toadstools that I found growing under a log, but I never was much on salads. And the toadstools made me feel all light-headed. I seem to recall that the fish started talking to me. Even I knew that wasn't right."

Maybe the fish stopped talking or maybe it was hunger that finally drove him back to the mine, leaving the brook trout swimming and him stumbling like a prophet down the rocky slopes. Men were crowded around the boxcar. The sauna train smoked in the clearing with the storage car backed against the ridge. Everyone was jumping up and down as Uncle Jack wandered down in his blissful, toadstool-induced reverie.

"They seemed anxious to be gettin' on their way, but I didn't see any sign of Ernie. I figured he was taking one more crack at the brown trout in the swamp before we called it quits for the year – figured that's why the men were so jittery."

"But you figured wrong," said Ernie.

"No, I figured right. You just never got a chance to get your rod out of the case."

Uncle Jack spied Ernie on the slopes outside the pump house. Uncle Jack's instincts had been true. Ernie was indeed planning to take one more shot at the brown trout of Taconite Creek. But now his fishing gear was scattered in a pile on the ridge, and Ernie was bent over and working furiously to start the pumps. Trickles streamed from the door, and the water level behind the dam had risen dangerously. The highest splashes had already knocked rocks from the top of the dam, and miniature waterfalls were spurting through.

Uncle Jack met Ernie on the mine ridge. They huddled together.

"Da pumps are seized. Dare are hoses cracked and pipes busted all da vay back to da dam. You vere supposed to vatch da vater!"

"I was watching the water. For the last two days that's all I been doing. I've been sleeping in the stuff!"

Uncle Jack spread his hands apart in estimation of the brook trout, telling tales of lost water that that had never before seen a man standing over it. The men milled nervously below, leaning on pick axes and shovels, apprehensive about the meeting of the minds on the slope above. The train stood waiting.

"I told Ernie to come back up with me, right then and there. I knew he could tie a fly to match what those brookies were after. I couldn't have cared less about the train or the rest of the crew wanting to get on back to Ashland. I was a little crazy in the head."

"You knew the pump house was in trouble, and you still put your fishing gear inside?" I asked.

Ernie whistled sharply like a cuckoo clock. "Da pumps and da pipes and da hoses, day ver all shattered like da inside of his head. But it vasn't collapsed yet. Da real collapse vas still coming!"

"I remember it started with a low rumble," said Uncle Jack. "It reminded me of Ernie's stomach after he helped himself to third portions of your mother's meatloaf, but it was even more ominous than that. There was something unsettling in the autumn breeze off the ridge. Water curled over bedrock, and the creek appeared to shift, like the coils of a snake getting ready to strike. Then the whole side of the mine caved in on itself."

Uncle Jack kicked at a boulder blocking Ernie's train. It was nearly as big around as the stove. "Rocks came down, and men ran, and shovels flew through the air. Ernie and I almost got caught in the downward slide, but the foundations of the pump house were solid. Despite his shortcomings, when Ernie builds something, he builds it good! It was nip-and-tuck; the whole ridge was shaking. Ernie was petrified, and it was only my quick thinking and reflexes that saved our fishing gear from the landslide. I grabbed it and pulled it all back inside the pump house. The back shelf was the handiest thing still standing, so that's where I stowed it."

"Quick reflexes! Hoo-boy, dat's a dandy part of da story I don't remember." Ernie plucked a mayfly out of the air as it cruised through the shadows. "And dat's a dandy bug!" The afternoon shadows had fallen without me realizing.

"Too bad the train and the boxcar didn't have the same reflexes," said

Uncle Jack. "They ended up buried to the axles. Luckily, the men were all unscathed, but I think some of them had wished they'd perished by the time we hiked into Ashland. I don't think it was Christmas yet when we finally trudged in, but that late-autumn rain had turned to snow, and it sure was cold enough to be in the holiday ballpark."

I looked over at Ernie, but he didn't have anything more to add. He was busy studying the mayfly. I knew the spell of the Taconite Creek story was broken, just as I realized it was still writing itself.

It was pretty simple to figure the lay of the land for myself. I knew that the dam and the pump house had been built to cage the water, built to prolong a taconite mine. The water had just as easily ended it. But it hadn't been the taconite, and it wasn't the water, either. Those were just means to an end. It was the obsession of what swam in the waters that built a mine back here.

"Have you ever seen a trout shoot out from below the bank to suck one of those mayflies in?" asked Uncle Jack.

"No," I said with a grin, "I haven't. You should have stored your fishing gear in the box car. It would have made more sense, and it would have been a lot dryer."

"But den ve vouldn't have needed you," Ernie said, giving me a good-natured poke in the chest.

Uncle Jack stood up and stretched. "We came back for the gear in the spring, but the winter had frozen it up good. By the time it thawed out, Mother Nature had done quite a number on the pump house. I figured I knew one small miner that might make it inside, though. And as they say, the rest is water under the bridge – or through the pump house – or whatever."

"I guess you knew what you were doing, then," I said. "But how did you know exactly when the pump house would crumble?"

"I studied such tings at da Finlander University of Rock Study," said Ernie. He looked proud.

I widened my eyes and tried to look impressed.

"You are so full of shit, Ernie, that even the boy can see it now," said Uncle Jack. "It was sheer bad luck, and that trumps a university degree every time."

"What about that mayfly?" I asked, changing the subject before the circular arguing started up again and darkness found me watching a heated debate instead of fishing.

"Let us get reacquainted with our long-lost weapons of war," Uncle

Jack said, pointing to the bundles. "Then I reckon me and Ernie can show you a thing or two about that flying bug."

"I get first crack at them." I picked up my fly rod and the cigar box full of flies and headed for the brushy creek bottom.

"You may be young and full of vigor," said Uncle Jack, scrambling to unroll the bundles, swatting away Ernie's own attempts at pawing through the canvas cases. "But you still got to learn the places where the big ones hide. There are trout in this creek that can swallow the one you caught this morning like a minnow." He waved a knowing finger, like a master who still has the upper hand on his student.

Uncle Jack unfurled a fishing vest from deep within one of the bags. "Damnation Ernie, quit tugging at that rod case and give me some room to breathe." Ernie was donning a hook-marked and faded hat. The two of them looked like kids trying to grab presents at Christmas. In all the excitement, it didn't seem to make much difference whose name was on the tag.

"Give me back my fishing vest. I have da special flies in da side pocket, and I vill not see dem fall into da wrong hands."

"Well then, take off my lucky fishing hat that you just put on your thick head. I don't want you to jinx it."

I'd tried to keep the fire from starting, but I only succeeded in containing it. At least the blaze was headed in the general direction of the trout stream. Boxes of flies were flipped back and forth like trading cards before we finally walked into the shadows of the Taconite Creek bottoms. I could not see my two friends in the gloom of the alder tunnels, but I could hear their lines floating and their reels clicking.

"What about the mine company?" I asked into the darkness.

"Vell, as long as ve are coming clean and telling da truth, ve are not really retired." Ernie's voice came from a watery thicket.

"So they're still expecting you to bring in iron from Taconite Creek?" I asked.

"Not really dat,"

"But you're still working for them?"

"Not really dat, either."

"Quit playing twenty-questions. You're scaring the fish." Uncle Jack's voice drifted from upstream. "Fact is, after we marched all those men through the sleet and snow and rolled into Ashland, no trace of a train and no trace of any mining equipment – well, let's just say there were a lot of unhappy stories and a whole lot more unhappy people drifting around the frozen ore docks. We got fired. But those suits and ties aren't so smart. If it was me, I'd have fired both of us years ago. Now, if there are no further questions, I've got a date with a big trout."

There came the steady pluck of mayflies hitting the surface and the slurping of trout taking them down. I thought about holding it in, but I still had to ask.

"Uncle Jack?'

"What?"

"Won't the company want their mine back?"

There came the sounds through the brush of a singing reel and a fat plop. Uncle Jack sounded busy. I figured that's why he didn't answer. There came a tightening along my own line, and it was all I could do to turn my own fish away from a sunken brush pile. I forgot all about Uncle Jack not answering. When my trout broke water, thrashing his head to try and spit the fly, I forgot that I'd even asked the question.

CHAPTER 25

Mornings and evenings, we fished the bottoms of Taconite Creek. The first few outings found me fishless more often than not, but the thick tangles were a fine classroom to learn in. Woodpeckers drummed, and crows echoed calls from across the rocky slopes above; but the jungle of green below, where we fished and where I learned – *that* was an isolated spot of existence.

Giant ferns brushed my head as I crawled along the stream. Willows arched in dark tunnels, and mighty logs crossed the stream. The logs seemed fallen from the ages, possibly some of the very same giants that drove the first white men back in here. Spider webs clung to my neck when I ducked beneath to find the darkest and deepest banks. Piercing shafts of sunlight came through the thickest trees and shone like beacons into the dark water. I learned to tie on flies in the sun beams. It was like using a natural flashlight.

I waded in pants and shoes, the sand and silt bottom sucking at my ankles. The cold water was always a shock, even on the hottest afternoons when the rocks baked high above, and the magnificent steam showers rose like clouds.

Ernie always waded in just his clothes, too. The cold water never seemed to bother him. The first few times out he stuck close, showing me how to cast gently without wrapping in the brush and how to let the current wash my fly beneath the banks. He got down on his belly in the water until only his head showed above, pointing slowly and patiently to the dark and watery places. He looked like a waiting predator, hunkered down and scanning the stream with watchful eyes.

"Ya got to be sneaky and tink like da fishes." He was neck deep in water and peering over a fallen log. "You got to get right up to da doorway of da trout's kitchen before da trout comes home to your kitchen and into da fry pan." I bounced my fly off Ernie's left ear. It might have made a good earring and given him a swashbuckling-pirate look, but instead, the fly stuck fast to the log, and I splashed in to retrieve it. We looked at each other and laughed in the shadows, brushing spider webs from our hair, moving on to the next hole and the next lesson.

It was always me and Ernie together through the first days. Uncle Jack was gone for hours at a crack. I'd see him crawling up the rocks high above in the early morning, wearing his hip boots with his taconite-dusted map in tow. He had the map out constantly, marking a bit here with pieces of charcoal left over from the nightly sauna train stove fire. Sometimes we all met up and fished together, but usually we wouldn't see Uncle Jack coming down from the ridge till way after dark, the moon waxing fuller by the hour, and him silhouetted and looking like a solitary ghost gliding down.

Where does he disappear to all day?"

Ernie shrugged his wide shoulders. "If you vould get inside his boots and know vie he go and vare he go, den you vould know vun of da great mysteries of life."

I asked Uncle Jack the same question, and he told me he was doing missionary work with a band of savages.

"How high up the ridge do the savages live?" I asked one morning. My hair was tousled in knots from nights of sleeping outdoors. My skin radiated a dark brown from the sun's reflection off the rock face above. I was still wiping sleep from my eyes, but Uncle Jack looked to have been up for hours.

"Oh, the savages are right here. In fact, I'm looking at one of them now." Uncle Jack chortled and banged away on top of the sauna train. I needed a haircut, and Ernie's beard was full-blown bushy. "I'm just trying to help you both out of pure sympathy and the goodness in my heart."

He always started the morning off banging on the side of the sauna train, stoking the burner with kindling, and firing a pot of coffee. There he was, in the early morning dew, boiling coffee and singing his favorite song to wake us. Uncle Jack loved "Praying River"; said the song had been around near as long as Taconite Creek. Said it had meaning as wise as the water itself. He stood in his boots, banging time on the side of the train with a religious fever in his eyes:

> "Let's go down to the river to pray; studying about that good old way;
> Who will wear that iron crown; Lord, show me the way;
> Oh brothers let's go down; let's go down; come on down
> Oh sinners let's go down; Down in the river to pray."

After his morning wake-up song and after breakfast, Hip Boot Jack was off like a shot, not down to the river to pray, but climbing the ridge with a fly rod in one hand and his beat-up parchment in the other, pebbles raining down behind him as he disappeared into the tree line. The gravel that fell off the ridge behind him as he disappeared was only a morning wake-up call, too. Rocks pelted down in waves when the sun started heating the slope, giving me and Ernie something to do when the trout stopped biting during the heat of the day. It was a constant game of nine-pin bowling when the big ones started banging into the boxcar. Shovels clanged to the floor, and stacked lumber went over like dominoes. Barrels of nails and spikes teetered precariously, and the threat of flying shrapnel loomed heavy in the shadowed corners. We strategically moved crates and barrels, shoring up the fortress against the rock assault. It kept me on edge and was more than a little unnerving.

"How did you ever work out here with all those men and all the rocks coming down? It's a wonder nobody was smashed to pieces."

Ernie looked up at Taconite Creek, pouring down from two directions around an island of rock, the water pushing harder with every passing day to reclaim the whole thing. "After da pump house sunk and da creek busted, it has started getting bit wilder. Every year, we took more rocks and pushed da water back little more, It vas like tightening drag on a reel with da big fish on da udder end. You could see it stretching da tension of the whole ridge. Now, line has got so tight dat da fish is about to break off."

"Is any fish really worth all that?"

Ernie picked a big chunk of taconite rock from the top of his buried sauna train and held it to the sun. The rock glared red and orange like fire. It reminded me of the flashing spots on my first brown trout as it struggled in the water above the dam.

"Your uncle always tought dat it vas. I reckon I always tought so, too. Da big people who own mineral rights tought da rocks ver plenty big enough – long as da money kept rolling in and ended up in da company bank."

"What do the mine owners think now?"

"Day fished enough from here for now and moved on to easier fishing someplace else."

Another boulder smashed down the ridge. It echoed off the side of the boxcar, seeming to call out to me that there was still much to learn about the business and the obsession that shook the iron core of Taconite Creek.

"What happens if the line breaks?"

"Vell, I guess ve duck and hope dat it don't snap back and take our heads off."

CHAPTER 26

The day started perfect. It sure is true what they say about the calm before a storm.

I pulled a heavy brown trout out of a log jam. Ernie said I was nailing my lessons, drifting below the logs and twitching the fly just enough to avoid sticking the hook in the tangled wood. The fish cleared water above the sunken logs, pulling hard for the safety of the dark hole. I gave line and took line. Ernie splashed up and down in the water next to me, cheering and barking like a big, wet dog that was happy to be alive on such a morning. I turned the fish into the pool above and tired it out in the quiet water at Ernie's feet. He netted it with the look of a proud parent

"I tink you got da game figured. Now, even da big fish is gonna tink tvice about playing 'round vit you."

I'd slowly become a part of Taconite Creek, falling into an easy rhythm, and it was like being in a trance where the whole world around me became sharp and clear. I could count the purple and white flowers that grew along the moss without brushing a trace of line into the shadowed arches of the streamside gardens. The creek and the very essence of life that teemed from it; all those lessons sucked in through my soul.

We returned with our catch to find Uncle Jack already waiting. He'd come down early from the high ridges, whistling a tune and looking satisfied and secretive, like he'd discovered a buried treasure and simply needed to go back to the spot with a pick axe and a shovel. We found him putting the final touches on a cake he'd baked in a makeshift reflector oven.

He was spattered with flour and covered with bee stings that stood out red and angry through his white-sifted arms and face. "Top of the morning, gentlemen," he hailed us with a wave of uncharacteristic joy, considering he also had a bandage wrapped around two of his fingers and was crouched over a hot stove, while we stood watching and unscathed and holding a nice stringer of trout.

"Those are some dandies. It's a fine thing to have a couple of first-rate meat hunters in this camp. Me, I like the business of staying back and holding down the fort. I should have been a chef – leave all the nonsense of rock mining and swamp fishing to the youngsters."

The smell of cake wafted in the air. Flour drifted around his feet with a gentle breeze, and Uncle Jack grinned like an albino Cheshire Cat. The bandages on his fingers looked like they had been wrapped by a blind doctor. Something was up.

Ernie and I squinted in the glare of the sun bouncing off the reflector oven. Ernie caught a whiff of the cake, and his stomach rumbled.

"It's a rutabaga cake. We had the flour stockpiled, and I found a stash of wood duck eggs up above. I left most of them – only took a couple. Maybe we should build a nest or two for them when we move our camp up there."

"Move our camp?" I started to interrupt, but Uncle Jack waved me off.

"In due time, in due time," he said. "I'm talking baking right now. Listen and learn from a master."

"Rutabaga cake, did you say it vas?" slobbered Ernie. I'd never seen him more transfixed by one of Uncle Jack's orations.

"Yep. I got some sweetener from a hole in a lightning-split hickory down the way. It was a big hive, plenty of first-rate comb honey." Uncle Jack itched at a red welt along the side of his face. "Of course, the bees didn't exactly see it that way.

"I ripped some sheet metal off the side of the truck for the reflectors. I figured I might as well salvage what I could before the dang thing sinks into the ground completely. I hammered and bent it with a rail spike and shined up the metal with some gravel from the stream. You should take some lessons from me, Ernie. I'll turn you into a design mechanic in no time."

I probably should have been worried that our only way out was slowly sinking into the swamp bottom, dismantled piece by piece, and turned into parts for an oven. But the spell of Taconite Creek was on me. Uncle Jack had sliced his fingers on the sheet metal while beating it into fabrication. With bee stings welting and covered in the glories of his baking majesty, he looked like he had been in battle.

We fried trout and demolished the rutabaga cake. Ernie rolled around in the dirt, rubbing his stomach in contentment. It wasn't exactly a scene out of a blue-ribbon restaurant, but we wouldn't have had it any other way.

In the afternoon, the sky boiled up like a dark omen and Uncle Jack's baking class came to an end. Thunder clouds slid down the ridge and hung heavy over the mine clearing. The alders and birch were soon dripping immense droplets of rain while the high-rushing reaches danced in the glare of crack-bolt lightning. We were forced to repair into the shelter of the train car, Ernie licking the last of the cake crumbs from his fingers.

The day still seemed to shine bright over Uncle Jack. His face was glowing red, and there were still patches of baking flour in his hair. Every time a lightning bolt shredded through the doorway, it turned him into the semblance of a crazed spirit. He waited between thunder claps with a serene stare that was a little eerie. He hadn't even made fun of his partner for eating half the cake. I think his tranquil demeanor even began to unnerve Ernie.

Uncle Jack took time lighting a kerosene lantern and dusting off his map. The lantern cast a warm circle over the faded parchment as the rain hammered the tin roof. Slow leaks dripped from the shadows, and we shuffled small pots and bowls to catch the water. The drips struck metallic music into our traps. Uncle Jack kept time with the music as his bandaged fingers drummed out a steady plan on his map.

"I have finally found the perfect spot of ground."

"If I had vun of dem Indianhead pennies for every time I hear you say dat, I vould be rich. Dat's vut I tink," Ernie said.

"This is different. This is the end of the rails. I ain't going to speak for all of us, but as far as I'm concerned, my wandering days are over after I set up right here." Uncle Jack traced a line on the map. His finger started at a small pen-drawn train car that had an etching of a fish jumping over it and a pick axe scribbled below it. I gathered, easily enough, that it was the Taconite Creek mine clearing. He continued up curved, contour lines that spread apart in ever-tightening arcs. His finger wound up and over the ridge, stopping at a point that was void of any markings at all.

"When I get myself situated right here," Uncle Jack started, thunder rolling down from the ridge, and lightning illuminating the map in strobe-light flashes. "When I get myself situated at the top – then that's where I'm aiming to stay until St. Peter himself comes down personally to tell me that I got to move higher. Taconite mines and the whole world be damned!"

I thought that if Uncle Jack kept talking like that, he wouldn't have to worry about any one of the saints taking him higher. I held my tongue and didn't say a word, sitting cross-legged in the kerosene glow and staring transfixed at the old map.

"I finally cornered that brook trout, cornered it all the way to the top."

"You spent all those days up the ridge looking for one fish?" I asked.

As if to punctuate my question, a clap of thunder shook the train car, and a slide of rocks came down the ridge. Rubble pelted the roof, and a pick axe clanged off its hanger and onto the floor. Lightning danced through the gloom. Ernie furrowed his brow.

"Yep, and he's right about here," Uncle Jack wiped a bandaged finger on a spot of his map, dragging a trace of baking flour high above the contour lines, high up the course of Taconite Creek.

"I don't see nutting," said Ernie.

"That's 'cause there ain't nothing there yet, dummy," said Uncle Jack. "Nothing except the best brook trout fishing hole you ever laid eyes on."

It was just a floured finger print on a stained map. But it was the end destination. The boxcar we sat in, waiting out the rain and waiting for Uncle Jack to spur us higher, was a lot like the railroad tracks back home, the ones I crossed and marked as my starting point for fishing on the farm-pasture stream. Both were only sentinels standing guard. Beyond the boxcar, beyond the tracks, far above the mined out ridge of Taconite Creek – that's where the real secrets waited.

"When can we see it?" I blurted. It was as exciting as hooking into a big trout.

"Soon enough; there isn't any rush. We'll move slow and careful, like stalking the bank through the weeds. The last thing we want is a slew of mine company boys moving in on the best fishing hole ever."

I thought to myself that moving the mining companies into the best fishing holes ever was pretty much what Uncle Jack and Ernie had been doing since the start, but again, I held my silence.

Ernie himself was quiet the rest of the afternoon. He tied flies, meditating, sitting by the train car opening as the rain kept up. He stared above often, staring at the mine rubble wasteland. He was pondering those mysteries of life.

I kept busy stacking crates and putting things back into order every time a fresh batch of boulders pounded down. And Uncle Jack, he stared at the map. The rain kept on and it was still going strong when we turned into our cots for the night. The last thing I heard him say before I drifted off to sleep was, "Slow and easy... We'll take our time and ease up there, slow and easy." He mumbled it like a mantra, like he was soothing himself to sleep.

Slow and easy; trout fishing advice, good and solid stuff when it comes to wading a slow stretch like the bottoms of Taconite Creek. But when you hit a rocky and brawling run like the one that spilled down the ridge past our train-car camp; when you miss your step and slip on a wet boulder and the boulder shifts enough to flip you into the roaring water... Then slow and easy takes you for a ride.

CHAPTER 27

Come morning, we started digging the sauna train out of the rocks. It was after the snake had attacked Uncle Jack, and it was a breaking point. Uncle Jack's mantra of "slow and easy" was the thing that had broken.

"That's it! By God, I've had enough of this insect- and rodent-infested wasteland. It's high time you got that piece of twisted metal to do more than just bake trout and heat up coffee. My nerves have had all they can stand. We got to get the high hell out of here 'fore the whole place comes down."

His hands were still shaking from the trauma of the night as he drank his morning coffee. He accidently dropped the map into the warm ashes of the sauna train. It caught a bit of fire around the edges before he pulled it out and blew on it, which only fanned the burning parchment more. Finally he stomped and swore it into submission in the dirt. Uncle Jack was livid and ornery, cussing the map and cussing Ernie, and cussing the sauna train the whole while.

"It was this dang piece of junk paper that got us back here in the first place. That, and the no good, steam bath piece of wood-burning garbage over in yonder slag heap." Uncle Jack swore and stomped on the blackened map which, to tell the truth, actually looked better for the cindering. It took some of the taconite-red cast out of it.

Ernie smiled. His fly-tying meditations of yesterday had done wonders. "By yimminy it is a grand morning vit da sun peeking over da pines. Hard to imagine da horrible tings dat crawl 'round in da night in such a peaceful place."

This started Uncle Jack into a fresh fire dance on the map, cussing and muttering under his breath.

Ernie kept prodding the proverbial bee's nest and firing up Uncle Jack who, besides getting attacked by a serpent, was still in the process of itching and scratching twenty-odd bee stings of a real nature. But Ernie was right. It was a beautiful morning with last night's rain hanging heavy in the swamp and the creek twinkling down just as peaceful as could be. It was a slow and easy morning, just like Uncle Jack's mantra; a mantra that had flown the coop last night when Uncle Jack hollered us all out of a dead sleep, running in circles and screaming that he was being attacked by a giant serpent. It was quite a sight. I thought at first he was having an allergic reaction to the bee stings but, rubbing the sleep from my eyes, I saw that he really was tangled up and fighting a monster.

"It's choking the life out of me! Back off, you demon, and let me reach my knife. If I'm going down, I'm taking your slithering carcass with me!" Uncle Jack jumped and hollered, bouncing into the train car walls like a wildcat and flailing away at the giant snake. He finally plunged head first out the door and landed in a puddle of rainwater. He lay unmoving, and we thought the serpent might have done him in for good. A final flash of lightning came from over the ridge as the storm moved out, lighting up the scene in front of the train. It wasn't pretty. Uncle Jack groaned and rolled over in the carnage, twisted, wet, and glistening in the mud.

It must have been a good pelting of rocks on the car roof that knocked down a coil of heavy rope from its iron peg on the wall above Uncle Jack's cot. The coil had landed flush on his slow and easy dreams. Full-born terror beneath a raging northern storm but, in the morning light, the shape-shifting beast turned back into the reality of simple rope, along with the reality that slow and easy had never been a part of Uncle Jack's makeup. He wasn't born that way. He was hell-bent on finding the next piece of water or the next field of taconite rock. Uncle Jack had few equals when it came to moving fast and far in achieving a goal. That he found the snake in the rope coils more often than not just went along with the territory.

Ernie, on the other hand, followed to temper the situation. He tamed the coils of the snake like a charmer with a flute, winding it back down, slow and easy, until it became less and less a snake and more a functional piece of rope.

Yin and Yang: Together it was whole, but separate, well... There was Uncle Jack, lying in a rain puddle and wrapped in a rope coil.

We'd tried to sleep again after helping Uncle Jack back into the train. The tangled rope stayed put in the puddle throughout the night, but in the morning it was gone, with the sauna train's stove fired up and Uncle Jack fired up right along with it. Slow and easy out the window, the smell of burnt rope hanging in the early morning sun, and Uncle Jack cussing and calling for us to get the train dug out.

Ernie and I quenched the fire in the train's stove with buckets of water from the creek. Ernie was happy and laughing all the while. He seemed genuinely interested in the project, but he kept glancing over at Uncle Jack and making slow hissing sounds through his teeth, like a snake ready to strike. Uncle Jack stomped and sulked, setting Ernie off onto another round of good humor.

With the fire out, Ernie began lifting the big boulders that blocked the lower reaches of the train. I scraped the smaller stuff from around the wheels and pistons, shoveling sand and gravel into buckets like a kid playing in the sand, tossing it into mounds until it looked like the world's biggest sandcastle.

The shattered rocks mesmerized Ernie. His chuckling subsided as he entered a world of his own, kneeling and studying the particular bands of rock, turning them in his hands. He actually licked a few of them, tasting along the fragmented lines.

"Oh dat's good iron in dare," he crooned, tasting one to his particular liking. He muttered disapproval when he found one not up to his culinary standards. "I don't tink ve even make a fry-pan handle dat vouldn't melt down like da butter vit dis vun," discarding the rejected sample onto my sandcastle mounds.

"Does he look for iron like this in every rock pile he finds?" I asked Uncle Jack, who had been milling around with his charred map, looking abused and neglected, glaring at Ernie, and itching his bee stings.

"He's got a case of little hammers and vials of liquid that he uses to take samples with," said Uncle Jack. "But he swears he can taste the iron quicker than it takes to test it. I have to say, he's usually pretty accurate. He's tested more fields of iron than most geologists have ever seen in two or three lifetimes; gets the ore grade nailed down damn close, even before it's sent back for all the conventional lab tests. It may seem strange, but it's saved a world of time that was better spent in other pursuits, especially when the hatch was thick and the big ones were prowling the water."

It was the most words Uncle Jack had strung together without swearing since the snake incident. He seemed to be coming around, so I baited him some more.

"He doesn't eat the rocks, does he?"

Uncle Jack actually smiled at that. "Not unless they're shaped like rutabagas. Then he'd eat that train out of the rubble in no time flat."

That was the other side of Uncle Jack's nature: As quick as he rushed into being angry, he rushed right back out the other side.

Ernie didn't hear or, if he did, he didn't care. He was into the rocks like nobody's business. I believe that not only was he one of the greatest fly-tying experts who ever lived, he was also the best geological sampler, however unorthodox his methods, to ever ply his trade in the northern fields of iron.

"No use standing around and watching," Uncle Jack said, "Even though we ain't aiming to mine nothing more here, when he gets into that zone, he either doesn't remember or flat out doesn't care. Hell, he doesn't even know we're here. We might as well take a hike and leave him to his business. When he finally gets that contraption dug out, he'll be like a proud father getting his first born back home from the maternity ward. Then he'll forget all about playing around with them rocks. Then he'll start wrenching and pounding his steam-bath brain child back into shape, and that could take a hell of a long time – longer than that, even, depending on if it needs more pounding than wrenching."

"Where should we go?" I felt guilty leaving Ernie to do all the work, but Uncle Jack was right. The closer the sauna train came to being unburied, the more buried in rocks Ernie appeared to get. He really didn't seem to know we were standing right behind him and discussing his geological taste-testing.

"Ernie's got it covered below. We might as well go up."

Uncle Jack headed up the ridge along the broken banks. I started to follow, but he pointed me back to the boxcar where our fishing gear was stored.

"I ain't up to casting today – but you better grab your rod and a mess of flies. Where we're going, you're gonna need all of 'em."

Following Uncle Jack past the ruined pump house and over the dam, I realized it was the first time I'd been this high on the Taconite Creek ridgeline since the morning I'd tangled with my first trout. I balanced across the crumbling raceway with my rod held in both hands before me like a high-wire acrobat over Niagara Falls, the spilling sounds of Taconite Creek spread below my feet.

I followed up the creek through a gorged valley of leaning balsams, watching over my shoulder as the boxcar clearing got smaller with every step. Far below, I saw where the creek split, diverging on either side of a sand and rock island before coming together again and flowing into the swamp. The collapse of the pump house had created the island, and it was one of my favorite spots, with a yawning shelf of rock reaching over the swamp and calling the trout to lie in the shadows and wait for supper to flow down the slopes. It made a fine swimming hole in the heat of the day, and we'd dive off the rock island and take baths in the cool, deep water.

It was best in the evening, though, when the sun sat square on the crests of the pines, the early sounds of crickets calling in the coming dusk. Then the last rays glinted gold on the water below the island. I'd sit with my rod held high and patient, squinting into a glare that turned slowly red around the edges the pool; red turning into swimming brown as I waited to make my cast.

I stumbled over a pine root and almost went down. It was a long roll down the slope.

"Less looking back and more looking forward," Uncle Jack was moving uphill fast, as if being drawn by an unseen magnet. "Keep your rod over your shoulder in case you do take a mind to tumble back a spell. You might break a leg, but you won't break something more important. Don't ask me how I know – let's just say I've left my share of broken rod tips scattered across the hills."

"Never broken a leg, right?" I gingerly stepped over a rock and adjusted my rod over my shoulder.

"Nope, cracked my skull a few times though," he laughed. "Ask Ernie. I'm sure he'd be happy to tell you that it was the least important thing I could have damaged."

We wound through moss-covered boulders beneath the shadow of pines. The air picked up a sharp clarity that magnified distances. Hills and valleys rolled in endless succession through openings in the swaying branches. They looked like green waves, cresting and falling from one valley to the next. It seemed that if I held my fly rod outstretched, I might touch the farthest of the rounded swells. The pines got taller as we went higher, rising into a cathedral above with a red carpet of spongy needles spread below. Almost as a distant dream, the stained waters of Lake Superior stretched into a summer cloud horizon. High up on the Taconite Creek ridge, there was a coolness from the lake that you never thought existed on the hot rocks and scarred surface of the mine below.

The flow of the creek choked narrower. I leaped back and forth across it, landing and sliding on the pine-needled banks. The water ran shallow and clear, gravel bottomed in red pebbles of ore. It was like looking through a red magnifying glass. Shafts of light reflected the bottom like a stained-glass window as pebbles of quartz pieced together with red taconite rocks in an intricate puzzle. If it wasn't for the ripples along the edges and the murmuring whistle of water, you would think that it was only a stained sheet of glass that separated gravel from the air above. I wondered why on earth I'd toted my fly rod up here. The water was shallow enough to spear a fish with a table fork.

Crazy thing is, if I had a fork, and if I didn't mind eating small portions, I could have had a feast. Over the gravel and quartz swam hundreds of small trout. They flashed silver in the riffles, purple tracks spreading across their backs like dark lightning. They were all brook trout. The bottom was alive in a rainbow of color.

Uncle Jack sat down on a boulder beneath the pines. He had his compass in his hands, spinning it around in small circles. He'd paced like a nervous jackrabbit up the ridge but, as he stared into the creek and watched his compass, a look of total ease came across his sharp features.

I stood, fly rod in hand, listening to the water gurgle. The small trout darted over the glittering streambed shallows. I noticed that along the far bank, the water's force had eroded the quartz and gravel into a cut of shadowed darkness. It might have been my imagination, could have been a trick of the sun, but there were flashes holding in the deeper current that looked to be fish the size of small logs.

"This is where you disappear?" I asked.

Uncle Jack twirled the compass and pointed it up the ridge. "It's along the track-line direction. This is the high-road route to the pinnacle; the pinnacle of my life, anyways."

I watched small ants scurry along the crevasses of rock and up the vertical faces of the stream-side boulders. The breeze from the far-off lake blew up the ridge and swept them from the rocks and into the creek. As quickly as one ant was swept away, another took its place on the iron rocks above the water. It was an unending cycle; a miniature drama that had played out for untold years up here without a witness, except maybe Uncle Jack.

I pondered the ants and I pondered my fly rod. I fidgeted in my pocket and found Ernie's cigar box, plucking a small black floater and tying it on. The breeze whipped the end of the line, and the fly danced in the air. It sure looked like a falling ant to me. I cast to the seam along the far bank, expecting greatness on every curl of the line.

Time and again the small ones would bump it, but no big trout so much as looked at my ant. I tied on a creation that Ernie had designed to look like a stonefly living on the rocky bottom. The results were the same.

Uncle Jack looked at his compass and held his silence.

A bright streamer was next through the current, twisting and dancing and alive. Ernie was good at his art. The streamer was tied with feathers from a peacock, and where he'd ever found a peacock in the northern woods, he never bothered to say. The trout in the deep current had obviously never seen one. They were oblivious to the blue-and-gold creation.

I lay down my rod. "I don't know what they want. I guess they're just not hungry."

"Told you to bring a lot of flies," said Uncle Jack. "A dilemma like this brings a ton of practice with it. You got to sit here and figure in your head, really think it through. It's just like one of them school problems, only this classroom ain't near as stuffy."

"You figure it out?" I asked.

"Not without doing my homework. I spent a lot of stubborn pondering, a lot of days and nights up here working it out."

"My fingers are getting sore from tying on flies. It wouldn't be cheating if you just gave me a little hint."

"I'll give you a hint, but it won't be as much fun as figuring it for yourself."

"Hooking up with one of those bigger flashes would be more fun than figuring it out," I said.

"The hint is, you could sit here for days and watch these brook trout. You could tie on every fly known to man and fling it in the creek. You could invent flies that have never existed and fish mornings and evenings, the black of night or the high-noon sun. All they'll do is laugh at you."

"They have to eat sometime," I said. "They don't come down the ridge to do it. I've never seen one, and you said yourself that you'd never seen one until last autumn when the pumps seized up, remember?

"Ernie would never let me forget. But they do come down there. Big ones, too – the really big ones – but only once a year, every autumn, laying their eggs before running back up here to hide. When the little ones hatch, they run back up here just as fast. Just look at these swirling beauties."

"The brook trout you chased? The reason you were gone when the pumps failed. You chased it here?"

"I chased it through here. I chased it all the way to the top."

"But you never caught it? You've never caught any here?"

"Guilty as charged," said Uncle Jack.

"Why chase all the way up here when you have such a good thing down below? All the trout you care to catch. Maybe not brooks, but so what? The swamp below is loaded with trout that you can catch."

"I'm stubborn," said Uncle Jack. "I didn't say I was necessarily smart."

He tossed his compass in the air with one hand and caught it in the other. He held it up to his eyes. "I've used this thing so much that the degree markings and numbers are darn near worn off. It's gotten me places, but when I get to the places, when it comes to matters like these here brook trout – then I've always had to rely on my internal compass. I'm not like Ernie. He looks at a problem and sees the solution in his mind right off. For me, it takes a while, and sometimes I got to have a little luck. I have to go hard and long at a problem to find what I'm after."

"Maybe the brook trout are scared. Maybe they stay up here where it's safe." I said.

"Funny you should mention that. I had the exact same thought when I first came up here. With that thick swamp below, why, the sun never completely hits the water. Disconcerting, that's what it is, like living in the Arctic where the sun don't shine for months at a time. Makes a man – or a fish for that matter – either want to hole up and hibernate or get on a fast train out of Dodge."

"I was thinking more along the lines of the trout hearing all the blasting and mine digging going on below." I said. "You said yourself that they come down there to spawn, but only in the autumn when you were done mining for the year. Maybe the little fish, when they hatch, come up here to tell the bigger ones that they're sitting above the biggest taconite mine in the country, so they better stay put and hide."

Uncle Jack slapped his knee. "Now you're thinking like a trout! "

"If I were a trout, I'd be a pretty hungry trout if I didn't eat sometime," I said.

"That's the answer! Keep along those lines of reasoning and there won't be a fish alive that you can't catch."

"That's the answer?'

"Not the whole answer, but damned if it isn't one hell of a thought."

I was confused. It sounded like a riddle, maybe even one of Ernie's mysteries of life. "What's the rest of the answer?"

"Do you see Lake Superior shining way out there in the distance?" Uncle Jack asked.

"I saw it through the breaks in the trees as we walked up here. I can feel the cool air coming over the ridge."

Uncle Jack handed me the compass. "Superior lies directly north. The compass arrow ought to point straight that way – straight across the lake, into Canada, and clear up to the North Pole. True north is the magnetic pull that makes the compass arrow work."

I palmed the compass rather smugly. "I remember all that stuff from science class."

"So you tell me. I guess that *was* the only class I wasn't worried about you failing this spring." Uncle Jack said, as I slowly turned a shade of red to match the iron-rock boulders along the stream. "Now use the compass to *show* me." He added.

I lined the faded dial with the arrow. Standing tall on a boulder, determined to prove that I knew exactly where I was and what I was doing, I pointed towards the distant lake. The needle stayed put for a second, then slowly began to spin. It didn't exactly go nuts, but it was as if the needle had a mind of its own, twitching erratically before finally swinging all the way around. Instead of pointing north towards the lake, the needle settled in the opposite direction, up the ridge and out of sight along the rushing creek.

I tried it several times with the same result. The compass started north, but always it made a slow swing back up the ridge. "Maybe I should have failed science class, too." I dejectedly handed the compass back to Uncle Jack.

"No. You're smarter than you give yourself credit for. You proved it. You're not in summer school right now, are you? Instead, you're up here, using your mind in a place where no one in your school has ever been."

"You helped me though all of that school stuff, you and Ernie both – I couldn't have done all that myself. I'll just get all confused again when school starts back up in the fall. I'll be just as confused as I am now. I don't understand at all what a broken compass has to do with brook trout."

"But you did do it yourself," said Uncle Jack. "You were the one going off and doing the work. You maybe didn't get it right off – you had to work at the problem. Life would get boring if you knew everything there is to know without the fun of solving the mysteries. It's no different than me sitting here for days at a time, staring at these brook trout, before I finally got it. All me and Ernie did was help you find your internal compass."

Uncle Jack continued. "This here compass won't point north right now, but it's not broken. In fact, without it, Ernie and I couldn't ever have found Taconite Creek. We couldn't have found any of the iron ore except maybe by blind luck. It's almost like magic, except it ain't that, either. This compass will only get you close, and when you get close, the only real magic is here." Uncle Jack pointed a finger at the top of his forehead. "And in here," he added, pointing his other finger at his heart.

It dawned on me. It all came together, and I blurted it out excitedly. "When you get close, that's where the compass starts pointing! The magnetic draw in the ore – that's how you find it!"

"Now you're not only thinking like a trout," said Uncle Jack, "now you're thinking like a taconite trout fisherman!"

I pointed up the creek, winding higher and higher and finally out of sight through the boulders. "So there's an even bigger deposit of taconite up there, and the brook trout are drawn to it like your compass?" I asked.

"You saw for yourself where the compass arrow pointed, and it wasn't down below. That's a mighty big mine that we dug out down there, still plenty of ore left. But it's nothing compared to what's waiting above. As for the brook trout... They don't feed here, because they don't live here. The few bigger fish that you see in this run are just standing watch, waiting to show the little ones what to do when the time comes."

"Time comes for what?" I asked.

Uncle Jack stood up. "You asked for a hint, not the whole answer. Too much knowledge at once can seize up the mind of a growing boy. We'd better get back down there and see if Ernie is done swearing and pounding his steam contraption out of the rock pile."

I started following him down. I stopped and looked back at the ants crawling along the boulders. "You're going to tell the mining company. You're going to come up here and take the iron, aren't you?"

Uncle Jack turned around and slowly walked back. "First you start thinking like a trout, now you start thinking like a man. I reckon you're learning more than just fly fishing."

"Has Ernie been up here?"

"Nope," said Uncle Jack. "Ernie is happy with the way things stand. He takes things as they come. He eats and enjoys whatever the day happens to set on his table. That's a peace of mind that is hard to come by. Herb in Popcorn Corners has the same thing. The mysteries of life they go on about, those mysteries aren't really mysteries to anyone but people like the movers and shakers in the executive boardrooms, people who need the steel – not so much for what it stands for – but for what it can get them under the banner of progress. You see, when it comes to money, for some people there ain't no such thing as happy with the way things stand."

"Ernie will follow you here if you ask him. You know he will."

"That's one of those mysteries of life that's hardest to comprehend," said Uncle Jack. "I couldn't have got here without Ernie. I would have been run out of the taconite business years ago. We moved over the next ridge, on to the next mine, the next piece of trout water. The scenery changed but was always me and him. I don't tell him to follow, and he doesn't tell me to stay put. It's a bond that runs pretty darn deep."

Uncle Jack knelt by the stream. He watched the trout swimming. He picked up a pebble and tossed it into the water. The ripples extended outward in a series of rings.

"The thing is, I've never been satisfied with enough, either. I'm not a whole sight better than the mining companies. I went along hand-in-hand with them, bringing them taconite in exchange for what I could get for myself. The only difference is, with me, it's always been the allure of the places: the waters and the tunneled valleys and the rising hills, the places where the iron piles up, where it's been piling up ever since the glaciers pounded a mile high and drained into the dark basin of Lake Superior. I should have been satisfied with the way things stood, but it was always what might lie around the next bend, what kind of escapade waited over the next rise of timber – that's what kept me moving. Ernie followed, out of friendship or out of feeling sorry for me – who knows? I'd like to think it was friendship, but the fact is I've dragged him into plenty of messes, and he's always been able to get us out of them. For a lifetime of *that*, I figure I owe him something."

The ripples died in a slow ring where the pebble had gone in, spreading outward and gone. But looking back, I could still make out the center of the vanishing rings, like something imperceptible coming to the surface before quietly vanishing into the waters of Taconite Creek.

CHAPTER 28

Halfway down the ridge, Uncle Jack stopped and sniffed the air.

"What's that?" He paced nervously like a deer, trying to get a better vantage with his nostrils flaring.

"What's what?" I asked.

"Smoke and steam. We better get moving! And to think that Finlander gets nervous when I'm left in charge."

We double-timed it down the slope to find steam billowing. It shrouded the clearing in a whirling cloud of fog. The smell of wood smoke dominated. Taconite Creek itself seemed to live in the rising smoke, breathing it in, carrying it on its rushing waters, and curling it into the swamp.

Ernie shouted and pounded his fists like a wild man on his perch atop the sauna train. "Come on, you beeg engine! Give dem pistons hell!" The stack whistled, rubber-bottomed wheels spinning rocks and gravel high into the air. It sounded like hail hitting the top of the box car. Ernie saw us descending the line of the creek. "Ve need more steam!" He shouted.

"Come on!" Uncle Jack said. "He's almost got it out of that rock pile. Drop everything and grab some timber!"

We ran to the side of the train and hefted armfuls of oak from the woodpile. The train's stove was how we cooked, and it was part of my daily routine to find and drag logs into the clearing where Uncle Jack would split them up. He might not have been capable of designing a train engine, but he could sure split wood enough to fuel one. Ernie had already decimated half the woodpile into the sauna train's burner. It was glowing red hot. Uncle Jack whipped open the stove, and we threw in as much wood as it could handle. Then, for good measure, we jammed in some more. Ernie shouted something I couldn't make out, because the whole train crackled with split-oak fire.

Pistons jammed forward, stuck for a moment, and then popped back the other way. The wheels were trying to break loose as Ernie throttled the train, but they were caked with gravel and soot and bacon grease and fish bones. They seemed to be having trouble remembering that they were a part of a train and not a camp stove. Ernie shouted over the noise, hollering in Finnish. Trout bones flew from the wheel bearings and spattered the clearing like an ancient graveyard.

"Calm down and speak English, Ernie!" shouted Uncle Jack. "You're bellowing like a bull moose!"

Ernie leaned down the side of the train and pointed to the set of steel tanks that hung down from either side of the rocks on top of the burner. He pointed to a fill spout on the side of the tanks.

"I said ve need more steam! Da fire is already burning hot enough to melt da rocks!"

"Got it. Now we're getting somewhere," said Uncle Jack, grabbing a cast iron bucket. "Why didn't you just say so!" he yelled back as we ran for the creek. "The word steam don't sound like the word water to nobody's ears – no matter what language you're using!"

We made a bucket brigade from the creek to the train tanks. Uncle Jack filled buckets from the rushing stream, and I ran to the train and poured them in. Ernie opened a valve high above the stove, and the cold water of Taconite Creek spilled down on white-hot rocks. Jets of steam hissed from either side like whales blowing sprays of water. Ernie jammed a lever forward, spinning the control gauges with quick turns of his wrist, and steam shot evenly through copper tubes and down to the pistons. We poured in more water, and the pistons turned harder.

A high whistle finally vented from the stack atop the train. It echoed from the ridge. A deer bounded from its swamp bed by the creek. Flocks of crows shot into startled flight. "Dare she blows!" Ernie shouted as the train broke from its iron-rock prison and moved into the clearing.

The billowing clouds dissipated as the train found its rhythm and started chugging around the clearing. I chased the moving sauna like a wild puppy. Ernie resurrected a worn, checkered engineer's cap from under the seat, flagging the cap into the air and hailing us with a victory wave as he took the train through its paces. It rolled over the rocks with ease, crunching the iron-graveled rock. It spun through the mucky swamp bottom, past the red truck that was still stuck and now sprouting moss. The train passed so close to the mired vehicle that it spattered mud upon the growing green life of the sunken windshield. Steam vented from the train's valves, shattering the air with a piercing cry until you swore that every trout in Taconite Creek might poke their fins out of the log jams to see what was going on. I howled right along with the train's whistle.

Ernie finally eased the train alongside the boxcar. The stove glowed hot, and the train sat hissing softly and smelling like fresh wood smoke on a clear night.

"Vell, vut do you tink?" Ernie asked me.

"It's amazing!"

"You are a fine mechanic and one hell of a back-woods railroader," said Uncle Jack. "And that engineer's cap is a great touch. I had one just like it, but I lost it somewhere. It was a nice complement to my hip boots. I'd almost offer to trade you my fishing vest for it. Now, come to think of it, where did you get that cap anyway?"

"Come to tink of it, vare did you get dat fishing vest? I had vun like dat vit a bunch of flies in da pocket. But it got lost somevares, too."

"On second thought, I think you should keep the cap. It looks better on you, anyway." said Uncle Jack.

"Vant to try it?" Ernie questioned.

"Try what?" I asked.

"Try da train!"

"You mean me drive it? Really?! It looks complicated. I don't think I'll be able to work the controls."

"It is very simple. Climb up and I show you. Dis dial in da middle make more steam to both sides – den you go faster. Dis dial on da right make more steam to one side and you turn dat vay – same vay on da other side dial. Very simple, now you are trained. Have fun. I am dirty from all dis verking in da rocks. I am going to take a bath now." He jumped off the train and walked away.

"Does it go backwards? How do I stop?" I hollered.

"I have not figured dat one out yet, and very carefully," he called back.

"You can't bash it up anymore than it's already been bashed," added Uncle Jack, "but don't get too close to the boxcar. That confounded wood-steam contraption has a tendency to burn things down, and we've got all our fishing gear in there. Less important stuff, like rail spikes and rutabagas, too."

Uncle Jack followed Ernie to the deep hole below the rock island. Soon they were swimming and bathing and splashing and laughing, while I sat alone atop a steaming train.

It was intimidating – gauges and hoses and the tall frame of wood-burning steel beneath me. But it turned out to be nearly as easy as Ernie said. I rolled pressure into the valves with the center dial, and the train lurched forward. I nearly toppled backwards off the seat, hastily turning the dial back down; too much steam, I decided. I tried again with a slow and easy turn. This time, the train rolled into a gentle crawl.

I got the feel of the valves, swinging left, backing off the dial, and turning slowly right on the opposite side. I ran slanted courses across the clearing and circled the slopes of the mine. I throttled the pressure dials another notch and kicked up whirlwind clouds of taconite dust. Scant weeks ago, I was worried about failing in school and now, by God, I was driving a train.

I headed along the creek towards the swimming hole to show off. I ran flush on the edge of the water, and I felt the trouble happening as soon as I heard the squelching of the springy ground. The train bogged down as the wheels sunk low in the ferns and found the mud underneath. I felt the train sliding down the sloping banks and shot a panicked glance at my companions in the swimming hole.

"I need some help here!" I yelled.

They floated on their backs, spouting water and kicking up large wakes. Neither of them paid me any mind. "It's going to tip right into the creek and end up as the biggest trout hideout on the entire stretch!" I shouted.

They just floated, oblivious to my cry of help. I'd seen them twitch their ears and catch the splash of a rising trout a half-mile away. Now, they just kept talking and floating.

I pulled the chain that vented the steam to the stack, and the train gave a piercing whistle. Unfortunately, it also took power away from the pistons. The wheels gave a lurch, and I sank deeper into the bottoms. The whistle did finally catch Uncle Jack and Ernie's attention. But instead of panicking, they leisurely paddled to the edge of the rocks, breast-stroking through the pool like there was not a care in the world.

"Open da beeg valve over da stove and give her more vater! Give her more steam! She'll roll right out of dat clay hole!" Ernie was seemingly unconcerned that his train was heading for a watery grave.

"No, No, No. Abandon ship and let her go!" Uncle Jack laughed. "And if it's going to be the best trout hole on the creek, I call first dibs on fishing it."

They had more faith in me than I had myself. I took a deep breath and found the lever to let more water onto the stove rocks. Steam rose thick. It hid the clearing in ghostly waves of vaporized water. I could barely see Uncle Jack and Ernie floating in the pool ahead of me. They were like laughing phantoms springing in and out of existence in the fog. I focused on the dials and levers. Ernie's engineer cap rested on the seat beside me. The train tilted ever closer to the swampy water.

A little more steam and a turn of the dial, spitting red clay, ferns, and watercress into the swamp. The train gave a mighty lurch and grabbed purchase from the edge, shooting over the rocky ground and coasting to a stop next to the swimming hole. I peeled sweaty hands from the train dials. Ernie and Uncle Jack sauntered over, cheerily toweling off after their baths.

"Dat vas mighty good train verk." Ernie said, dripping water from his shaggy hair and beard.

"I have to admit, Ernie, for an over-engineered sauna that's been sittin' in a rock pile for a year, the thing still has some spunk," said Uncle Jack.

Ernie lifted the iron casing from over the rocks and felt the heat of the stove. "It is cooling down good. But it is still hot enough to cook someting to eat, I tink. Boy, dat swimming is good for da appetite."

"Should I catch some trout for dinner?" I asked. "I'll fry them up." I was anxious to make atonements for my near miss with the train.

"No fishing tonight," said Uncle Jack. "We've got a sack of potatoes and some beans that we brought from Popcorn Corners. We might as well eat what we can from the stockpile. It'll lighten the load on the train when we leave. I bet there's still a crate of rutabagas here somewhere, too, unless Ernie's been cutting into them on the sly."

"We're taking the train home?" I asked.

"You got to get home somehow," said Uncle Jack. "It appears the truck has gotten mighty comfortable in the swamp. I suppose we might pull it out, but I never really cared for it all that much. That leaky radiator is thirstier than Ernie's steam engine."

"But I'm not ready to go back. I'm just getting the hang of fishing, and there's still so much else. I can learn to work on the train – Ernie can show me all about the mechanical things. What about the brook trout up on the ridge? You told me I needed to figure it out. I'll help you mine the ore, if that's what it takes. I bet I can! I need more time. I really don't want to go yet!"

"Take it easy. Take it easy," said Uncle Jack.

Ernie didn't pay attention to my rambling. He was heavily occupied in the boxcar recesses, looking for his crate of rutabagas.

"I told your mom that you'd earn your keep, and so far you've held up to that and then some. You've come a long ways, and she'll be darn proud. I know I'm proud. I know Ernie is proud, too, but he's too busy worrying about his stomach right now to say so. Now comes the tough part; we've got a hard spell laid out in front of us." Uncle Jack said.

I stood stoically. I didn't want to leave. But thinking it through, I also didn't want to ruin everything I'd experienced by acting out a tantrum. Uncle Jack said it was a hard spell, and he was right.

"Should I pack tonight?" I asked.

"No, leave everything in the boxcar until it's time. Tomorrow, we'll start pulling the timbers and rails out of there. Of course we'll need tools and lumber and ropes and a few hundred rail spikes. It'll take a while, but I figured it through while I was taking my bath. Not only is swimming in that cold water good for the appetite, it also does wonders to help a man organize his thoughts."

"How can we take all that stuff and still leave room from for us?" I asked.

"We'll have to make a few trips." Uncle Jack said.

"Won't that take a long time?"

"Once we get a few rails down, it'll jump us over the worst of the rock slides. The bridge will take more time. Granted, it will be a work in progress once we get there." Uncle Jack said it like it made the most logical sense in the world.

"I have no idea what you're saying. I thought we were taking the train." I said.

"Vare are ve taking da train?" Ernie sat on the edge of the boxcar, the rutabaga he'd scavenged going down in mighty swallows, skin and all.

"We're leaving, out the way we came, except not with the truck," I said.

"Who said we're going that way?" asked Uncle Jack.

"Vut is da matter vit da truck?" Ernie munched away, swinging legs over the side of the boxcar and looking at the sunken relic in the swamp.

"The truck is sunk to the windshield, and Uncle Jack said we were taking the train," I answered both of Ernie's questions at once.

Ernie yawned in the glory of the afternoon sun. "I could eat rutabageys and trout right here for da rest of my life. Dat vould be heaven."

"I said you had to get home eventually. I didn't say which way and when." Uncle Jack said.

"Maybe backvards to go forvards," Ernie added.

"Or maybe up to go down," said Uncle Jack, pointing far up the creek.

I'd experienced their misdirection before, but it had never shown clearer than that moment, sitting by the sauna train with Uncle Jack refreshed from his swim and talking in riddles, Ernie eating a rutabaga and talking in riddles; up and down and backwards and forwards. They created havoc. It was clear to see how they had finagled their way past the purse-string holders and executive boardrooms, and onto every trout-stream taconite deposit in the Superior hills.

I took a deep breath. "Let me get this straight. We are leaving this mine site on the train."

"That's what I just told you," said Uncle Jack, matter-of-factly.

Ernie just licked the remains of his snack from his fingertips.

"Even if they did fire you – won't the mine company want their boxcar and equipment back – won't they wonder what happened to you – won't they wonder what happened to their taconite mine?"

Uncle Jack dug in the boxcar and pulled out a sack of potatoes. He sat down with his knife and started peeling. "They'll come looking eventually. Maybe there are even some of the fellows who can remember part of the way in here. I'm sure some of 'em still haven't forgot the pleasure of walking the whole way out. I imagine they'll find it again when the stakes get high enough."

Ernie lifted the steam tanks off the stove and back up on their hinges. He waved a hand over the rocks, opened the burner, and looked at the glowing coals. He gave the side of the train a loving pat. "Vitout a train like dis, it's a long time coming 'fore day find a vay to come back and take more iron rocks here. Oh, boy! It smells yust right for dinner." He rubbed his belly and took the cooking rack from where it leaned against the train.

"We'll clean the place up when we leave – there won't be a hell of a lot left to find," said Uncle Jack, finishing his potato peeling and opening another crate. "Whoa, that's not the beans."

The sun sat low on the ridge, throwing the clearing into shadows. Uncle Jack hastily put the crate lid back on and shoved it under the boxcar before plunging back in and continuing his search.

"On second thought, you might as well try to wrestle a trout or two out of the swamp. I can't find the beans, and we need something to go with the 'taters. Don't stay too long; we got a big day ahead of us."

The sun was just about down when I made my first cast. I saw living color flash from beneath the bank and got ready to set the hook. There was still enough light to see the amber spots and searching jaws of the trout as it sucked in the fly. And there had been plenty enough light to see that the crate Uncle Jack opened was stocked to the top with dynamite.

CHAPTER 29

My arms were falling off before the sun fully broke the pines. Trout still rose in the swampy shadows, and I could see the ripples as I shoveled up the ridge. The heavy splashing of trout kept a steady rhythm with my labors, their feeding noises receding deeper into the swamp tunnels with every dawn arrow breaking through.

Another bucket of gravel scooped from the bottom slopes, mine scatterings crunching beneath my boots as I hauled it higher. Building the rail grade, bucket by bucket, as the sun moved down to greet me and the trout slurped breakfast in the swamp. It went on like that for the longest of three days.

It was nearing the summer solstice. Nights were short and presided over by the brightest moon imaginable. The rocks reflected like waiting eyes in the moonlight, the faintest glow coming in the east. The ridge was alive with glowing red minions of taconite.

"Roll 'em out! It's time to kiss the moon and dance with the rising sun!" Uncle Jack was the picture of life, standing at the cusp of dawn, hip-booted legs and a religious fever in his eyes. My sleeping blankets were warm and soft. Outside, the cruel iron gravel waited, and Taconite Creek rushed cold. I buried my head deeper, ignoring Uncle Jack's alarm-clock hollering and trying to ignore my stiff muscles. If I didn't move, maybe he'd forget.

He'd start into singing church hymns: "Amazing Grace," with a boisterous and out-of-tune emphasis on the stanza: "I once was lost, but now am found; was blind, but now I see." Invariably, he'd bellow "Praying River." It was always his personal favorite, and then there was no help for it but to get up and start another long day.

Ernie was slumped over outside, the moon throwing shadows across the sauna train's stove. He'd beat Uncle Jack's summons, his hulking frame brooding over bubbling coffee. He moved like a roaming grizzly all day, lifting and climbing, head swinging, and powerful legs striding. He'd turn into a tireless machine once the sun was up, but he simply wasn't a morning person. Maybe it was a product of his long, dark winter days in Finland, where hibernation was a standard practice. Or maybe it was that he didn't so much mind being up early, but preferred to have meditative silence in the dark before the dawn. I know for a fact that he hated Uncle Jack's witching-hour vespers.

"If I hear dat prayin' river vun more time ven it's still too dark to even see da river, I vill stuff both his boots in da organ pipes."

By the time I crawled out of the train, one pot of coffee was already gone; Uncle Jack gulping his share between songs of jubilation, rubber-booted feet pounding jig steps in the clearing; Ernie, fortifying himself morosely over the stove, shooting withering glances and kicking wads of gravel at Uncle Jack if he ventured too near Ernie's early-morning personal space.

The light of setting moon and rising sun fought each other's reflections in the river as I knelt down – just like in Uncle Jack's favorite hymn – praying, working the stiffness from my body, and filling the empty pot from the cold water. I fortified myself with an equal share of coffee and headed for an equal share in the labor of another day. It was a labor designed around running the sauna train up the pinnacle of Taconite Creek itself.

I filled the biggest spaces between the crags with gravel. Ernie and Uncle Jack came behind and laid down rails and ties. It wasn't a conventional train track. It was cobbled together with a minimum of cross-ties and spikes and spiraled like a switchback trail. Ernie's train didn't need rails on flat terrain, but the ridge was steep and rocky. We needed to give the moving sauna a boost over the rockslides.

The sun beat down, and the glare from the rocks was intense. By mid-morning, it was hot enough to make Uncle Jack shed his boots. Gravel and rock stuck to our sweat. The sun turned us brown, and the dust turned us black. The threat of rockslides was imminent. It was my responsibility to watch for the biggest ones.

"Avalanche!" I'd shout, as another slide came down from a creek bed that was still trying to find equilibrium. Uncle Jack and Ernie dropped the rail they were lifting and dove for cover. They'd slowly pick themselves out of the spattering rocks after the threat had passed, pulling gravel from beneath their fingertips.

"Dammit, Ernie! You don't have to move out of the way so fast that you drop the rail on my toes. You know I don't have my boots on!"

"I am moving no faster den da last time. It is you dat is moving slower, even vitout da boots. I tink you vould go faster if you did not sing like da vounded duck every morning."

There were bacon sandwiches topped with fresh watercress for lunch. We took a cooling swim in the island hole of the creek before starting again, filling gravel and laying rails until the shadows were long in the pines, and the rocks raised their evening mist. Through it all – the sore muscles and the early morning singing, the pots of coffee in the gray dawn and the hourly rockslides – we moved higher. By the third day, we'd progressed up to the tattered dam.

I fished above the dam with Uncle Jack as darkness fell and the moon rose full. He caught two nice browns right away. He was humming a victory tune and wiggling his eyebrows at me when my rod bent in half. Uncle Jack's melody stopped short, and he got down on hands and knees for a better look at the fight.

"Whoa, got a hold of a dandy one there! Don't let him get away. I'm starving, and these two little one's I've caught aren't going to make a dent in my appetite, and we've still got Ernie's appetite to contend with after that. Speak of the hungry devil himself, here he comes now."

Uncle Jack took his eyes off the battle long enough to watch Ernie winding the train up the filled-gravel crevasses and wood-laid tracks of our labor. He stopped just short of the dam, which was the only obstacle left before the train could chug up the gravel and pine-needled banks of the upper creek.

I wrestled with the fish. The moon rose higher, and line sang. I gave the trout slack, and the fish sank heavy into the water at the face of the dam, charging at once to the surface, up and up, breaking water and gliding through the moon's reflection. I lifted my rod with the fish as he jumped, keeping the line from snapping. He fell back into the pool with a deep splash. Ernie sat on the train and Uncle Jack sat by the dam, both watching in silence as the trout sulked down to the bottom for a game of tug-of-war. I patiently lifted and prodded, wearing the fish down, and all the while pulling him closer to the moonlit surface. Soon enough, the moon glistened cold on the flopping, wet sides of a brown trout that was longer than my forearm. It was the biggest trout I'd seen taken on Taconite Creek.

Ernie applauded from his steaming perch while Uncle Jack lifted the trout and admired it in the glow of the train. "This one's enough for us all to eat on. The two minnows of mine are a shame compared to it. Stop the train and fire up the grill – I've been shown up, and supper is served!"

I gutted the three trout and fried them over the stove as Uncle Jack surveyed the dam in the moonlight. "I figure we can cut cedar posts to drive into the creek bottom on either side of the dam." said Uncle Jack. "Hammer in some cross-ties and use the dam for a center brace. The train will glide right across."

Ernie pondered quietly. He stepped out on the dam, bending his body up and down and testing his weight. He stomped, and pieces of mortar crumbled into the water. He got down into the water, waist deep next to the dam, and inspected the bottom by digging his boots in. Wavelets of water spilled through broken mortar.

"I don't much like it," he said.

"What other choice is there?" Uncle Jack asked. "The creek is flowing too hard and fast above and below. I don't think the train can shoot those rapids."

It had been three days of labor to get the train up to the dam. It should be said that both Ernie and I were still not certain why we had to get the train up to this point at all. Uncle Jack had a plan. He'd refused to say more. He was excited, and Uncle Jack's excitement always had a way of being contagious. His excitement alone had been enough to get us this far.

"Can't we just keep to this side and go to the top?" I questioned.

"Not unless you want to walk hunchbacked the rest of your life from hauling gravel," Uncle Jack answered. "I don't think Ernie and I have enough gumption to lay a track through it. I don't think Ernie can survive that many mornings of my singing."

I was preoccupied with flipping the trout off the sauna stove, or I might have answered my own question. The down-slope side of the creek was where the yawning mine had been opened. It had been blasted into countless gullies. Unless we wanted to spend the rest of the summer leveling a path over a treacherous network of Badlands, it was out of the question.

Uncle Jack speared a trout off the stove with his knife, pulled the backbone, and crunched it down in a single swallow, tail and all. "Nope, this is the easiest spot. The creek runs level enough – it's why we picked it for the dam in the first place. We gotta go over here, or we don't go at all."

Ernie picked at his own trout without really eating. "I don't know vie ve go at all. I never ask. Maybe, I tink to myself, you yust vant to make a rail line for old time's sake – but I know dat it vas too much verk, even in the old times ven ve ver still full of da vinegar. So I know it vasn't dat. You showed us da spot on your map, vay up high, so it is not too hard to figure dat it revolves around da trout and da iron, but again, I never ask and you never say. But I know vun ting for sure. I do not like da looks of dis dam. Maybe ve should yust be content vit da moments given to us."

Uncle Jack paced with his hands in the air. "It's like this. We need to make one last push. Maybe then we can live out the rest of our lives carefree without having to search around the next bend. And maybe we can live without having to look over our shoulder and wondering who's chasing around the bend behind us."

"This is a wonderful place!" I said. "It's as carefree as it gets. Just look at all these boulders, with steam falling down the ridge in late afternoon and the creek flowing dark through the swamp and trout rising beneath the alders. A train car to sleep in; what more could anyone ask for?"

Uncle Jack opened the stove and dumped the bones of his trout into the fire. "They're going to come when the other pickings lean out, and then there ain't going to be any carefree to go around. They might not know the exact place, but they've seen the ore, seen the rock we hauled out of here and piled on the docks. Maybe the freighters set sail and hauled for another shore – but they're not going to forget – no matter how many years go by. They're going to come back, and when they do, it's going to make what we did here on Taconite Creek look like child's play."

Ernie spread his hands in the rising moonlight. "And vut vill ve accomplish by crossing da creek and going up da ridge? Day vill come, and ve vill be chasing trout dreams somevare else. Day vill follow us dare, too. Ve cannot run forever. Ve cannot stop time from spinning."

Uncle Jack walked a step onto the dam. He stood with his hands folded behind, like a ship's captain surveying a broken shore, the splitting rush of Taconite Creek spilling at his feet over the causeway. Insects hummed unseen in the still summer night, and nighthawks swooped into the bottoms to chase them. The air was alive with wings.

"You're right. This was a perfect place long before we ever set eyes on it. Even after we did our best to mess up the whole affair, it's still about the most perfect place under the sun and the moon and stars. There ain't nowhere better." Uncle Jack smiled gently and pointed to the heavens. Despite the brightness of the moon, there were still a million lights twinkling along the ridge top. "Almost nowhere better," he said.

"If this is where we stop, then I guess I can live with it. You know, I don't think it was ever about catching that brook trout up the ridge. I don't know if it was ever about the trout at all. It was more about me running away from myself, running after phantom shadows in the water."

Uncle Jack rested an arm on Ernie's shoulder. "Maybe I should have stayed on the farm like my old man told me."

Ernie smiled gently. "Ya, and maybe I should have stayed back in da rock university in Finland. I maybe vould have made vun hellova teacher."

"You sure would have, Ernie – teaching the mysteries of life to everyone. Hell, you could have been paid for lying and slept nice and comfortable instead of being paid for lying and tramping all over the country."

"You bet," said Ernie. "And if you had stayed on da farm, den maybe you vould have burned down da barn instead of da bridge."

Uncle Jack chuckled. "I just might have at that."

Uncle Jack rested his other arm on my shoulder. "It looks like you're the only one here who still has all his mistakes ahead of him."

He hummed a few bars of "Praying River," and then he spoke.

"I'll make you a deal. If we're going to call a halt to this operation, especially after your endless, and shall I say tireless, and shall I say outright backbreaking efforts, risking avalanches and heatstroke – then the least I can do is show you what it was all about. Tonight, the three of us will make the pilgrimage. I want to show you something."

Uncle Jack clapped me on my back. "Then *you* can decide for all of us."

CHAPTER 30

If I could paint the night on canvas, it would be a masterpiece, but the medium I drew in life was to paint with words. Words are all that remain to explain the night that was given to us. Words are the only witness to tell I was there on Taconite Creek.

The lifeblood of a taconite giant sprung beneath a summer moon. Boulders and crags arched a network of shadows across the stream, broken only by flashes of trout that scattered like glass, fading from silver into nothing and reappearing on the other side of the dark webs. The shadowed bridges were frail and wispy at first but, as the rocks got bigger, the complexity of the bridges grew. They put illusions in my mind as I trudged upward in silence. If Uncle Jack and Ernie would have walked out over one of the shadowed bridges and into the tumbling rush, I would have followed without hesitation.

After miles in the moonlight and shadows to reach Uncle Jack's camp, where he'd climbed so often, in his own words, "reaching towards the pinnacle of life and chasing phantom shadows in the water," we could go no higher.

It was set beneath pillared white pines. A peeled ridgepole was lashed between the two trunks, evergreen branches angling down from either side. A small ring of stones surrounded the charcoaled remains of campfires past. There was pebbled gravel beyond the stone ring and the looming red shadows of a cliff face. But the centerpiece, pouring from the rock above Uncle Jack's camp, was the headwaters of Taconite Creek. They arched gracefully from the rock face itself, falling in a ten-yard swath, not careening or crashing, just a curtain of water as if someone had turned on a giant garden hose without a spray nozzle attached. The water poured down and gathered itself in a pool before shooting past the pine camp and under the shadowed rock bridges.

I stirred pine kindling to life in the fire ring, not so much for warmth as for the welcoming glow that it threw onto the rocks. I wanted to see the surroundings in more than moonlight. Pine branches crackled and popped.

Uncle Jack stood behind me as I built the fire. "The fire ring was already here, you know. I built the shelter myself, but the ring of stones was here long before me. I found a chipped arrowhead in the ashes. I wouldn't doubt that generations of Indians sat and pondered here. It wouldn't surprise me one bit if it was a shrine for medicine men, some kind of holy place."

Ernie stood transfixed at the foot of the rising wall, marveling at the heaving fissures. The blaze rose higher. Shadows of red reflected from the rocks.

"See what you were missing, Ernie?" Uncle Jack asked. "All the while nibbling on them small rocks along the creek bottom, and here you could have been gorging on a whole damn mountain."

"Vater springing from da rock itself!" Ernie murmured. He seemed to be talking to the wall of rock. He picked a burning piece of pine out of the fire and brought it to the rushing pool of water for a closer look.

"It vashed down, all da iron, everyting from here. It must have took 'bout hundred or more centuries, one little bit at a time, dribbling down da creek to pile up above da swamp."

Ernie's torch flashed across the pool. The burning light and the moon's reflection in the water showed hundreds, maybe thousands, of silver flashes. The pool was alive with fingerling brook trout.

"Dat is more brook trout dan I have ever seen in vun place. I tink, dat is more brook trout dan I have ever seen in my life. Day are not big, but day sure are pretty."

"There are so many of them. It's a fish hatchery. Even more, it looks like a fish factory!" I exclaimed.

"That, my boy, is exactly what it is," said Uncle Jack.

"Where do they all come from? And where do they go?"

"Where do they come from? That's a question of countless campfires and countless casts," answered Uncle Jack. "And where they disappear to? That is a question that's taken a heavy toll on my mind."

"Not to mention it is a question dat blew out a pump house," said Ernie.

Uncle Jack leaned back against the taconite wall. The moon settled above the looming rock. He took a rock that had fallen from the heights above and tossed it into the pool. The last of the moonlight caught the ripples, and then the moon sank above the wall, and the ripples disappeared.

"You squeeze out your mysteries of life, Ernie, and I squeeze out mine. The pump house just got squeezed in the middle."

Ernie tossed the burning pine branch back into the fire ring. Sparks flew high into the air and followed the last of the moonlight fading over the rock face. "Ya, maybe ve both yust squeezed too hard."

I crept to the edge of the pool and lay flat. The fire danced in the ancient stone ring. There were schools of small trout higher up, but I saw longer bursts of lightning below. They were skittish, like real flashes of lightning can be, burning your eyes quickly, and then gone. I knew the deeper flashes were big trout.

"What's the secret, Uncle Jack?" I asked. "You wouldn't be aiming to mine this wall if there weren't trout that could be caught, right?"

Ernie kicked at the fire's coals, and a fresh plume of sparks rose into the summer night. He looked uncomfortable. He was Uncle Jack's partner. He held the mysteries of life deep in his mind but, alongside those mysteries, he was also the only one standing atop the pinnacle of Taconite Creek who had the mechanical knowledge to open a mine this high up. I knew Uncle Jack hadn't asked him. But when it came down to it, I figured Ernie would follow.

Ernie spoke to Uncle Jack. "You have da iron in your blood and da trout fire in your belly. It vill not go out, othervise ve vould not be up here tonight."

Uncle Jack shrugged. "There's enough trout and taconite up here to span a lifetime. Without your help, though, I don't think we can even make the first cast."

Ernie knelt by the rocks of the fire ring. He brushed ash, running his hands across the smooth surfaces of pure taconite. He looked up at Uncle Jack. "I am like you. I have da trout fire, and dare is da iron in my blood. I know da rocks like you know da brook trout. You say you found an arrowhead? Dis stone ring has sat here for a very long time. Dat vall of rock above has been here longer. Me and you, ve have torn much rock from da earth. But now, I don't know dat I have it in me to dig no more."

Uncle Jack paced over to the water. I was still on my belly watching the trout. He stared into the water with me. "I'll be honest, Ernie. When I first trekked up here, when I first saw all of this iron ore, saw all the brook trout, I'll admit the thought crossed my mind to tear up the whole thing and make it a fish pond, just like back on the farm. Spend enough time up here listening to the water and staring at a trout – you start to hear voices. You don't know if it is the rocks or the water or the trout itself that's trying you tell you something. A lot of things weigh through your mind. I finally reached a stalemate. The trout looked up at me, and there was no higher for them to run, and I looked down at them and couldn't catch a single one. And do you know what? That stalemate bothered me. I like to come out on top, but I don't mind getting skunked if I've given it my all. I've been beaten plenty before – played enough cribbage with Eddie Barker to bear that one out. But a stalemate, well, that's like kissing your sister! Not that my sister isn't a lovely lady, a great mother, and an all around miracle," Uncle Jack said hastily, patting me on the head.

"Also she is vun heck of a good cook," added Ernie, wistfully rubbing his belly.

"Absolutely!" chimed Uncle Jack, jumping up from the pool, pulling me to my feet with him. "Come over here – right next to the waterfall. Stay right there. I'll show you a thing or two about worming out of a stalemate!"

He trotted to the fire ring. He was excited now, and when he got excited, he couldn't move slow if he tried. He grabbed Ernie's smoldering torch from the coals and waved it to life like a Fourth of July sparkler as he ducked inside the leaning shelter. The solemn scene was charged in an instant. His torch brushed the evergreen branches and started them to smoking. I thought for a moment that the whole shelter might catch and go up in flames.

Ernie winced. He'd seen it often enough over the years, waiting for the excitement to spark into flames, waiting for it to happen like he was expecting it.

Uncle Jack crawled from the boughs of the overgrown opening as quickly as he'd gone in. He had his compass and his map in one hand and the torch still lit in the other. He started out at a run, sniffed the air, and stopped in his tracks momentarily. Almost as an afterthought, he retreated back to where the slightest flicker of flame was crackling. He beat the growing flames into submission with his map, whacked the charred edges of the parchment against a hip boot to keep the map itself from starting alight, and nonchalantly, as if it were a matter of course, continued on to where we waited by the flowing water.

His eyes glowed in the torch light. "Hold out your hands." Uncle Jack laid the compass in my outstretched palms. Ernie peeked over my shoulder, looking at the simple magnetic machine that had taken both him and Jack to the far reaches of the taconite rails. The arrow spun steadily.

"That's a whole lot of taconite staring us in the face, huh, Ernie," Uncle Jack said.

Ernie lay down on propped elbows and looked up at the wall. With the moon down behind the rock wall, the stars popped out brighter. "It is mighty, you betcha," he answered.

Uncle Jack gave me a gentle nudge in the direction of the wall. "Take the compass and see what answers lie yonder."

I walked along the rocky wall, turning along the creek and back towards the fire ring. I turned in circles, and the compass turned with me. I'd been explained the facts of the matter, but I still swore up and down that the magnetic arrow was broken. "I don't know which direction is which by looking at this thing. It's like you said; all this iron ore has the compass in a stalemate."

Uncle Jack spoke to me in a whisper of conspiracy. He tapped the top of his head with his finger. "North and south don't matter. You need to use your head to figure which direction takes us out of this stalemate."

Moving back along the rock face, staring at the compass, I began to see the wild swings of the arrow take on a chaotic reason. The bulges of rock attracted the magnetic needle. The bigger the outcrop, the wilder the needle danced. If I moved away from the wall, the needle drew back with me. I'd seen the swing of the compass when Uncle Jack first walked me above the boxcar clearing. Up close, the taconite ore magnified the effect a hundred-fold.

"Ernie, you know iron better than anyone this side of the Ore Dock Saloon," said Uncle Jack.

Ernie nodded. "I tink dat after all my years spent tromping after your boot prints and digging out samples from da rock piles – after all dat, maybe I know da iron better dan da udder side of da saloon, too."

Uncle Jack grabbed Ernie's arm and pulled him from his contemplation of the stars above. He solicitously brushed pine needles and gravel dust from Ernie's back. "Both sides of the saloon it is! I'd even go so far as to say inside the joint itself, but the boys through those swinging doors are rough and tumble – not really proper company for a grade-school geologist."

"It *vas* university," Ernie said, indignantly stepping from Uncle Jack's clutches and brushing off the last of the pine needles himself. "Rough an' tumble, you should know, you vas inside da place enough!"

"University or saloon, it's a horse apiece and boils down to the same thing. They both have doors to get inside. Now get over there and use your higher learning to help the boy find the door."

Ernie ambled over, and we stood together at the waterfall. I looked at the compass and the ore veins. My heart danced along with the shimmering arrow and the pulsing torch light.

"Is this what it was like, always finding things like this, you and Uncle Jack?"

Ernie breathed deep the summer air, splashing an upturned palm into waters that poured from the rock itself. "Not always tings like dis. Not always sights to take da breath away." He splashed water contemptuously at Uncle Jack "Not always da drama and mystery, neider."

Ernie ran fingers along the rock. He licked his fingertips. "I'd say dat's good ore. Vut's his ding-dang compass tell us?"

I waved it along Ernie's wall section. The arrow jumped like it was charged with electricity. "I think it is good ore, Ernie. Uncle Jack's compass seems to agree with you."

"Vell, at least dare's vun ting ve agree on."

"I heard that!" shouted Uncle Jack. "I don't need to snack on rocks to pull my half of the business. My compass brought us here. Keep eating on those mysteries of life, Ernie. You might find your half eventually."

Ernie hunched over and whispered to me, "I don't really eat da stuff, but I taste da ore yust da same. It is heavy in da air."

I took a deep breath. The spray from the water came out of the cliff and sank deep through my nose and into my lungs until I felt it in the pit of my stomach. It was as if the water itself was magnetized. Ernie was right. The iron was in the water. It was in the very air itself. It was like sucking on a handful of pennies.

Uncle Jack cheered from the shadows. "You've almost got it boys! You're getting warmer, but before you get hot, you'll have to get cold and wet."

"You know what, Ernie," I said. "I'll take your mysteries of life over his riddles any day."

Ernie swatted a mosquito. The torch wavered in his hand. "Da riddles are minor, yust a tiny sting like a 'skeeter. As long as he don't start singing – it is da singing dat bites me like da big horsefly."

I walked up to my knees into the churning pool. Numbness and fire spread upwards. The spray from the falls soaked strands of hair into my eyes, and I wiped them from my forehead, breathing in wet mist, and trying to keep my footing along the rocky bottom. Something cold and wet brushed against my leg at the foot of the falls. In the flickering light of Ernie's torch, a trout darted. It was a silver phantom shooting into the cliff shadows.

I stood still, peering into water that was boiling like a kettle from the falls, running up my spine with the temperature of ice. There were more phantom shadows in the water. I also noticed that the needle of the compass had quit dancing. It banked away from the waterfall. The needle acted as if there wasn't any iron ore at all behind the flowing rush.

"Does water affect the compass like the iron does?" I asked Ernie.

"How do you mean?"

"The waterfall is playing games with the needle. I'm as close to the rock wall here as you are on the bank. I've seen how the compass acts when it's close to the ore. But it seems like there's nothing at all behind the water. I saw a big trout disappear beneath the falls."

"Water don't have any effect. It should be no different dare as vare I'm standing here. Dat compass probably scares trout away yust like its owner."

Uncle Jack stood with arms crossed expectantly. Normally, he would never let a comment like that one go unscathed. He would jump all over it. But he stayed silent. I was close to Uncle Jack's answer.

I stuck my head into the waterfall, taking a shower in ice water from an iron-ore showerhead. The current washed strong at my feet, almost as if there were two rivers coming from the rock, the one above my head and an unseen one below. The moon had set above the wall some time ago, but I could see moonlight now. I thought it was just a reflection of the fire, but the more I peered, the more I became convinced that there was actual moonlight coming through the water.

Cool currents of air stirred through the falls, and I shivered. It reminded me of standing outside the Lake Superior cave when we'd first driven in to Taconite Creek, the air warm outside, and the deepest holds of Lake Superior drafting upwards. I shivered again, but it was not because of the cold. I shivered with realization. I knew what Uncle Jack had searched for and how he had found it. Another cold shadow brushed my leg, then another, tailing beneath the waterfall itself. I took a deep breath and followed. I hung the compass around my neck, just like Uncle Jack. And just like Uncle Jack, I followed the brook trout into the origins of Taconite Creek.

CHAPTER 31

Cold moonlight funneled down. The summer air outside had been humid, but it was a natural ice chest in the passageway beneath the falls. The cavern angled up, and I knew there were two outlets to the headwaters. Unlike the pump house split in the mine clearing far below, the diversion above was a natural product of untold centuries. Water ran knee deep in the bottom tunnel, while the rushing waterfall passed directly above in its own passage. It crossed my mind that this was what deep-earth miners experienced, thousands of tons of rock above, with enough water flowing to sink an ore freighter if the roof took a mind to collapse. The water above echoed like a rushing train.

Startled trout flopped like salmon against the current. I cornered one of the fish in an eroded pocket and tried to lift it. It thrashed through my grasp and swam upward towards the moonlight. The brook trout was fat and heavy-sided.

I stuck my head back out to call for Ernie and Uncle Jack, but they were already wading into the pool. They carried a balsam branch torch that roared like a funeral pyre. Sparks lit in Uncle Jack's hair and in Ernie's beard. The torch sputtered through the falls, coming back to life in the cool draft of the passage.

We climbed – torch light flickering on heavy veins of red, and water dripping from above. Ernie and I scrambled, trout glistening before us in splashing wakes. Uncle Jack followed leisurely. His eyes glowed with the waiting expectancy of a parent watching his children open a silver-wrapped present; a package unwrapping into full moonlight and a bubbling spring pond.

A stunted-tree landscape stretched back through a glen. White birch with roots upturned stretched like fingers into the water. Lily pads and watercress dotted the surface. Shelves of rock stepped out over the pond. Twenty yards over, the waterfall outlet broke over rocks and sucked below on its own course. We crawled ashore and stood in awe. Ernie summed it up.

"I have seen da midnight sun in Finland, hanging on vun horizon vile da full moon looked across on da other. I have seen da ocean vaves pounding high as a mountain ven I first came across to dis country, and I have seen Lake Superior smooth as glass, like maybe you could ice skate across it. Dare are many vunders – but *dis* is someting!"

"The top of Taconite Creek and the top of the taconite range. Any higher and we'd be fishing with angels." Uncle Jack crawled out behind us.

Sweet fern and grasses grew as tall as my chest. It was easy walking. Despite the lush surroundings, the surface beneath our feet was solid rock, a hidden garden springing up through the cracks. I got down on my belly. It was like looking across the surface of a distant and foreign planet surface, dark red and cracked, the color of Mars viewed through a distant telescope, but it was a rock planet that had let green life come through.

Uncle Jack produced his map. It was battered and worn as ever. Taking a piece of charcoaled pine from the torch, he drew a rough circle above the reaches of the wiggling scratch that represented Taconite Creek. "I wanted to wait 'till you both were here to make it official." He smudged a large X in the circle. "I reckon Herbie would trade a gross of rutabagas for this mark."

I turned my head in circles. "Has this always been?"

"As long as the iron and as long as the water," answered Uncle Jack. A fat plop sounded from the middle of the pond as a trout rose to take a night bug. Silent rings spread on the surface. "It's been here as long as the trout," he added.

Another trout rose from beneath a lily pad, then another. From the tangled roots of a fallen tree, a silver flash cleared water, hitting on the other side of the submerged log like a beaver tail slapping water. "It is da lifeblood of Superior itself," said Ernie. He was either breathing hard from the watery passage climb or from the sight of trout rising beneath the moon. It was impossible to tell.

"That's exactly it, Ernie. Lake Superior is stained deep with iron blood. We both know it. You've loaded enough freighters, and I've loaded enough trains. We've dug into the pulsing arteries of that lake for a lot of years. But this," Uncle Jack spread his hands, "this is the heart."

"How did you know?" I asked.

"I found the way up through the waterfall the same way you did. Used the compass, thought about the map, pondered in my mind; and all the while I followed the trout. It was the lake caves winding down into Superior that finally broke me through. It was those caves, and thinking about Eddie Barker hooked to a big lake trout in that dark lake hold, maybe still fighting, with no lake trout above the caves, but plenty of browns, and above it all?"

"Brook trout," I said.

"I figured if we could split Taconite Creek in two by digging out a bit of iron, then Mother Nature could probably do it better, of course, without all the blasting and landslides and such. She hid the trout above like we buried a bundle of fishing gear below."

"Mother Nature yust covered her tracks better," said Ernie.

Uncle Jack strolled to the edge of the spring pond. "I reckon this has been bubbling up here going on forever. I reckon before any white man set eyes on this country, back when my ancestors still talked as strange and funny as you do, Ernie. Well, maybe not that funny – but long before anyone but the Native Indians knew this country existed. How long it took to trickle through this iron rock, splitting the seams and soaking the swamps into Lake Superior – it makes the mind stand still and spin around at the same time."

"Deep mysteries for da pondering," said Ernie.

On the shores of the hidden ridge, as Taconite Creek crept down from its hidden berth to evolve, we stood on the foundations of life itself. Uncle Jack watched me, my mouth open in awe. It was as simple as water flowing downhill, yet it was so complex that I knew it would remain forever beyond the reach of my mind. It was not like school. It was not something you could study or learn in a lifetime of books.

"Those ants we watched," Uncle Jack said. "Crawling the rocks, trying to mine into them, blowing into the creek and washing away, but still they keep going, trying to find a crack, working to get some purchase in the soft ground to start digging in."

I nodded my head.

"That's how it is," he said. "We're them ants, except now we found the crack. Now we found this."

"What," I asked. "What do we do with the crack now that we've found it?"

"This is ground worth digging into. And take my word for it, this is water worth fishing. Those brook trout might not be interested in eating down below, but that's 'causc thcy got a natural dinner table all set for 'em up here. There's a hatch of bugs that comes out of these trees and grass every day. But I said that you should decide, and I meant it."

Ernie looked around the clearing. The trees and the grass, the rippling pond and the iron rock beneath our feet. He looked at me.

"You are young. You see vit different eyes. I have dug out a lifetime of rock, maybe caught more fish den two lifetimes. Vut does da heart say?"

"It feels like when I dropped the offering plate in church once," I said. "It slipped out of my hands and, as soon as it did, I wanted to take it back, but it was too late. All I could do was watch it go. It made a booming clang.

It was loud, but it sounded louder because of where I dropped it. I could feel the noise right into my soul. It feels like that. It feels holy up here."

"Dat is said vell. Ven you run across Herbie someday, him sitting behind da counter and tinking deep toughts, you tell him dat vun. Dat vun should be vorth many rutabagas."

"It is like the ants," I said, turning to Uncle Jack. "Like you've been saying all along about others following. Maybe other ants will crawl up here eventually, but if we start digging ore, then the other ants are going to hear the crash of the offering plate. They're going to get here that much sooner."

Another trout broke water and fell heavily. We turned to watch the rings of the rise, flowing steadily outward, like it had always been.

"Well put," said Uncle Jack. "But you've got the right concept and the wrong idea. I'm not saying we should mine anything. I've about run out of map, and the compass won't show us any finer place. I'm all for setting up and letting the world move on without us here. How would you feel, Ernie, watching the rising sun a stone's throw from the first rays, drinking coffee from the doorway of a little shack, watching the morning hatch, watching the rings of the rising trout sparkling? By God, I'd probably beat you up and already be at it. No singing to wake you, either. You'd have to figure your own alarm clock."

It was then, listening to Uncle Jack's plans unfolding in the moonlight... It was then that I really learned. I learned what books and newspapers can't teach you. Visions. How to snatch them from the air, to see them in your mind, and to put them down onto paper for others to feel: The sun slanting across a shack on the ridge, a pond with the sudden pull of a trout breaking the morning stillness. I could see the vision clearly. I knew then how Uncle Jack and Ernie lived. It wasn't the iron ore, and it wasn't even the trout. It was the burning flame of a dream.

"I tink dat vould be as close to heaven as I am going to get," Ernie said.

"Then we ought to take the train across the creek and make it so," said Uncle Jack, slapping us both on the back.

The burning flame of a dream; a decision made so quickly that I didn't even know I had played a part. All these years gone by now, and I'm still not sure. The decision was made as Uncle Jack knew it would be.

We went down the way we'd come up, but instead of inching tentatively, we slid down like otters. The pond above had cast a spell. We saw the shack in our minds: built from the base up, rails and cedar logs, spike-driven floor built from the very boards of the train car below, sloping roof cut from the boxcar siding. There was plenty stockpiled. There were even rolls of tarpaper in a back corner. I'd set them back up enough times against the rock bombardment. I'd asked Uncle Jack about using some of it to seal the leak above my sleeping cot, but he'd waved me off.

"A little night water never hurt a fellow. It's better than a warning siren – gets you up early to get at the fishing while the trout are still on the prowl, before the whole creek floods and turns to quicksand. Did I ever tell you 'bout the time I got a train stuck? 'Course, it wasn't my fault...."

I'd moved my sleeping cot and continued setting up the tarpaper rolls like bowling pins after every tremor. There obviously hadn't been enough to stop a tiny drip below, but I knew there was more than enough to waterproof a shack of Uncle Jack's fancy.

"We can even build a fireplace out of all the taconite chunks that are cluttering up the place," Uncle Jack orated as we stumbled into his camp below the cliff. "That would serve twofold. It would help cover our tracks, and it would be darn good exercise for you, Ernie. Of course, I could engineer the whole thing: building a train bridge across the dam, moving the necessaries up here and such. But I hate to rob you of a last chance at doing some physical labor before retirement."

Ernie said nothing, chin nodding onto his chest. The coals sparked into a blaze in the fire ring after an armful of wood. We were damp from our excursion. I had been filled with youthful exuberance coming down the water passage. I was all for going below to the train clearing and getting underway. But I yawned as the fire's warmth hit me.

Ernie crawled into the shelter and was snoring in an instant. I vaguely recall Uncle Jack disappearing into the shadows and dragging a night log onto the fire. He crawled in next to Ernie and mumbled a final benediction: "The other ants will crawl up here eventually. But if we do it right, it's going to be a long time coming." Then he was snoring alongside Ernie.

I heard the crackling fire. Sparks from the night log rose from a ring of stones that had been there long before we'd come. They were stones that would be there long after we'd passed. The embers rose over the water, over an iron wall standing watch above Taconite Creek.

Late-staying fireflies brushed the top of the wall, mingling with the rising sparks until it was impossible to tell the flashing bellies from the sparks themselves. It was like the Fourth of July, and then it came to me in the lonely nostalgia of night that my mother expected me back, and I wasn't even sure what day it was. I wanted to stay forever, but I knew my time here had to end. Summer wasn't endless. I thought these thoughts as a child, but the dawning glow of adulthood was peeking around the bend.

As I curled into a ball between Uncle Jack and Ernie, a firefly drifted down from above and settled on a rock of the fire ring. It sizzled to the ground. It got too close, attracted by a burning flame. I tried to hold my eyes open. I simply couldn't.

There would be no dreams. We were all living a waking dream on Taconite Creek. But I know now that I should have held my eyes open. I should have been like the firefly, burned my hand on a hot taconite rock to stay awake if that's what it took. I should have taken it all in a moment longer.

CHAPTER 32

It's still hard for me to fathom, after all the years gone by and so many advances in construction technology; booms, cranes, industrial-sized bulldozers and payload trucks... I'm still in awe of how we built the shack so quickly with nothing more than trout-fevered sweat and a sauna-bath steam engine.

The first robins had just started chirping when Uncle Jack and I untangled ourselves from the shelter, crawling bleary-eyed and stiff through the ashes of the fire ring and over to the waterfall to splash new life on our faces. Ernie was nowhere to be seen. The morning was thick with clouds of mosquitoes on the prowl for their breakfast. We took turns swatting as we washed up.

"Where in blazes did that Finlander run off to already this morning?" Uncle Jack dunked his head fully beneath the spring pool water like a bear chasing a salmon. He came back up for air and shook water in the air, trying to drown as many of the droning pests as he could. "Probably scared him off with all that talk of work, and he snuck out the back door to go fishing. Maybe he lit out like a screaming girl when he saw all these mosquitoes. Either way, it amounts to the same thing – he ain't here, daylight's wasting, and that fishing shack won't build itself!"

The pines drooped in the humid air. There was no hint of a breeze, but I noticed the slightest tremor beginning along the lower branches, like unseen hands shaking a sifter. "Is it just me, or is the ground rumbling?"

A sharp blast pierced the morning air. Clouds of mosquitoes lit off from the low grass around the pool. I saw white steam coming over the lichen-covered boulders, and heard the steady chug-chug coming and another steam blast shooting up the ridge. Uncle Jack stopped in mid-swat of a mosquito on his neck. His ears perked up, and his eyes shone. It was not so much the sight of the train that stirred him. It was the sound rising above it all.

The train was loaded down with timbers and ropes and tarps. Sitting atop it all, like Santa on a steam-engine sleigh, was Ernie. He was waving his fly rod, singing "Praying River," and blowing his steam whistle in time with the stanzas. I swear to God I saw a tear cascade down Uncle Jack's cheek. Ernie pulled the loaded train up to the waterfall pool and tight to the high rock wall. He throttled the engine down and sat smiling and surveying the morning.

"Vell, dis is good looking sight. It is barely daylight in da swamps below, but da sun is poking good up here and da work crew is vaiting."

Uncle Jack's lips moved, but no sharp comeback issued forth. He stood looking at the loaded train, silently mouthing the words to the favored hymn that Ernie's train had delivered.

"How did you get the train across the creek so fast?" I asked.

"I yust got up little early," he answered.

Ernie wound down the ridge before first light. Putting a makeshift bridge across the crumbling integrity of the dam had troubled him the day before. Yesterday, it had been a bridge with no purpose. It had simply been another crossing in a life of wilderness rambling, following Uncle Jack on the never-ending taconite rails. Ernie was gone at first light because now the last station had appeared around the bend, and it was a fine and welcome paradise.

He shored up the dam with sacks of rail spikes, pinching both sides of the crumbling mortar together. He heaved boulders into the creek to anchor the sacks. The offshoot branch of the creek that had bubbled up with the collapse of the pump house sprayed stronger as the dam held back more water. Ernie took what timbers remained from the pump house and spiked them in the mix for good measure.

The sound of his axe carried over the heavy, dawn dew of Taconite Creek. Ernie chopped down two lodge pole pines that towered above the creek. They fell with a crash on either side of the dam. Uncle Jack and I might have heard it in our dreams, but neither of us remembered.

The trees were stripped and laid across either side of the dam, rail timbers nailed across in a neat row. Ernie wasn't a morning person, and he hated Uncle Jack's morning reveilles, but he'd beaten both the early song birds and Uncle Jack. He was a mechanical genius, fully capable, but it still must have been a construction world record.

That world record was consistently shattered in the days that followed. They were good days. The shack issued forth upon the bubbling headwater springs of Taconite Creek. The climate below was hot and sticky. The height of summer beat down on the rocks. Even in the shade of the pines, there was no air moving. There were mosquitoes and biting flies and standing-water sweat on every inch of my body. But atop the plateau, the western breezes rolled white clouds of cotton, and it was heaven. I felt like I could reach my hand up and swipe a handful of glory. No... I take that back... they weren't just good days. They were the finest.

Ernie dismantled Uncle Jack's shelter and built a pulley with half of it.

The rest of the wood went to feed the insatiable appetite of his steam engine. Ropes hung down from above the waterfall, and Ernie hooked them like a belt around the wheels of his train. Unless we wanted to carry everything through the waterfall passage, it was the only way to get the construction material up top.

I started the day below, slowly backing the train down the slope, winding the rope around the train wheels, and lifting the building supplies over the pulley and up to Uncle Jack and Ernie. When one load had gone up, I wrapped the ropes back around the wheels, tied on a new load, and added an armful of wood to the sauna before doing it all again.

When it got too hot, steam from the train stack sweating over me in a sauna-bath fog, and after I'd been bitten by enough flies to make my arms look like they'd gone through a meat grinder, then Uncle Jack or Ernie would come down and take over and I'd plunge through the waterfall and up the tunnel to take their place. The shadowed and dripping walls of the passage knocked the heat and insect bites down. By the time I came out atop the ridge pond, the breeze raised goose bumps on my arms. It was like coming from the bowels of an active volcano and finding a glacier field on top.

The shack was raised on stilts in a small grove of cedar trees along the deepest edge of the pond. The water in front was not fast flowing, nor was it without motion. It bubbled in a gentle upwelling before pulling in the direction of the waterfall outlet. The cedars swayed shade along the water on both sides of the shack. The slightest breeze dropped high-flying insects out of the branches and down to waiting swirls of brook trout.

The trees also served as anchors, lashed with heavy rope from their trunks to the shack's stilts in an array of angles and knots. Sheets of tarpaper crested the flat-board roof, shingled over with cedar boards that were trimmed from other dark groves along the edges of our taconite-mountain paradise. Thus fortified, the shack could withstand the heaviest storms that Lake Superior might whip across the ridge line.

We fished the afternoon hatches of blue-winged olives, and even Uncle Jack was hard pressed to find fault with Ernie's goose-feather creations. The sun rested flush on the ridge top horizon like a fiery eye, watching us strip in brook trout by the bushel basket. Most of the basket got dumped back in the pond – not even Ernie could eat that many – but we still cleaned and ate our fill every night.

We rode the train down the slopes and over Ernie's bridge on scheduled runs. The old camp in the train-car clearing was slowly dismantled.

Everything that could be carried, pulled, or pried was stripped out of the boxcar and put to some use above. We ripped a long section of siding off the boxcar and wrestled it up the ridge. Spiked to rail timbers that were driven through cracks in the rock, the siding became a front porch.

Myself, I was somewhat nostalgic about our old camp below; the swamp and the sunken truck, the dam where I'd caught my first trout... Even the rockslides down the mine ridge didn't seem so bad. Uncle Jack and Ernie had put so much sweat and blood into the mine that I think they were happy to leave it behind. Ernie still looked a bit wistfully into the dark swamp holes as we cleared out the boxcar, but Uncle Jack never gave it a second thought.

"Quit lollygagging and start loading, Ernie! If you want to make pilgrimages down this godforsaken rockslide to catch them browns, I'll be more than happy to sit up above in peace and be rid of you for a day – all the more brook trout for me! But you'll want somewhere to come back to at the end of the day, your tail dragging, and none of them browns even close to measuring up to my fish. And unless you start loading your share, there ain't gonna be no such place!"

We loaded up the train and rolled back over the bridge.

Once the porch was finished, Ernie spent less time staring below. Truth be told, he didn't even spend as much time fishing as me and Uncle Jack. He roamed the high ridge, picking up odd feathers and bits of fur from rabbit holes. He came back with anything and everything that struck his fancy. He even fashioned a camp chair from birch logs, lashing ropes for a seat and, for a final touch, putting down the canoe cushion that had once saved my bottom from an agonizing jolt of rail spikes. He spent a lot of time just sitting there on the porch, tying flies and teaching me to roll cast in order to avoid tangling in the rope anchors and cedar-branch coverings of the shack. He commanded a full view of the pond, and he watched us fish, never missing an opportunity to heckle Uncle Jack every time he missed a strike. There was a peaceful smile on Ernie's face, and it was plain to see that, while he may have still been pondering the mysteries of life, he no longer searched for them.

Somewhere in those wonderful summer days, between moving out of the boxcar, lifting everything we could salvage from the mine site, and putting it to practical use in the spring-pond paradise; somewhere in the lull of the casts and the rising of the trout, I discovered a notebook and pencil tucked in a corner pocket of my pack. I figured my mom packed it to remind me that I'd have to come home eventually, back to reality and school in the fall. She'd seen the spark that Uncle Jack and Ernie had started in my mind, and I reasoned the notebook came along because she didn't want to see the flame falter.

I started carrying the notebook through the groves and to the far cornered logs and rocks. I sat and watched the sun angle the water, refracting endlessly into the depths. I watched water bugs skittering the surface film, weightless on skating legs with no apparent purpose in life except exploring the hidden pond. The taconite foundations of our summit were streaked with red. The rock was solid beneath my feet as I walked. It felt like it ran down to the core of the earth, racing the welling water back up through its veins. I started writing, trying to capture in words the thoughts that exist in far and secret places.

I watched Uncle Jack wading to his chest in the cold water. No shiver crossed his wiry frame – only the constant motion, forward and back with his arm like a pendulum on a clock that runs forever. The clock only stopped with a subtle shift in the line, a quick thrust, jumping its gear tracks in a rise from the depths of the pond. A trout would be stripped in or a trout would escape, sometimes with fly and leader broken. Either way, an escape would be met with a low grunt and a single "Damn it."

A caught trout was a different story. Uncle Jack would wet his hands with a splash, and a brook trout glistened above the surface. If the trout was big enough, Uncle Jack tucked his fly rod beneath his chin, bending his head to the waterline, crimping the rod to his neck with line splayed in loops and both hands lifting the worm-tracked back of a fish that measured in pounds. Always he admired the silver fins and the pulsing sides, holding the fish high in the rays that shone upon the ridge. He admired it all with a smile and a look in his eyes that approached reverence. I wrote that down, too.

I wrote how the spots of the brook trout blended red against the rocks of the pond, shining veins of ore against the banks; how the spidery tracks on the backs of the fish reminded me of Uncle Jack's map, its twisting lines in random patterns and no given destination but to find a certain rock and carry it away to the forge – piling it on a skyline empire of city mountains; how cities were far away, cities might never have existed. There were only the endless iron ridges, silent and waiting. There were only the waters of the trout. I wrote the truth as it unfolded, scrawled in the margins of my notebook and etched into my very mind:

The iron ore and the water and the trout – in and of themselves they were nothing. But the taconite rock, together with the water and the trout... Together, they created a whole. For Uncle Jack and Ernie, together, they transcended life itself.

CHAPTER 33

The shack was fully vested atop our hidden iron ridge as we sat the last night gathered around the porch. Only a faint glow of pink still shone in the west as the pinprick of a million galaxies came to life in the darkening sky above. All around, as if we were standing on the highest brink of the earth, the northern lights began flashing across the ridge like searchlights.

Ernie contemplated the growing darkness from his birch-chair perch. A family of chipmunks had become very comfortable with him, and they scurried around his feet. He fed them pieces of dried rutabaga, and they ate right from his hand.

Uncle Jack sloshed happily through the flowering lily pads of the pond with a stringer of trout in tow. I'd just kindled a fire in a new ring of stones by the shack. The cooking grate had been dismantled from the sauna train and was set firmly in the rocks. My notebook and pencil lay in the dirt as I fanned the flames.

Uncle Jack swung the stringer of brook trout in a circling jig of victory and dropped the fish at Ernie's feet. Chipmunks scattered in fright. "It sure is nice to have a home-bound soul around the camp to do the cleaning and the cooking. I never would have believed it, sitting on the porch with your furry little pets while I do all the wet work. You remind me of one of those monks who sits on a mountain all day doing nothing. Might as well get some exercise and clean these fish, because pretty soon you ain't gonna be able to squeeze out of that chair."

Ernie grinned and took the fish to the pond side. There was a look of contentment on his face. He began cleaning but soon became distracted, stopping in mid-knife to watch the northern lights and the dance of small midges and mayflies over the water. The surface was still. It was a polished mirror reflecting the lights and reflecting the bugs flying over the pond.

A water beetle crawled along the shore, its casing evolved into red-hewn camouflage for the stained waters of the pond. Ernie plucked it, studying it for a moment, taking something small and dark from his shirt pocket and comparing it to the beetle. He flicked the beetle with his fingers into the deeper water, and a large trout broke the placid surface to take it under. Mayflies and midges scattered for cover as ripples splashed against the shore like a ship's wake. Ernie nodded approval and gently placed the small object back in his pocket. The smaller bugs resumed their flight patterns over the water, and all was still again. Ernie continued cleaning fish like nothing had happened.

"That was a hell of a trout!" exclaimed Uncle Jack. Came right up after that beetle and ignored all the small bugs. What's that you stashed in that-there shirt pocket, Ernie?"

"You vould not be interested. It is a fly... It is for catching da trout."

"You don't say?"

"I traded pieces of rutabaga to da chipmunks for some red fur. I only got tiny bit, enough for single fly. I have not named it yet, but I tink it looks like a beetle – not so bad for sitting on da porch all day, anyvay."

"On second thought, why don't you come back up here and take it easy. I caught the fish – it's only fair that I clean them. Say, if you sit real quiet, do you think maybe them chipmunks will come back?"

We fried trout and ate trout. We talked and laughed. Uncle Jack paged through my notebook.

"This is some mighty good writing. I was about to start in on *you* about sitting around all day and neglecting your duties, loafing on a birch log and writing notes. I was thinking to myself that you're getting as bad as Ernie, that's what I was thinking. He's a bad influence for a growing boy. But now that I see what you been doing with your idle hands, I'd say that you have some real writing potential. Everything you've seen in the last weeks, everything we've all seen. I'd say you got it down just right."

"I am proud to have crossed your path," said Ernie. "You got da back cast and da forward cast yust right. Now, you are starting to set da hook." He belched in contentment. "And you fry da fish good as your mother, too."

Uncle Jack continued reading my journal. "I can't believe you're the same kid we picked up a few weeks back. I'd take the credit for it, maybe even give Ernie a share, but I think you pulled this talent out of the water on your own."

He stopped and re-read a line. "I don't ship water over the top of my boots and swear like a sailor every time I miss a strike, do I? And do I really chase brook trout rises like a startled deer? And it says here that Ernie's eyes are as keen as the nighthawks that soar above the pond at night – that he can smell out a fish like a perceptive bear, and can dream up a fly to catch that fish in his sleep. Why...after all I've done for you. I told you he's a bad influence!"

There was more talk and more laughter. When I used to sleep, when I used to dream – I lived that night over a million times.

"Know what tomorrow is?" asked Uncle Jack.

"It is da day after today," Ernie said with a straight face.

"It is the day before the next day," I added.

"Bad influence – I mean it – you should be ashamed of yourself, Ernie! And you!" said Uncle Jack, a finger pointing in my chest. "You should be careful about hanging around with the wrong crowd – the foreign crowd that wouldn't know a patriotic holiday if it bit him in the nose. Tomorrow's the Fourth of July!"

A distant memory floated in on the night breeze. It swirled around my head like a mosquito. I tried to ignore it, but it buzzed on just the same. "I told Mom that I'd be back. I told her that we'd all be back for the fireworks."

"So you did," said Uncle Jack. "It's a wonder how time flies by up here, isn't it? It's also a wonder that we still have one responsible member left in our party. I reckon a promise is a promise, especially to your mother. What do you say, Ernie? We're about out of rutabagas to trade with the chipmunks anyway. I'd hate to think my sister would send a search party – she wouldn't for me, but she just might for her son. It'd be a sorry waste for a whole party of searchers to get lost and sunk in the swamp."

Ernie smiled, but he spoke seriously. He shook his head. "You two should go. I vould be honored for you to take da train out. But I tink I stay. I tink I vill sit in dis birch chair, tinking on dose mysteries of life. I tink I vill yust sit and vait vile da world spins vitout me."

Uncle Jack jumped to his feet like he'd been stung by a wasp. "But Ernie, we're a team! I can't drive that thing without you! It's a steam bath on wheels, and you know how temperamental it is. We'll be back before you know it! The top of this mountain has been here forever, and it's not going anywhere. Besides, Herbie will want a full report from you – you got to tell him about the chipmunk flies – you got to help me navigate – you got to come with!"

Uncle Jack was genuinely concerned. There was a look about him of a forlorn puppy that has been thrust out the door and into the cold. I thought at first it was because Ernie was the only one with the mechanical aptitude to reel us out of a jam if something went wrong, that Uncle Jack was the searching, tapered leader and Ernie the fly line. Uncle Jack led and Ernie followed. But over many years – fishing, reliving, and dreaming – I have come to understand what has always been. A fly line and leader work together. Iron rocks are nothing but rough chunks on an endless range without the steel fire of a forge. Trout without water are simply dead fish. Uncle Jack and Ernie –Ernie and Uncle Jack. Together, they were a whole.

"You have da engineer," said Ernie, clapping me on the shoulder. "He vill do yust fine for da partner." Ernie looked at Uncle Jack. "Besides, I don't trust you to remember by yourself. Dis vay, ven you all come back, you'll for sure bring me some more of dem rutabagas."

"We might make it," said Uncle Jack. He was thinking quickly, and the wheels of the train were already moving. "If we start early, maybe we can make it through the Lake Superior clay to Popcorn Corners by afternoon. I reckon we could borrow a truck. You threw a wrench at me, Ernie, but I'm fast, and I can duck."

"What then?" I asked.

"Why, I guess you have a life that needs living. Me, I suppose I'll come back up here and fish next to Ernie. I don't understand half a word he says, but I'll be danged if I'm going to trust him alone with all these brook trout. I guess we'll both sit up here and let the world go on without us."

I sat in silence. I felt myself slipping away.

"Nothing is forever," said Ernie. He felt what I felt. "You vill alvays have a place in da iron range. Ven da spring breezes visper, summer vill alvays follow. Ve vill come for you again."

"Promise?"

"We both promise," said Uncle Jack.

There came the slow and steady rings of rises on the pond. The trout of Taconite creek had taken a mind to feed in the growing darkness. "I say we all go fishing together, one last hurrah," said Uncle Jack.

We cast in the darkness, split across the pond with the singing of line and the thrashing of water. There was blue lighting in the sky as the northern lights flashed down. It was if we stood on the very iron and earth that spawned them. Magnetic iron was heavy in the air and in the water. There was only the iron and the trout and a blue rain of light coming down. Only steady casting in the flashing darkness to tell there were three of us.

"I been thinking..." Uncle Jack's words hung like shadows across the pond.

"Dat's been da problem as long as I can recall," Ernie's words echoed back.

"We've still left a lot of crumbs down below for the other ants to follow."

"Day von't find us tomorrow."

"It may be sooner than later."

"Da iron don't matter to dem no more."

"It will again."

"Da world spins."

"Tomorrow's Independence Day."

"I vill celebrate by feeding da chipmunks."

"Sure, after our train leaves to Popcorn Corners, you and the chipmunks can both hole up together and celebrate. I expect a pile of red-furred flies when I get back. But tomorrow, before we leave, I was thinking that we should have a show."

"Vut kind of show?"

"A fireworks show. A track-covering fireworks show."

I didn't say anything, and there was no answer from Ernie. Only the steady casting of three lines, forward and back. There were two heavy splashes as hooks were set. I don't know to this day what was landed and what was lost. I kept casting in the darkness, and it seemed like an eternity. Fighting a trout is a chancy blur; endless, gentle casts, before the line pulls rigid and the silence breaks.

Life surfaces from a deep pool, and it moves fast. It comes in an instant, and it goes in an instant. Then it is gone, disappearing like flashes of blue lighting from the northern heavens.

CHAPTER 34

Uncle Jack set the first one flush on the dam beneath Ernie's bridge. He wore his hip boots and, when he crouched along the creek bed to place it, their slick and worn rubber reflected the water below. It was a solitary stick of dynamite, and it was the calculated top of a pyramid of destruction.

"It'll be more than enough to open the gate and slap the mare on the tail," he said. "We'll spread the bigger fireworks further down. After the first horse takes off, the whole herd's gonna follow."

Ernie leaned against the sauna train with arms crossed and an apprehensive look in his eyes. "Long as da whole herd don't stampede us into da dust."

They let me take the train across the bridge and down to the far side of the clearing before the show started. It was packed with my gear for the trip out. I parked it next to the creek alongside the mud hole, and there really must have been quicksand, or some northern Wisconsin variation, because all that remained above the swampy ground was the red top of the truck's cab. I picked my way back up the grade and crossed the bridge.

"I vant you high up da creek and hiding behind dose boulders," Ernie lectured. "You stay down and covered, and I don't vant you moving an inch. Dis is not playing around games like crawling into da pump house or climbing da vaterfall. Dis is as real as it gets."

"Where are you going to be?"

"I vill stand right here on dis bridge and make sure dat da crazy vun don't blow his head off."

Uncle Jack rolled the starting fuse back up the ridge to the shelter of the boulders. "Quit worrying, it's only one case of dynamite, not an atomic bomb," he said.

"Dare's a reason God put a picture of da trout in your head instead of da plans for such a bomb. And I don't tink me *or* God likes dis plan vun bit."

Uncle Jack shook his head stubbornly and cut the roll of fuse off at my boulder shelter. He pushed my head down. "You stay down like Ernie told you, don't move a muscle. When we get set below, we'll come back here to start it off. You do exactly as Ernie says, and I might even let you light the fuse."

He took the roll of fuse, walked across the bridge, and connected it to the other side of the first charge. His hip boots slogged heavily as he headed down the mine slope and went to work. Ernie stood atop the bridge in heavy meditation. He muttered silently. "I say let dem come and have dare mine back. I vould give dem my train even. I say da hell vit all of it."

I snapped a twig as I crept around the boulder for a closer look at what was going on below. I had to see. I paused, hoping Ernie hadn't heard, hoping he was preoccupied with Uncle Jack's demolition set-up. But Ernie could hear a trout rise around a bend in a rainstorm. He could cast to a rise behind him without looking. "You stay hunkered behind dat rock or I vill tie you dare myself vit my best fly line!" His head never flinched in my direction. His eyes never wavered from Uncle Jack, crawling down the ridge, trailing fuse behind him, and cradling enough explosives to turn back the clock on a taconite mine.

Uncle Jack talked incessantly and nervously as he went, placing charges in the rock crevices. "Yes sir! If I have anything to say about it and the dynamite holds out, this mine is about to look like nobody's ever dug a bucketful of ore out of it. It'll take a little pop to blow the train car, but I think we're going to make it. It's a good thing we're only using one stick on the dam... Shoddy craftsmanship – that's what it is. The whole thing would crumble in a stiff wind! That bridge is the only reason to use any nitro at all – pounded together with enough spikes to build a fortress, for crying out loud."

"Da bridge I built! Da dam you helped vit! Figure out da shoddy craftsmanship for yourself later. Pay attention now!" Ernie shouted.

Uncle Jack continued setting the explosives down one by one, bantering to himself like a rooster. I inched my head above the shelter, and I could see veins popping on his arms as he carried his burden. The morning sun was already hot and hitting the mine slopes, and there was sweat wringing down his face.

"The good Lord gives and the good Lord takes it right back, Ernie. When it's all said and done, the only difference between my craftsmanship and yours is that we can use whatever's left of the bridge for firewood! Get your head back behind that rock!" Uncle Jack hollered, placing the last and biggest charge in the doorway of the stripped-out boxcar.

I slunk behind my boulder, fingering the starting fuse. Uncle Jack could cast without looking as well as Ernie. He could also foretell a mayfly hatch before the first set of wings appeared on the water, but he hadn't foreseen the hatch that came next. The starting fuse was unlit, and I never saw the first explosion. I only felt it deep in my chest.

The world began moving like a dream where legs pump furiously and the body goes nowhere. The heat from the rocks must have done it. It was sauna rocks without cooling water, and it didn't create steam. It started in the middle of the slope, and it created fire. Uncle Jack ran for the upper creek as fire and rocks rained down. He was running in slow motion, and he was running for his life.

Ernie spanned the bridge in a single leap. He had his knife out, and he was in the rocks trying to cut fuse lines and sever the pockets of explosions from reaching the bridge. It was like trying to sever the heads off an erupting hydra. Rock fragments pounded like iron shrapnel, and clouds of red dust mushroomed and folded back along the creek.

I lost sight of Uncle Jack and Ernie in the dust, and without thinking of the consequences, I ducked out of my hiding spot and tried to find my way down to them. Another explosion, a fresh wave of pebbles, hit me square in the face. I breathed dust, and my face bled from flying gravel. It was dark as night – and the night was blood-red and came in a choking cloud. I panicked and fell face down into the rolling creek, and I'll go to my grave remembering that.

"Move! Make for da bridge!" Ernie's voice boomed over the explosions.

"It's caving fast!" I heard Uncle Jack. The cold water cleared the fuzziness from my head and washed away the stifling heat of the dust. I tried to regain my feet and move towards the voices, but the pebbles along the creek bottom kept slipping beneath.

I heard Uncle Jack again. "It's a tightrope! It's shaking like a whip!"

The dust settled enough for me to see the situation clearly. Uncle Jack teetered on the rail ties of the bridge with arms outstretched for balance. His hip boots were black and smoking, but he looked to be in one piece. Ernie was on hands and knees, leading the way across. The bridge tilted to one side, and the dam was cracked open in the middle with sheets of water sucking through.

It turned dead calm. Ernie must have cut the rest of the fuses, and the charges had run their course. I held on, digging my feet into the pebbles and fighting to keep from sliding down the rushing creek. Ernie and Uncle Jack had almost crossed to the other side of the bridge. *We're going to make it*! I thought. Then the world went white.

The boxcar erupted below in a roar of twisted metal and splintered boards. The entire ridge line jumped. Ernie was knocked flat on his belly, and Uncle Jack cracked through the bridge with one leg wedged tight between the rails. The vacuum pull through the broken dam became too intense, and I lost my battle with the sliding bottom and tumbled down the creek. My ears were ringing as I slid downstream. I grabbed wildly and caught a root from a fallen birch, watching as a heavy brown trout rolled from beneath the tangles. All the chaos, and still there were trout in Taconite Creek.

The bridge gave another lurch as more of the dam gave way. Taconite Creek rushed down the grade at a furious pace. The birch root tore from its bank mooring and pulled half the fallen log with it. I went sliding down, clinging to the tree. I never saw what became of the trout.

Uncle Jack saw me coming first. Ernie was still flat on his belly and trying to pull him free from the splintered rails. Uncle Jack pushed him away. "Don't bother with me! Grab the boy before he slides under!"

Ernie acted quickly. He shifted position and reached his arms down. Uncle Jack held Ernie by his suspenders as I rushed closer. Ernie's engineer's cap slid from his head as he reached down. It hurled down the slope in a torrent of the water. I held onto the birch like a gnarled life preserver. "Hold da arm up! Hold it higher!"

He had me. I can still feel his hand gripping like iron and pulling me from Taconite Creek. I can still feel it as sure as I feel my fingers digging across the rings of this stump. I feel it across all the years. He could easily have hefted me onto the tilting bridge. Uncle Jack holding onto Ernie, and Ernie holding on to me; we might easily have been all together. Instead, Ernie roared like a wounded bear. He pushed me back, and I slid beneath the bridge and over the cracked dam.

I washed down the ridge in an instant, my head tumbling and rolling, the garbled underwater noises of the rocks and pieces of the dam coming down with me. I hung up finally on a boulder alongside the swimming-hole island. My shins were cut raw. Blood ran down the side of my face from a flapping gash. Blood mixed with stained water, and it tasted of iron and hot powder. It was where I'd spent afternoons enticing trout from the deep runs. Now, I lay like a spent fish on its hard bank.

Ernie roared down from above, and I twisted my body to see. He was still kneeling on the bridge. His arms hung loosely at his sides, and Uncle Jack still held him by his suspenders. He seemed to care not if he toppled off the bridge. My eyes locked on his, and I saw a flash-flood of emotions in the span of a heartbeat: nervousness and fear until he saw my head surface down the run; anguish when he saw the blood flowing down the side of my face; and relief when he'd seen me surface far enough down to suit his purpose. Then there was only courage. Courage was the last thing I saw.

The fuse to the single charge of dynamite on the dam sizzled within feet of its destiny. I'm sure Ernie cut the fuse. He was too calculating to make that kind of mistake. He'd just cut it too far down the slope. There was too much fuse and too many fireworks going off. It was a tangled gauntlet of hooks and lines that even the wariest and wisest trout couldn't have negotiated without tangling. When the boxcar went up, a burning piece of rubble must have relit the uphill section of the severed fuse. Ernie had sensed it, like he sensed so many of life's mysteries, and he let me take my chances on a downward plunge. I saw courage in his eyes, because he knew that he'd finally been hooked, and he knew the hook had been set deep.

He tried to shake the hook up to the last. He was stronger than iron, but he was tied to another, and he was tied with a devotion and bond that ran deeper than forged steel. Ernie wrapped his arms around Uncle Jack and ripped him from the splintered hole in the bridge. There was a crack like a snagged line breaking, and I heard Uncle Jack scream with his leg bent at a right angle, one hip boot still dangling beneath the bridge and flopping in the current.

The fuse burned with a final pop as Ernie tossed Uncle Jack from the bridge. Uncle Jack hit the water as the bridge and dam exploded, spreading itself wide down the waters of Taconite Creek. That final blast burned into my mind. Then there were only the waters that had been there forever, rushing over me and reclaiming the iron rock that had been there longer than that. The island was gone in the flood. I went down with it. I washed past the sauna train, and I remember its stack was still steaming as I passed into the swamp.

CHAPTER 35

I awoke to the sounds of thunder and water, instinctively covering my ears and curling into a ball, burying my face in the swamp bottom, and breathing in the rich mud. I braced for the next explosion, the next shower of hot gravel on my neck, and the next tidal rush of water as the creek righted itself from above. A brilliant flash penetrated through the cakes of mud and dried blood around my eyes. There was a final, crashing roar before the water came down.

It started like the soft patter of chipmunks on a tarpapered roof, plopping louder like the rise of a thousand trout; and then, with a final rumble, the summer rain showered down on Taconite Creek with the rush of a steam engine rolling from the rocky heights. The rocks of the ridge cooled and misted, and I knew it was over. I buried my head in the mud and cried.

I found Ernie's engineer cap floating in a half-circle in a back-current pool. Uncle Jack lay in the water below, washed against the upturned roots of a cedar tree. His eyes were open and fixed on the cap. His face was blackened with ash, and he blended in with the dark roots of the cedar. One hip-booted leg swung lazily out into the current like a tree root. I might have walked on past him except for the whites of his eyes. I saw the whites of his eyes staring at the cap. He never spoke a word as I came upon him. I desperately wanted to hear something, anything. I wanted him to holler, wanted him to tell me what a fool I'd been to not stay in the cover of the rocks. I wanted him to yell how lucky I was to be standing before him as the rain pattered down on the pool and Ernie's cap circled in the eddy. He never moved and he never said a word and I remember the whites of his eyes staring at the cap. I can still feel those eyes burning across the years and into my old soul.

Half the front axle of the boxcar train lay buried across the creek from Uncle Jack's final fishing hole. The warped shaft was down in the muck, the upturned iron wheel looking like a set table with nothing but crumbs of blasted, taconite rock powdering the surface. The axle was dusted red, and mud bubbled from below. It was sinking into the swamp, inches at a crack.

The rocks misted solemnly along the ridge. There was no trace of the pump house and no remnant of the dam. The only things moving were the raindrops and the creek current and a thin trail of wood smoke rising over the swamp line. Ernie's train was all that was left. Taconite Creek flowed into the swamp, and the air was still charged with the smell of blasting powder, but the rain was settling it slowly away. The whole of the boxcar had been hurled into the swamp, and all that remained were pieces of iron sinking into nothing. They would be gone soon enough. Uncle Jack may have been mistaken and misled on many things, but covering our tracks, on that point, he had nailed the target squarely. There was nothing left to tell that an iron mine once stood here.

I sat down in the water next to Uncle Jack. I shivered in shock for a very long time. Bruises rose on my body unaware, and the gash on my cheek stiffened and numbed in the cold. I looked through the rain without seeing.

"You need to move now. Da rain vill catch you your death." I heard Ernie's wisdom faint in my head; faint as if across a far river. Still I sat, unmoving next to Uncle Jack, his eyes white and forever staring at the circling pool and the circling cap.

"He is gone far across da ridge. Ve can't follow him. Ve need to move now." Ernie's deep voice resonated clearer into my shocked stupor, not far across the river now, but closer, as if wading along the shallows of the rain-soaked creek. "He covered his trail. He covered all of it before he left."

I looked above the circling water and the engineer's cap was gone now. And there he stood, straight out of my dream from the first night on Taconite Creek. His beard was burned to stubble, and his suspenders were burned clean off. He teetered unsteadily, holding his soaked cap in one hand and Uncle Jack's missing hip boot in the other. The boot was melted black, and Ernie was a torched wreck, but still he smiled gently. He put the drenched cap on his head and held out his hand, the hip boot still dangling.

"He vouldn't vant us to follow. He vaits on da high ridge for us to come later. Maybe not so long for me, but he vould not vant to see you up dare for long time. Ve must get out of the rain now."

I got unsteadily to my feet and would have gladly fallen into Ernie's waiting arms, but I would have knocked him down. He was burnt and hurting, and so was I. We would have both fallen, and neither of us likely had strength left to rise from the water. We leaned on each other instead and made our way up the bank. Ernie's train was still steaming, battered by debris but still standing. It was all that was left to tell we had come to Taconite Creek.

Ernie slumped over in the compartment and fell into an unsteady sleep. Heat radiated in waves from his burnt skin, but he was shivering at the same time. He mumbled in his sleep.

I tore open my pack and shredded a flannel shirt, soaking the strips in water and placing the cool rags on Ernie's burns. I used the last of my strength to haul some wet logs from the streamside debris and throw them in the stove. The sauna fire was hot enough, and I knew they would burn. The train cab warmed slowly, and the rain hit the roof in gray pellets.

I must have slept some. I faded in and out with Ernie as the sky darkened with thunder. Lighting danced down the ridge and into my heart as we spent the night in the train. I remember bits of conversation, stolen verses back and forth. I think they were real, but as the years rolled by like the rings on this stump, I've become less sure what was said and what was imagined.

"It keeps running in my head, Ernie. It was my fault."

"It vas not."

"Uncle Jack was wrong about me."

"He vas not. Mistakes he made, but judging character vas never vun of dem."

"Why?"

"Da ending for us all is written. It is only da mystery of ven."

"What are the mysteries of life? Are they in the rocks? Can you taste them when you taste the iron?"

"Mysteries are tasted in da rocks, but day are also seen in da sky and felt in da vater. Day move vit da seasons – change vit da years. It is only important to remember dem ven you see – to hold dem in your heart ven day disappear."

"That's how Uncle Jack looked at it?"

"He did. He knew you vould come to see it, too."

"The iron weighs heavy on me, Ernie. I'm empty inside. Was it worth it? Was it worth it for all of us?"

"It is only rock. Rock is an empty nutting. Da life ve choose – to fill up da emptiness vit life – dat is vert more dan cities of steel. Dat is vert more dan all of it."

"What now?"

"Ve go on. Your uncle saw da fire in you. He knew dat you vould remember. He saw enough inside your soul. He saw enough to bring you to Taconite Creek."

"Will the mine companies come again, like Uncle Jack said?"

"Dey vill come. It is not important. Vut is important is dat you vere here and dat you remember."

"He's gone forever. I feel lost. It hurts."

"Dat hurting is da mystery of life. It vill pass slowly, but it is da mystery to keep close inside of you forever."

"I think I need to go forward. I think I need to go home."

"I am already dare," said Ernie.

CHAPTER 36

We started early in the morning after the rain had passed. The earth was fresh and wet, and the sun glistened on leaves of dripping green. If Uncle Jack had been there, the day would have been full of promise.

It was a solemn and unconventional funeral procession up to the waterfall entrance where we buried him. We floated him across the creek where the dam once stood. The water was shallower now, and you would have thought the hand of man had never laid a finger upon it. We rested many times along the path up. I was stiff and sore, and Ernie's skin was broken in angry blisters. Rushing water pulled off layer after layer of mud and ash as Ernie cooled his burned body in the creek at every stop.

Ernie said that if Uncle Jack had a last will and testament, he couldn't have written a better ending. "He vould tell me I look like da baked rutabaga stewing in da water, dat's exactly vut he vould say."

Lake Superior shone dark red in the distance. Taconite Creek ran over its ore-stained bed, and brook trout flashed the bottom into life. "He would have wanted to have one last look around," I said.

"He vas da iron miner and explorer, a better fisherman and da finest friend. He vill finally get da chance to ask Eddie Barker. He vill be hearing a big story if Eddie Barker hooked dat Lake Superior trout. I hope day don't have da cribbage board up dare. St. Peter himself vill throw dem both out ven day get to arguing."

Those were the last words Ernie spoke before we laid Uncle Jack to rest. We wrapped him in evergreen boughs cut from his shelter and piled taconite stones from the ancient fire ring for a grave marker. It seems morbid, a burial like that. But Uncle Jack was laid to rest at the end of the taconite rails and beneath the entrance to his finest hour. We buried him with his compass and with his cindered and black hip boots on. The boots looked like they'd been to the iron forges of hell instead of the finest of hidden trout waters. The compass jumped as we piled the rocks around his final resting spot. But as we laid it in Uncle Jack's folded arms, it swung steadily toward the waterfall. It pointed ever upward. Only Ernie and I knew. We made an unspoken pact to keep it thus. Uncle Jack would have wanted it that way.

As we limped away from the freshly-turned grave, we heard a heavy splash. By the time we turned around, there were only waves in a ring below the waterfall where a mighty brook trout had risen. The circling ripples of the rise were ancient music. They faded slowly against the bank to where a pile of red rocks marked the passing of an age. The rippled splash of the trout blended with falling water from above, and it was the finest hymn ever sung.

CHAPTER 37

We cast out of Taconite Creek in ever-lengthening loops. We took the sauna train as far as we could. I engineered us through the swamp while Ernie slept. He was blistered and burning with fever. We followed the water out. The train got us as far as the caves dropping down to the Lake Superior shore before it sputtered and died in a mass of red clay, seizing a piston or throwing a rod – or some other technical term that only Ernie could fully comprehend in his mechanical mind.

"Da train is tired," Ernie said. Maybe he could have fixed it, but his heart wasn't in it anymore. The pulley we'd used to build the shack atop the taconite ridge now served to lower us down through one of the biggest caves. I lowered Ernie to the sand below, clambering down after him like a monkey. All my years of climbing trees served me well, but I still don't know how we managed it. As Uncle Jack was fond of saying, "Sometimes you just got to go hard and hope you have a bit of luck."

We left the train above, sitting in the clay and water with the waves from Lake Superior calling up to it through a darkened and wet passage. I could still smell wood smoke burning as we lowered ourselves down. I never saw it again.

I shouldered my pack and fly rod, and I still had Ernie's box of flies. Ernie limped behind empty-handed. He possessed the strength to move a ton of ore and a mind that could build a train and a ridge-top paradise out of nothing. But he'd been crushed in his body and in his soul. We plodded through the shifting sand. Before we made Ashland, we camped three nights, driftwood shelters and fires on the shore. There were tributary streams coming out of the iron hills, and I waded up from the lake to catch enough for us to eat. It was easy enough. Ernie watched without saying a word, but there was approval in his eyes as I set the hook on heavy-sided trout. He knew I'd learned, and he didn't need to speak of it anymore.

The doors of the Ore Dock Saloon called us in. We stumbled in after nightfall to smoke and laughter and Uncle Jack's brook trout hanging in splendor behind the bar. Drinks were placed slowly down and chairs turned to face us; there was steady, watching silence as we stood ragged in the entryway. I stood with a pack on my shoulders, a pack that had come full circle to its origin. Ernie leaned, spent, against the wall. The patrons took the situation in at a glance, and there were no questions asked. The newspapers might not have remembered, but Ashland was an iron ore town, and it never forgot. The town remembered, and we were taken in. We were taken care of.

A doctor came out of the night, and I was led to a soft bed. Ernie, likewise, was led away. Phone calls hummed over the wires. To this day, I don't know who took care of me until my mother arrived. I slept for a very long time, and I remember dreaming and waking and dreaming again. Taconite Creek rushed through my mind until I couldn't recall what was real and what was imagined. I saw my mother standing in deep conversation at the door of my room. She was talking to Herbie from Popcorn Corners. I wasn't sure until years later if he was really there, because when I awoke for good, he was gone, and so was Ernie, and there was only my mother sitting with tears in her eyes. I didn't have to speak a word, because somehow she knew. She took me home. The iron hills and Taconite Creek faded behind as we went.

REFLECTIONS

All that is left now are the rings on an oaken stump and the fading rings of a rising trout that has circled across the years – counting, watching, and marking. This tree was as much a sentinel as the rail tracks, as much a silent guardian as a high-ridge waterfall. It might seem only a stump, a shadow from the past, but it remembers when Uncle Jack and Ernie flowed out of the iron hills to shape my life. It remembers when a trout stream met a taconite mine. It has seen paper boys come and go, and countless news stories are wrapped in its rings.

Ernie stopped by once or twice in the early years. He was older and slower, but his beard grew back, and the smile never left his eyes. He still helped himself to seconds and thirds of my mother's cooking. Taconite Creek might have crushed a part of his soul, but it left his appetite unscathed.

As I grew, his visits became less until, one day, he was just gone. I think he'd come by just to see, just to make sure that what he and Uncle Jack had started in my heart and soul was going to take seed... He wanted to see the *Sisu*.

I still felt empty, but it was not like after my father had been killed. I'd changed. The dam had broken, and the waters were flowing down from the ridges in a natural destiny. There had been tracks laid down for me to follow. School was still a challenge, but it never bothered me much again. I held onto those tracks and to my cow pasture stream. Eventually, I held on to life. I held on to it like it was a monster trout in a wild current. I splashed after it.

It's just me left now; me and the squirrels and an old stump and newspaper stories; stories of digging into the northern hills to find a fresh mine. It won't be easy, even with modern equipment, but I believe in my soul that Taconite Creek is still flowing and waiting like it has always been. I remember the steam from a wood-burning sauna mixing with clanging shovels and falling boulders. I remember a hand-laid stone dam and a rough-hewn bridge. I know of a hidden place where an old compass pointed, and the sound of singing fly lines rose above it all. If the modern mine companies have the *Sisu* to try, they just might make a go of it, but it's a bitch to get in there, and it's harder to get out. By God, taconite can indeed sprout over quicksand, and when the water gets a mind to flowing, they'd best dig carefully.

As far as the environmentalists go, damned if they shouldn't give their best shot at stopping the mine companies. The course of any river can be shifted with enough sweat and blood. There's always a path to the summit if you believe and, too, there's always Mother Nature. She's a powerful ally, and she can't be bribed no matter how high the stakes.

Regardless of how it shakes out between the two parties, it won't be the first argument that broke over those northern hills. Uncle Jack and Ernie were there first, and there isn't a lot those red rocks haven't heard. They've been there forever; they'll hold their silence and listen.

I once lived a dream in a place, the real mother-lode high on a ridge, and I don't rightfully know if that one was ever closed down or not. It was wild and hidden, and the biggest brook trout you ever laid eyes on called it home. The tracks up into it were wiped clean, so if you want to take the taconite rails to the pinnacle, you've got to use your internal compass to find the way. Don't believe the newspapers – they only see the little fish rising in the shallows. There are bigger secrets hiding in the deep pools. Go see for yourself – it's the way that life was designed to work.

Myself, I've come to realize it will always be there. It was my high school graduation day when I got the envelope. No real return address on top, only: Popcorn Corners. It was addressed to me, with the title of "Keeper of Life's Mysteries."

It is not where you are bound. It is how you remember the moments given and the path you choose to get there. Go down to the river to pray every chance you get.

The note was wrapped in Uncle Jack's map with a single fishing fly pinned in the corner. The map was worn and iron-stained as ever. The fly had been used and chewed, and it smelled like trout.

I'm at the outer ring of the rise now, but I was young when the iron trout of Taconite Creek first surfaced.

I kept the map and the fly all these years. I chose the least trampled river paths, and I tried to remember, but I don't know that I ever measured up. I don't know that anyone could. There was steel-fire in their eyes and iron ore running through their veins. I'll see them both again soon, high above Taconite Creek. I'm going to tell them that I spent my life trying.

John Luthens is a freelance writer from Grafton, Wisconsin. He rambles along the back roads, exploring country and writing of his outdoor travels for various publications. The family cabin in Douglas County, near the storied Bois Brule River, is a favorite starting point for his trout angling adventures along Lake Superior's South Shore. His column, *Fencerows,* appears online at OnWisconsinOutdoors.com.